Rovers Return

Edited by
KEVIN WILLIAMSON

First published in Great Britain in 1998 by Rebel Inc.,
an imprint of Canongate Books Ltd, 14 High Street,
Edinburgh EH1 1TE

10 9 8 7 6 5 4 3 2 1

British Library Cataloguing-in-Publication Data
A catalogue record for this book is available on
request from the British Library

ISBN 0 86241 803 8

Rebel Inc. series editor: Kevin Williamson

Typeset by Palimpsest Book Production Limited,
Polmont, Stirlingshire
Printed and bound in Finland by WSOY

Contents

The Line-up

ANTHONY BOURDAIN: New York chef, and author of two renegade mafia-cuisine novels, *Bone in the Throat* and *Gone Bamboo*, both available from Canongate Books. Currently resides in Manhattan. Regular patron at the legendary Siberia Bar, the Big Apple's only drinking den hidden deep in the bowels of the New York subway.

LAURA HIRD: Original Rover, whose first book, *Nail and Other Stories*, was published by Rebel Inc. (1997). Currently resident in Edinburgh's Gorgie district next to the stadium of an Edinburgh soccer club. She frequently frequents the Tynecastle Arms to purchase Stella and lime and nippy nuts from Frank, the unfortunate Hibee.

JOHN KING: Author of best-selling trilogy, *The Football Factory*, *Headhunters* and *England Away*. Well-travelled and a committed Chelsea supporter. Recently supported establishments of note include the Falcon Bar, Battersea (home) and the Dubliners Bar, Stockholm (away).

GORDON LEGGE: Original Rover, and author of two novels, *The Shoe* and *I Love Me, Who Do You Love?* and two collections of short stories, *In Between Talking about the Football* and, most recently, *Near Neighbours*. Currently resident in

Edinburgh after a long stint in ArabStrapLand. Has occasionally been spotted in the internationally renowned Robbie's Bar, a pub described by the *New York Times* as being the hang-out of the 'New Edinburgh Beats'. Aye, right.

EMER MARTIN: Irish emigrant in New York whose first novel, *Breakfast in Babylon*, was Irish Book of the Year in 1996. Her second novel, *More Bread or I'll Appear*, will be released in the United States in January 1999. Patron of Nightingale's Bar in Manhattan's Lower East Side, which is a must-see for every tourist, laden with electrical gadgets and expensive jewellery.

JAMES MEEK: Another original Rover, and author of two novels, *McFarlane Boils the Sea* and *Drivetime*, as well as a collection of short stories, *Last Orders*, which won a lot of accolades and a lot of new fans to his surreal, sharply observed stories. Currently living and working in Moscow, drinking whisky in the Sixteen Tons and working as a reporter.

Introduction

It's been two years since the Rebel Inc. side of Canongate Books kicked off with the now (unintentionally) notorious *Children of Albion Rovers* anthology. In that short time, twenty-four Rebel Inc. titles have been published featuring such underground and counter-culture icons as Nelson Algren, Charles Bukowski, Richard Brautigan, Alexander Trocchi, Thomas Pynchon, William Burroughs, Howard Marks, John Fante and Knut Hamsun as well as a fair whack of top-notch contemporary writers such as Laura Hird, Barry Gifford, Jim Dodge, Joel Rose, Ray Loriga and Michael Guinzburg.

And not forgetting the original *Albion Rovers* squad. As far as the aim of providing a vehicle for quality, non-mainstream writing it wouldn't be too self-aggrandising to say it's done no' bad.

Children of Albion Rovers featured half a dozen novellas (or whatever these things are called when they're at that awkward length somewhere between short stories and full-length novels) by Irvine Welsh, Alan Warner, Gordon Legge, James Meek, Laura Hird and Paul Reekie. Yet despite having six of the hottest young Scottish writers strutting their funky stuff – and with the type of publicity and hype that any publisher would kill for – shortly after publication the book was unceremoniously hit by an Exocet missile of the legal variety which removed it from the shops for the crucial first few months. So much for freedom of expression.

Anyway, the book eventually came back out and was hailed by many as by far the best anthology of new Scottish writing around. *Loaded* magazine described it as 'a fistful of Caledonian classics' and even the highbrow *Literary Review* heaped praise. Now, you can hardly move in bookshops for anthologies of Scottish writers. In the publishing industry, like the movie world, one thing is guaranteed: if there's a bandwagon of any sort then lazy publishers are the first to try and cadge a lift. You know the sort of hype: 'This book is the new *Trainspotting*/the Irish *Trainspotting*/the Geordie *Trainspotting*', or 'A harrowing tale of football thuggery', or 'Drugs, drugs, drugs', et cetera. Never looking for the original slant on the whole thing, just copying for the sole purpose of making some unoriginal profits.

With 1998 fading fast and the whole Millennium non-sense about to go into overdrive (unofficial soundtrack: K Foundation's: 'Fuck the Millennium, We Want It Now!'), the need to keep moving on is relentless. So with this sequel the original 'Scottish' identity to *COAR* has been widened out a bit. Three of the original members of the squad, Gordon Legge, Laura Hird and James Meek, are now teamed up with London's John King, Dublin's Emer Martin and New York's Anthony Bourdain. (And whilst Welsh and Warner have moved on from the thrills and spills of the Scottish Premier League to the lira-laden Serie A, Paul Reekie is still working off a red card.)

Gordon Legge's riotous story of sports reporters and weather girls set in a fictitious Scottish television studio confirms his growing reputation as one of the best short story writers around. His two collections, *In Between Talking about the Football* and *Near Neighbours* are classics in their own right and essential purchases. It just wouldn't be a Rebel Inc. publication without Gordon Legge (who has featured in all but one of the *Rebel Inc.* magazines as well as both Rovers anthologies). Laura Hird's story 'Hope' shows yet again that, just as in her first collection of stories, *Nail*, she has this uncanny ability to get inside the head of a surprisingly diverse range of characters. This time it's inside the head of a young gay man whose one-night stand turns into his worst nightmare. Her debut novel, due out in 1999, is definitely one to look out for. James Meek weaves his magic here with a bizarre yet moving story (of . . . a fisherman? Death? Hard to describe, really). Like Gordon Legge, James Meek seems to produce his very best work when he's writing shorter fiction. After the surreal landscape of *Last Orders*, his first short story collection, a new collection in 1999 is another one well worth keeping an eye out for.

And so to the three newcomers. Anthony Bourdain's 'Chefs' Night Out' is the perfect appetiser for the first UK publication of his mafia/chef novels, *Bone in the Throat* and its sequel, *Gone Bamboo* (both published at the same time as this collection by Canongate Books). Deadpan wit and colourful Italian gangsters abound and all three read as sharp as a chef's number-one blade. And this guy knows his food. Emer Martin's ambitious 'Teeth Shall Be Provided', with its nuclear fallout, Japanese cross-dressers, Indonesian tribes, and a crazy Irish dominatrix, is a sort of detour from within the narrative of her second novel, *More Bread or I'll Appear*. Her first novel, *Breakfast in Babylon* (embarrassingly billed in the States as 'the female *Trainspotting*'), was a wild chemical ride across Europe from Dublin to Israel and most places in between and is definitely worth tracking down. And last but not least is John King.

Back in 1993 a short story of his, 'Millwall Away', appeared in issue 4 of *Rebel Inc.* magazine. It was ferocious, compelling, and heralded the arrival of a great new writing talent. The story eventually grew into *The Football Factory*, King's best-selling novel of football, violence, and growing up in working-class London. Three best-selling novels later, King's contribution here, a harrowing tale of incarceration in a foreign prison, is part of a longer work which will probably appear as a full-length novel sometime in the future.

So that's the line-up. Home and away. As can be seen, the days of Rebel Inc. being a vehicle *solely* for the voices of urban central Scotland are long past, if they ever really existed at all. Internationalism is the future, and narrow nationalist concerns, whether in literature, politics or whatever, will hopefully become the dodo of the twenty-first century.

Just like its predecessor, the *Rovers Return* is a collection of six 'novellas'. This longer format allows writers more space to develop their stories and characters than the normal anthology format of much shorter pieces. Also, from the writer's perspective – as many established writers have already discovered – trying to get a good novella-length story published can often be a bit tricky. Publishers aren't that interested in them.

Stand-alone novellas are becoming something of a rarity as books are treated more and more as standardised commodities with regards to cover price and number of pages. *'The books have got to fit the packing boxes, like, and we need to charge enough to make a decent profit, so give us 250–350 pages, and that'll do fine.'* God knows what some of the profit-margin orientated publishers of today would have thought if Thomas Mann had handed them his slight (in pages) masterpiece, *Death in Venice* . . . *'Aye, no' bad, son, but if you write us another couple the same length we could mibbe bundle them all together and make a tidy sum if it sells.'* It reminds me of how a talent scout once told a young Jimmy Johnstone, the legendary Celtic winger who could drink his height in nips, that he should maybe think about getting himself a trade as he was too small to make it as a footballer. As it was, Jinky turned out to be one of the greatest players ever to grace the Hoops. Or as *Coronation Street*'s Vera Duckworth once said to her husband Jack: 'Size isn't everything and just as bleedin' well.'

So, to cut to the chase, this sequel to *Children of Albion Rovers* is the second in a series of what will now become an annual publication every Autumn. While most of the stories featured so far have been commissioned, and will continue to be so, we'll still welcome any submissions for the 1999 anthology of *approximately* 10,000–20,000 words. The deadline for submissions is March 1st, 1999, and the address they should be sent to is: Rebel Inc., Canongate Books, 14 High Street, Edinburgh EH1 1TE.

Enjoy.

Kevin Williamson, Editor

The Weathers and their Famous Fathers
GORDON LEGGE

'LETTUCE, LASAGNE, LIGHTBULB, loaf.'

It was always Safeway. Always just the back of eight. Always Tuesday morning. This week, Piershill. Last week, Comely Bank. Next week? Who knows, maybe Morningside, maybe Maybury.

'Lemon, lemonade, lemon meringue pie.'

Nobody really seen you. At that time, anybody out had to be in a hurry. There was the odd glimpse of recognition, of course: like the mason's handshake, a moment designed to linger.

Sinclair smiled.

'Lentils.'

Sinclair Stevens always smiled.

'Leg of lamb.'

It made somebody's day.

'Liver.'

After all, in your local Safeway, at ten past eight of a Tuesday morning, you wouldn't really be expecting to see one of the most famous faces in the country, now would you?

'Lorne sausage.'

Last night had confirmed it. The Early Evening! The Six O'clock! Channel Four! The Nine O'clock! News at Ten! Newsnight!

The Big Six.

'Lime.'

He knew it would happen. Oh aye, Sinclair knew it would happen all right. For weeks now he'd been telling folk, had his video all set up, all primed, ready just to capture the moment, the moments. Last night had been the night, the night of proof. He'd got home and, before doing anything else, he'd checked it through – Yes! Oh, yes! Oh! Oh! Yes! Yes! – then edited it down. Just the proof. That was all that was needed. Incontestable proof.

'Leeks and, oh, what the hell, a low-fat spread.'

Sinclair finished unpacking his messages. He'd separated them into three piles: the breakfast and snack cupboard; toiletries; the fridge. To amuse himself, as he'd emptied the bags, he'd called to mind, and called out, a consumer good starting with the letter L. He'd taken out coffee and said, 'lager'. He'd taken out yoghurt and said, 'laxatives'.

Sinclair could do things like that. Straight off the top of his head, he'd come away with the idea and seen it through.

Sinclair loved pressure.

There was no denying it brought out the best in him.

Sinclair was the best.

The best at everything.

He could even influence the news.

Once the messages were stored away, Sinclair went through to watch his video again.

The boys were going to love this.

The Big Six.

Marina was putting double-sided tape under her breasts.

Across the room, MacAllister was still crashed out. With his right arm aloft, fingers outstretched, it was as if, in his dreams, he was poised, trying to attract some kind of subconscious attention. To be sure, a strange way to sleep.

Nor, it has to be said, was it the prettiest of sights. Everybody looked their age the morning after and, devoid of soft lights and shadows, MacAllister was easily, oh, say, what forty-six, with a pale, blotchy body that called to mind none other than an aging Bertie Bassett – without the life-long costume of confectionery.

Marina gave her breasts a wiggle, a serious wiggle. Good. No movement. In fact, they were so static, if you didn't know any better, you'd have thought they were silicon. Marina put on a tight sports bra to flatten them out.

For the now, that would have to do.

It wasn't even as if they were that big. If anything, they were what you'd call perfect, 34C. But no, according to MacAllister, you weren't allowed them. It was one of the rules, one of the written down rules. If you had them, then you were going to have to hide them.

Daddy had forked out for the outfit. £375 on a cream blouse and canary yellow skirt suit. Yellow was a bold colour. Bold colours, as Marina had guessed, and MacAllister had confirmed, were important, so a bold colour it was.

The outfit would go on later. In the meantime, Marina shoved on her 'Jesus'. Marina called her dressing gown 'Jesus'. She called all dressing gowns 'Jesus'. When she was wee, every time she saw a picture of Jesus, he was, like something out a catalogue, wearing a dressing gown. The two became one.

Marina checked on MacAllister. No change. Ah well, one down, three to go. Not that she intended sleeping with all of them, mind, but, thing was, Marina had to win them over. MacAllister had given her tips, pointers. Marina had taken notes.

Getting off with MacAllister hadn't been a problem. The man did have a reputation. Through a friend of daddy's, she knew where to find him. She called in and made like she was waiting for a girlfriend. MacAllister had spotted her.

It was that easy.

To be fair, he wasn't entirely without charm. All things considered, Marina supposed she'd had a good night. He'd never taken his eyes off her the once. He wasn't shy when it came to parting with the pennies either. Even at the end of the night, after some fairly serious spending, he was still left holding a wad that would choke a spin-drier.

Marina lost count of the number of times he'd been asked for his autograph. On each occasion, he'd came away with something different, some different message, always something personal. Yet it wasn't an intrusion. It was all part of the night out. All part of being MacAllister.

This guy was famous. Even though he'd no discernible talent, no obvious skills, no track record of worthwhile achievement. Simply famous for being famous.

Just like Marina wanted.

Still in her Jesus, Marina crawled over the top of him, over to the other side of the bed. On the bedside table was a napkin with a number written down. Marina picked up her phone then dialled.

Of all places, a ringing came from under his pillow. (Christ, to think, he slept with it under his pillow!)

What happened next was probably, well, normal.

Like a kettle of bricks clanging to the boil, the snoring stopped. As if conditioned to do such, the straightened arm, the poised arm, retracted and pulled out a mobile phone from under the pillow.

'MacAllister,' said a voice familiar to millions. 'What's happening?'

While the studious and conscientious Moses – not his real name, by the way, just a nickname – painstakingly analysed the sports pages, the world-weary Oracle contented himself with the charms of *The Scotsman*'s daily cryptic crossword. This was a task The Oracle set himself every morning, and a task he usually managed to accomplish before midday. The Oracle was never that busy, anyway. Sure, he still did the odd piece, maybe a couple of times a week, but, for the most part, he was content to live off his reputation, and earn easy money from writing the links for the man who put the 'W' into anchor, sports anchor Sinclair Stevens. And you couldn't really get started on that till later in the day, till you knew for certain what was going to be going out.

Mind you, that said, today's crossword was proving to be a bit of a scunner.

The Oracle just couldn't get the top half going at all. It all had to do with this 1 across. A,S (9,4). That was the clue, the whole clue. A,S (9,4). So far, all he knew was that it started with an A, the fifth letter was R, and the whole thing ended with S.

Even so, The Oracle would persevere. Cryptic crosswords were, he reasoned, not unlike life. The way he seen it, there always came this point when you were stuck, truly stuck. Yet he knew he had the confidence, the God-given confidence, to overcome. He knew that, given enough time, and making the most of his patience and experience, there was never a clue, a problem, that didn't have an obvious and exact solution. Just like life.

The Oracle was always coming away with these wee homilies. Indeed, he was famed for them. Equally, he was famed for the obviousness and exactness of his reporting. A fame which even stretched beyond his chosen field, to such an extent that his *Something Personal: Selected Journalism 1960–1990* had just, to absolutely nobody's surprise, been voted one of the hundred best books of the century.

While most of the articles in said tome were word-for-word reproductions of the originals, the studious and conscientious Moses – who, incidentally, grew up idolising The Oracle with the same sort of fervour his contemporaries reserved for the pop stars of the day – couldn't help but notice how the ever-popular globe-trotting extracts – following the national team's World Cup exploits, covering the Olympics, etc. – were missing certain key elements which characterized the original pieces. This was never more than a couple of paragraphs wherein The Oracle would do his Alan Whicker, investigating the local cuisine, say, doing something that would now be described as classically touristy. Within this context, The Oracle would come across some helpful individual, some local, and proceed to wax lyrical: praising their kindness, their looks, their cheery smiles. These were sweet little segments, free of bias, full of wonder. The young Moses used to love them. Indeed, as much as anything, these pieces, and those segments in particular, went on to form Moses, giving him a basis upon which to embark on his journalistic career.

When he first joined up at the station, Moses, once he'd got over the initial awe at sharing office space with his boyhood hero, had taken time out to ask The Oracle why these little touristy segments hadn't appeared in the finished anthology. The Oracle took a whitey. 'Eh,' he said, 'maybe, in retrospect, they were a wee bit patronizing; you know, a wee bit too of their time.'

Moses could see that. After all, not everybody could have been that obliging, that nice, that kind.

Unless, of course, as MacAllister – who else – was only too willing to point out, descriptions were simply nothing but thinly-veiled accounts of The Oracle's dalliances with the local ladies of the night.

Entering The Totem (from FAC totem, MacAllister's witty nickname for Forth and Clyde's cylindrical headquarters), it was as if Sinclair was walking on air. They were all looking at him, some even giggled, but, tellingly, not a one said a thing. Well, what if he was a wee bit over-dressed. Surely that was the point. And definitely the point that, before the day was done, they would all be talking about.

He'd got the six – the Big Six – so Sinclair was wearing the six.

Sinclair Stevens was wearing six ties.

At every set of traffic lights, and at every junction, folk had stopped to stare. Even bombing along the M8, Sinclair was sure folk had noticed.

Just like last night, it was that obvious.

Sinclair took a wander round The Totem before going to his desk. They were all going to see him, the way he was dressed, the way he was carrying, brandishing, the evidential video. Sinclair wanted to be talked about. He went to one photocopy machine, then another. Then one coffee machine, then another. Then the snack machine. Then the canteen.

Nobody said a thing.

Sinclair Stevens was wearing six ties and nobody said a thing. Yet they were all dying to. They were all dying to know why Sinclair was wearing six horizontal stripey ties. They were all dying to know what was on the video.

Course they were.

Eventually, Sinclair made it to Level Six. (Six? Level Six? Everything was Six! Six on the brain!)

Station Controller Bob Sutherland was in the video room, no doubt brushing up on his management training tape. The sap that was Moses and the perv that was The Oracle were going through their morning papers, determinedly going out of their way not to notice or engage Sinclair. Such patience. Such mighty patience. It would be rewarded.

As soon as Bob Sutherland was out the video room.

Yeah, as soon as Bob was done.

Sinclair reached his desk.

There was a note and a blue folder there waiting for him; a note from Bob Sutherland.

'Study this. You've to meet and greet them off the lift. Reception'll phone.'

Sinclair picked up the blue folder. A yellow post-it was slapped on the front.

'The Weathers and their Famous Fathers.'

'Fuck,' said Sinclair. 'Oh, Jesus fuck.'

Finally, Marina had plucked up enough courage to try on her outfit. She checked herself in front of her full-length mirror. Just by looking, there was no way could you tell if she had breasts. There was no sense of movement, no tell-tale shape, nothing. Good.

The appointment was for half-one. MacAllister had said to get there early. Best to get accustomed to the environment. Some folk, apparently, just went to pieces when they were in a TV studio. Anyway, Marina wanted to get in early. She still had the three to work on: Sinclair, Moses and The Oracle.

Following Marina's wake-up call, almost straight afterwards

in fact, MacAllister had received another one. This time it was business, a tip-off, telling him to get to the airport. A quick call to the studio, to request a crew and, next thing, MacAllister was, as he put it, on the job. This, he said, was going to be big. Massive. He'd see Marina later. He promised he'd be at the audition.

Marina took one last look at the mirror. She looked great. The others didn't stand a snowball's. She was, to use daddy's favourite expression, a pound of fish in a factory full of liver.

Every reason to be confident, Marina gave it her best perfect-teeth smile. The smile that was going to grace tomorrow's papers, a glass of champagne in one hand, an umbrella in the other.

Yeah, it would be that easy.

The airport tip-off had been close – but, alas, no divine ponytail. The Mr R. Baggio that was booked on the incoming flight from Rome turned out to be nothing more exciting than a portly restaurateur who rejoiced in the name of Reinaldo.

Even so, MacAllister still decided to film the event.

Scene 1
MacAllister, with big banana smile, holding up a bit of card with Mr R. Baggio on it.

Scene 2
MacAllister (thrusting mic in front of portly person): 'Roberto, Roberto, can this really be you?'
Reinaldo (laughing, patting ample belly): 'No. No. No.'

Scene 3
Cut to long-shot of crowd with an animated MacAllister

and an amused Reinaldo very much the centre of attention.

Scene 4
MacAllister (close-up): 'So, for the benefit of all our viewers,
all our millions of viewers, can you confirm for once and for
all that you will not be signing in time for this weekend's
crucial clash?'

Scene 5
Reinaldo (laughing): 'No, Partick Thistle! Partick Thistle! The
Harry Rags!'

Scene 6
MacAllister (flanked by a couple of giggling stewardesses,
surrounded by a jostling crowd): 'Well, there you have it,
straight from the mouth of the horse's head, the Mr R.
Baggio on Air Italia flight 21578 from Rome was not Roberto
of that ilk, repeat not Roberto of that ilk, and will not
be turning out for the hoops this weekend. This has been
Gian-Franco MacAllister, for Forth and Clyde Today, down
at the airport.'

Big cheer from the crowd.

Cut.

And all that, which would, if used, make for nothing more than
a two-minute clip, had been timed by the crew – Kenny the
cameraman and Stevie the soundman – as having taken them
the best part of an hour and a half to script, set up and film.

*   *   *

Moses gave in.

'"Six horizontal stripeys?" "Six horizontal stripeys?" All bloody morning, phone's never stopped. "Why's he wearing six horizontal stripey ties?" "What's he got all those ties on for?" Okay, on behalf of the station, and probably the nation: why've you been wandering about all morning looking like something out of Bad Taste Uni's rag week?'

Sinclair's moment had arrived, the moment of triumph. 'At last,' he said. 'At last. Through you come, boys, through you come. This'll blow you away, this will.'

Moses and The Oracle followed Sinclair through to the video room with the big, comfy sofa and the big-screen TV.

Sinclair slapped in the tape, settled back and basked in the anticipated glory.

First up on screen was John Suchet going on about the volcano that was due to erupt in Malaysia. Then there was Martyn Lewis going on about the volcano that was due to erupt in Malaysia. Then Jon Snow, Peter Sissons, Trevor MacDonald, and finally, Jeremy Paxman. All going on about the volcano that was due to erupt in Malaysia.

Sinclair pressed pause.

'Well, impressed or what?'

'What,' said The Oracle, 'at a volcano going off in Malaysia? What's this, you taking a long-overdue interest in global affairs or something?'

'Now, Orca, don't you be sarcy. Think back, what did all the newsreaders have in common?'

'Eh,' said Moses, 'patronizing attitude? Distinct lack of regional accent? Nothing out of the ordinary there really. Funny thing with the news, the big news: ever watch it with the sound off? Should. Should try that sometime. Quite interesting. You really see how right-wing and pro-establishment the presentation is, the whole presentation. It's all about images, flags and all of that, respect for authority.'

'Moses,' said Sinclair, 'shut up, will you. We're not talking about that. Yet we are, funnily enough, in a more direct way, a more fundamental way, concerned with, as you put it, the notion of presentation.'

Moses went in the huff. He didn't like being called Moses. He didn't even know why he was being called Moses. Far as he minded, he was five minutes in the door, next thing somebody happened to overhear him talking about some obvious and blatant social injustice, and that was that – he was forever Moses.

'Just to get a move on,' said The Oracle, 'just so's I can get back to my crossword, could all this carry-on maybe have something to do with them six ties presently, and, in my humble opinion, rather regrettably, failing to strangle your tender wee thrapple?'

'Getting there. More, though. Come on.'

'*And*, the six ties you're wearing could all be described as being of a horizontal stripey persuasion.'

'Yeah. Yeah. I'll give you that.'

'*And*, the six ties as worn by last night's news anchors were likewise all of a horizontal stripey persuasion.'

Sinclair beamed. 'Exactly. No bother at all, eh? Always said you had it in you. Just waiting to pop out. Now, to take you back, way back, oh, about five, six weeks ago; if you would be so kind, remind me, tell Uncle Sinclair, what did you boys say when I first wore a horizontal stripey? Did you boys not say it was "stupid"? Did you boys not say, it would never catch on? And did I not tell you that within six weeks everybody would be wearing them?'

Sinclair rewound then replayed the tape.

'Now *that* is everybody. The Gods. Where Sinclair leads others follow.'

Sinclair was laughing. There was something else that probably deserved to be commented on, but Sinclair just couldn't bring himself.

He just stared instead, stared and pointed.

Because, today, John the postboy was wearing a horizontal stripey. Ditto Station Controller Bob Sutherland. And so, God bless him, was the wise and wizened Oracle. Thin stripes to be sure, but stripes nonetheless. Horizontal stripes. Only the sap that was Moses was stripeless. But then again Moses, the new kid on the block, all ideals and infallibility, would never be seen dead wearing something quite so decadent as a tie. See Moses was a rebel. Moses only wore collar-buttoned polo shirts. Black collar-buttoned polo shirts.

After the filming was complete, MacAllister and co. retreated to the chrome splendour of the airport bar. It was time to engage in some serious bonding (and, hopefully, blagging) with the portly Reinaldo and his Glasgow-based nephew Luigi – proprietor of the new and exclusive west-end restaurant which bore his name, an establishment some were already saying was well on its way to becoming the nation's finest purveyor of upmarket Latin cuisine.

First, not surprisingly, MacAllister and co. talked about football, then, once that was out of the way, they moved on to the far more serious subject of food, with MacAllister – surprise, surprise – being offered an invitation round to the fore-mentioned eatery.

MacAllister, though, all umm-ing and ah-ing, said that tonight was looking to be a special night. There was this girl, you see, a friend of his – as it happened, a very good friend of his – and, well, today was kind of shaping up to be a very special day for her.

Reinaldo and Luigi were affronted. Was MacAllister saying that they couldn't prepare something special? That they couldn't make the young lady feel special?

No, said MacAllister, it was just that . . .

Well, that was that then, settled. Reinaldo and Luigi were adamant. MacAllister and lady-friend would be appearing at Luigi's. Eight o' clock. Only the best.

To begin with, MacAllister was looking sheepish, but soon a familiar mischievous grin came to rest on his fleshy face.

Who said there was no such thing as a free lunch?

Christ, if you were of a certain mind – like, say, Kenny the cameraman and Stevie the soundman – you could maybe even have thought MacAllister had planned it that way. Planned the whole damn thing.

MacAllister said he had to go and make a call, pass on the good news. He went out into the foyer and phoned Marina, telling her how the celebration dinner was already arranged. Luigi's, he said. Just think, Luigi's.

Marina had been in a taxi on her way to the studio. She was well chuffed. Luigi's! Wow! Even daddy would be impressed by that.

MacAllister wished her all the luck in the world – as if she needed it – then returned to the others.

The three new friends were soon giggling and carrying on like new lads. Reinaldo and Luigi anticipating the free publicity. MacAllister anticipating the free night out.

Before long, everybody in the airport bar was feeding on the good vibes coming from the MacAllister table. Tourists were aware that something was going on. Locals were saying, 'That's him! That's him off the telly! I'm telling you, that's MacAllister.' Youngsters were despatched to collect his autograph.

In fact, the only two folk present who weren't in on the atmosphere were Kenny the cameraman and Stevie the soundman. They'd buggered off to have a go on the arcade-style Formula One game, where Kenny was currently breaking all records, while Stevie, waiting his turn, was sipping from a trusty pint of iced tap water.

Marina introduced herself at reception. She was told to go to Level Six. Somebody, she was assured, would meet and greet her there.

To set her at ease, a leafy, tropical pot plant was resting in the corner of the mirrored lift. A million miles from home, it didn't seem the slightest out of place. Neither did the in-house muzak, a cheesy children's choir doing 'Soul Man'.

Just as Marina was beginning to feel totally relaxed and in control – this place was just so her – the lift stopped at the sixth floor.

The doors opened.

And there was Sinclair. (Marina remembered to gush.) Wow!

And he was wearing six ties. (Marina remembered to gush.) Wow!

'Hi. Pleased to meet you. Sinclair, Sinclair Stevens.'

'I know,' gushed Marina. 'Marina, Marina Wilson.'

Sinclair checked his big blue folder. The Weathers and their Famous Fathers. 'Ah, yes. So you're one of the lucky candidates then, yeah?'

Marina nodded.

'Come here,' said Sinclair. 'Before we get started, and I show you round a bit, there's something very special I want you to see first. Something that really encapsulates what this business is all about.'

They went over to this side-room, the video room, with the big, comfy sofa and the big-screen TV. As they went in, Marina took time out to look around. She could see Moses, The Oracle and a man she didn't recognize but assumed to be Station Controller Bob Sutherland.

Marina smiled. She let her smile linger in the direction of The Oracle till she got a response, the merest of flusters. MacAllister had said to do that. In fact, according to MacAllister, The Oracle being The Oracle, that would probably be enough.

So far, so good.

Now for Sinclair. (Marina remembered to gush.)

Without so much as a word, Marina followed Sinclair into the side-room, and sat down, right next to him, on the big, comfy sofa, to watch all these snippets of all these newsreaders going on about the volcano that was due to erupt in Malaysia.

'See,' said Sinclair, once the tape had run its course, 'what all this is about, right: in a word, *presentation*. I was the first, okay, the first to wear a horizontal stripey. Six weeks ago. They all laughed at me. But I said no, just you wait, one day, one day this would happen – and now it has. This was just last night. Great, eh? You know sometimes, Marina, I go out at dinnertime and just drive round, just to see all these business types heading out for their extended lunches. I like to see what they're wearing. And you know something, I'll always see a few, one or two, whose hair, or shirt, or suit, is the same as mine was the week before. What a feeling that is, Marina. That's power. You know I get letters from hairdressers, old-fashioned barbers, telling me how folk, young lads, trendy young lads, the hippest of the hip, go in and ask for cuts like mine. They take in photos, out of newspapers – really, honest, they do – and say, "Here. This is what I want. I want a Sinclair." Marina, see, what I'm trying to say is – this is all about working on your *presentation*. If you don't learn anything else today, learn that. *Presentation*. The way you present yourself.'

Up until a few moments ago, Marina had still been acting out her script to win over Sinclair. MacAllister'd said that, in real life, as in his art, the guy was a rampant egomaniac. The way to woo him, to win him over, was to massage that ego. Go on about how great he was.

What Marina hadn't bargained for was how she would actually be into him. Not physically, not emotionally, not to fancy or anything, but into what he was saying.

That's right. Marina was smitten. Already smitten with the all-too-glamorous world of regional TV.

This was amazing. This was exactly what she was wanting. Power without responsibility.

Throughout her life, Marina'd had all these hopes and dreams, daft dreams, day-dreams, about the way things could turn out. Boys. Opportunities. Even books and films. But things never – *never* – met your wildest expectations. In the real world, nobody ever said what you wanted them to say. Nobody ever did what you wanted them to do.

Until now.

Marina was into this, well into it. She'd met a kindred spirit. Imagine her choosing something that would be seen by millions. Imagine her choosing something that would end up being worn by . . . Anna Ford! Jill Dando! No, this was better than the real world. This was the world where tropical pot plants flourished in mirrored lifts, where a cheesy children's choir could sing 'Soul Man', and where a well-known TV presenter could wander about wearing six ties.

'You see, Marina,' continued Sinclair, 'as you've probably gathered, it's all a bit larger than life round here. And, to fit in, to be successful, you've got to be prepared to be larger than life. To be bold. To assert yourself. Understand what I'm saying?'

Sinclair took Marina by the hand.

'You know, when I was young, Marina, all those years ago, only stars worked in telly. To me, to my generation, and I suppose yours too, there wasn't any difference between who was on the telly and who was in the films. Ena Sharples? Errol Flynn? They were just stars. They were just the same. It was what I always wanted to do, to be a star. I told my folks. I told my friends. I told my careers officer. You can well imagine their reaction. Yet I was determined. I wanted to work in that netherworld, where you can get to dictate your own reality, where you become so famous that everything is a direct response to you. And, you know something, Marina, I'm there and it's great. You follow, yeah?'

Marina nodded.

'Marina, I know what you've been through. The sneers. The laughter. Believe me, it was the same for Sinclair. I remember it well. When I left the school it was the dole, a scheme, uni or, if you were really, really good, and really, really successful — then you ended up doing the same crappy job for forty years that your dad had been doing for forty years.'

Sinclair stopped for a laugh before he went on.

'My dad was, and still is, a butcher. He browses through beef. That's what he does. That's what he does for a living. Browses through beef. You never want to do that, Marina. See the generation that our parents belonged to, they were stifled. In turn, they tried to stifle us.'

Sinclair took Marina's hand again.

'And what does your dad do, Marina? What crappy job does he do?'

Marina's mouth was open, but she wasn't saying anything.

'Marina?' said Sinclair. 'Marina? Don't be shy. Don't be ashamed. Tell me. Tell Uncle Sinclair. Come on. Blurt it out.'

Marina gulped. 'Well,' she said, 'since you asked, to be perfectly honest, he's just been appointed Chancellor of the Exchequer.'

Head of arts and entertainment at FAC TV (Forth and Clyde Television) was the redoubtable Lindy Anderson. Lindy produced and presented the weekly *New Impressions*, a late-night magazine affair which highlighted the work of local artists, writers and performers. Her annual remit also included responsibility for the high-profile coverage of the Edinburgh Festival, and the scheduling on Burns Night, St Andrews Night and Hogmanay.

That said, within the walls of The Totem, The Arts were dismissed as FAF TV, seeing as how market research – that most contemporary of gods – had shown how the only folk who ever bothered to watch *New Impressions* were the friends and families (the FAFs) of those who were lined up to appear on any given programme.

This being the case, Lindy worked away on an annual budget which was but mere pennies compared to the vast amount that found its way flying into the coffers of Lindy's avowed enemies – namely FAC TV's football reporters from the early evening news. To name names: the smarmy Sinclair;

the disgusting MacAllister; the pathetic Moses; and the kerb-crawling old git that was The Oracle.

When it came to her career at FAC TV, Lindy was far from the happiest of souls. An unhappiness which was further compounded by some news she'd just received that very morning. See Lindy had been in line for a presenting stint on the rejuvenated *Late Show*, the much-missed BBC2 arts and entertainment flagship. Such was the knowledgeable Lindy's renowned enthusiasm for all things arty, she was virtually head-hunted. Calls were made. Would she be interested? What were her ideas? When could she start?

All was going well, right up until the very last moment, when somebody down south, through some as yet unnamed source, had got wind of a certain weakness of Lindy's. Sure, she could present no problem, she could analyse and articulate with the best of them, at all times displaying a contagious enthusiasm, a keen curiosity and an expertise that was never bluffed. No, it was more to do with interviews. It wasn't so much that she couldn't interview, couldn't probe and promote debate; no, the problem was all to do with Lindy's body language – a body language which, once you took time out to stop and study it, was about as subtle as your average lap-dancer's, or, more accurately, about as subtle as your average lap-dancer's punter.

To put it bluntly, Lindy was in slavering awe, and consequently was known to fling herself at anything in trousers with product to promote. Being Lindy, painters and poets, those most tortured and oblique of souls, were the principal prey. Devoid of the petulance of actors and the politics of authors, such caressers of the canvas and masters of the pentameter projected an intensity which had an almost chemical effect on the essentially likeable Lindy.

Such attentions, mind you, though nearly always appreciated – painters and poets being notoriously obliging with
their affections – were not exactly, in the words of the
BBC, 'becoming for someone in line for such an esteemed
position'. Before she was even started, Lindy was bombed-out
and binned.

So, for the time being, she was stuck doing FAF TV at
FAC TV, with her *New Impressions*, her Edinburgh Festival,
her Burns Night, her St Andrews Night and her Hogmanay.

On a day-to-day basis, Lindy also made a series of shorts
for the regional news programme, *Forth and Clyde Today*,
focusing on community arts projects, and local folk made good.
This morning she was in Kirkintilloch, making a two-minute
feature on a promising new artist called Grant MacSwegan.
Self-taught, the young Grant had taken advantage of a deal at
his local high street chemist's and turned one of his paintings
into a series of a hundred postcards, which he'd promptly
sent out to his hundred heroes. One of whom happened to
be the popular singer and actress Madonna. Having received
the card, Madonna promptly responded, offering to buy the
original painting for £7000, a deal the unemployed Grant was
only too happy to accept.

Hence the story.

Something else Grant was only too happy to accept were
the amorous advances of the essentially likeable Lindy.

Currently, in the kitchen of the Kirkintilloch community
centre, the pair of them were chewing each other's faces
off.

Meanwhile, on the other side of the shuttered servery, in
the canteen of the Kirkintilloch Community Centre, waited
the ever-patient crew, Kenny the cameraman with his sidekick
Stevie the soundman. Kenny, sitting on one table, polishing his

lenses; Stevie, sitting on another table, combing the fur on his boom microphone.

The candidates had all arrived. Having been met by Sinclair – and granted the same sarcy intro – they were then given a brief tour which culminated in being shown to the waiting room, where they were presented with single-page A4 handouts. These handouts were the only instructions on offer. No questions would be allowed. No further guidelines would be given. There would be no interviews as such, just the auditions.

Marina stole a glance. On the face of it, the others were five very attractive young women. For all anybody knew, they could've been models. Very quiet. Very smartly dressed. Very pleasant.

Mind you, Marina could tell a lot from a stolen glance.

i) Shirley was the voice off *AA Roadwatch*. Sure she was pretty enough – pretty for radio, anyway – but she wouldn't get in with that hair. Trouble was, it was so curly and wiry, if you'd a mind to, you could easily've used it to scrape clean your week-old pots and pans. Nah, everybody knew you weren't allowed curly hair. Not a written-down rule – like breasts – just an accepted one. Shirley's father was the last but one moderator for the Church of Scotland. Only Moses, if nicknames counted for anything, would be impressed by that. And Marina still had to work on Moses.

ii) Jean had dodgy ears. Awfy big for such a young lassie. And then there was the dodgy nose, a bit too masculine. Nah, that wouldn't stand up to profile shots. Gave her a certain undue harshness. Jean claimed to be a direct descendant of Sir Walter Scott. Now that, it has to be said, sounded not only dodgy, but desperate.

iii) Nicola's fingers looked to be marginally inflated. If anything, they reminded you, ever so slightly, of the Incredible Hulk's. Marina stole another glance, looking for the tell-tale sign. And, sure enough, there it was — calves that only a mother could love. She might've been a size eight, but Nicola was a closet podgy. Nicola's father used to captain Scotland at rugby. Good enough background for being a loser.

iv) Madge's hair was really thick, and really dark. Black as tar, thick as tar. Her father was a former Liverpool stalwart of the early Eighties who, notoriously, was always injured when called upon to play for the national side. Madge had no chance.

v) That just left Iona. Iona was the problem. She had straight hair, a sweet name and an equally sweet face. She also had a really dodgy tooth, a squint one, right smack in the front. Normally, that would be a strict no-no but an old boyfriend of Marina's, her first karate instructor, had once told her how imperfect teeth were unbelievably sexy to the older man. Marina had been fifteen at the time and just out of braces. You can well imagine how she felt.

Iona might have been plain — straight hair, straight face, straight figure — but she was also very pretty, almost boyishly so. The Oracle would be into her. Marina would have to work on The Oracle. Unlike the rest, Iona wasn't born into money. Her father was one of the first big-money lottery winners, now a successful hotelier. The sort of person whose name meant nothing but who, when given a few prompts, would be an undeniable source of short-term media curiosity. Yeah, Iona was the one to watch.

So that was them, the contenders. Curly, Dodgy, Podgy, Tar-head and Squint-tooth.

The more Marina thought about it, the more the others could be discounted. The tooth was the problem. If Iona knew how to use that tooth, how to exploit it, then she could be a serious threat to Marina's career prospects.

But, Marina reminded herself, there was also one major saving grace.

The tooth.

The tooth itself – the problem – was also a saving grace.

They wouldn't let that tooth on.

No way.

Sure, you could be good-looking; but no way, absolutely no way, were you allowed to be sexy.

That was one of the rules.

One of the written-down rules.

Station Controller Bob Sutherland always stood up when you went into his office. He'd seen this on his management training video. According to the video, what you were to do to avoid Problem No. 1 – *Those You Don't Particularly Want to See* – was just to stand up, gather a few pieces of paper, then leave. And when you were management, you didn't even need to bother with giving an excuse, you just went for a wee walk round the corridors, in this case round the Totem, photocopied something, then, once the coast was clear, came back again. In response to any barked-out query or gripe, all you were to say was, 'Yeah. Leave it with me. No problem.' (The training video only mentioned 'Leave it with me.' The 'Yeah' and 'No problem' were improvs. Bob liked to improvise.)

So when FAC TV's head of arts and entertainment, Lindy Anderson, returned from her interview with the young Grant

MacSwegan, the Kirkintilloch Caravaggio, and stormed into Bob's office in best Katharine Hepburn style, Bob duly got up, gathered a few bits of paper, then made to leave.

Lindy blocked the way.

'D'you know what they're up to out there?' she said.

'Yeah,' said Bob. 'No problem. Leave it with me.'

(Shit, damn and blast! He'd got them in the wrong order.)

'No,' asserted Lindy. 'Problem! Big problem. Big, big problem. And d'you know what they're saying? They're saying it was your idea. They're actually saying that all this was your stupid idea.'

And, okay, if truth be known, so it was. It had been Bob's (stupid) idea to have today's auditions for the post of brand new weather girl adjudicated by the four sports reporters from the early evening news: Sinclair, MacAllister, Moses and The Oracle.

Overseen, of course, by the mighty Bob himself. Cause, when you stopped and thought about it, it was only fair and just that the head of FAC TV should be taking an interest in the appointment of his underlings. Besides, the attendant publicity would be massive. Just think. The four sports reporters in one photo! With a pretty girl! An umbrella in one hand, a glass of champagne in the other! The papers were gagging for it.

'I just can't believe this,' said Lindy. 'What d'you think you're playing at? The 1970s or something?'

Given Lindy's determination, Bob was forced to consider an option he never normally gave so much as a fancy to: Bob was going to have to try and talk his way out of this. Most times he could just rely on facts and figures and the god that was market research. Seeing as how, in those terms, Forth and Clyde wasn't doing at all badly. In fact, in the eighteen short months of Bob's tenure, FAC TV had not only maintained but actually strengthened its position as by far and away the most successful of ITV's regional outlets.

And by far and away the most successful programme, the station's crowning glory, was the early evening local news which, unless there was a disaster (for some unfathomable reason folk always watched their disaster coverage on the BBC) never slipped below the seventy mark. The god that was market research had shown that the right blend for local news was to have two female presenters (mid to late thirties), three female correspondents (early twenties) reporting on, respectively, crime and human interest, business and politics, and arts and entertainments – and, last but not least, at least four males to present expert and in-depth nightly analysis of the football.

Lindy, God bless her, was never entirely happy about any of this, but especially not the last bit.

'They're scum,' she said. 'Tell me, what are they supposed to be looking for exactly? Come on, tell me!'

Eh, thought Bob, no, maybe talking this through wasn't such a good idea.

The next thing in Bob's management training video (Problem No. 2: *What to Do When One of Your Minions Gets Really Stroppy*) was to say, 'I've made my decision. My final decision. Anything goes wrong, it'll be me that has to carry the can. That good enough for you?'

That should do the trick.

'Well,' said Bob, this time adopting a thoroughly more positive and potentially powerful air, determined not to get his words in the wrong order, 'I've made my decision. My final decision. Anything goes wrong, it'll be me that has to carry the can. That good enough for you?'

'Bull-*shit*,' said Lindy, this time adopting a thoroughly more negative and potentially knife-wielding air, 'there's not even an attempt at pretence. I don't know why you just don't go the whole hog, bring in Eric Morley, have them parade in bloody swimsuits and be done with it.'

Bob consulted his memory; there was an asterisked addendum to Problem No. 2: *When Minions Get Really Stroppy, Threaten to Call Security.*

'I'm afraid,' said Bob, 'if you don't leave the office this minute, I'm going to have to threaten to phone security.'

'Ih?' said Lindy.

Shit, thought the shame-faced Bob, you didn't say you were going to threaten to phone security, you *threatened* to phone security.

When he finally arrived back at the office, after his morning bonding with Reinaldo and Luigi, MacAllister made straight for Marina.

The six girls were sitting in the waiting room, silently studying their sheets of A4.

But, unlike last night, it wasn't Marina who grabbed the attention and stirred the MacAllister loins.

No, this time, it was the one with the tooth!

Yeah, the squint one. Right at the front. Jesus, it didn't even squint, like most folks, in the way; no, this one squinted out the way, as sure as a bunker-bound slice.

The sliced tooth.

God, was it sexy.

And, better still, its owner was giving him the eye.

Nice one.

Now all football reporters have this eternal problem: the public demand to know which team you support. If you express a preference, then you run the risk of alienating a huge chunk of your potential audience. However, if you don't express a preference then, well, folk just don't believe you, and history – market research – has shown how they'll go off and get their information from some other source.

Yet MacAllister, great man that he was, had managed to overcome this most complicated of concerns. Like the really annoying kid at school, he simply switched teams all the time.

And so it was with his women.

It meant nothing that last night, and this morning, he was with Marina. The girl with the tooth – Iona – was now the one he was pinning his hopes on.

The only problem was, to get rid of Marina.

Now, earlier on, back at her flat, Marina had been expressing her fears about winning over the support of Moses and The Oracle. So, what better to do than to point Marina in the direction of Moses and The Oracle. Then leave them.

Surprise surprise, that's exactly what MacAllister did.

A mere few moments later MacAllister was back in the waiting room, ostensibly introducing himself to the other girls, and instigating a blether.

Yet, in less than a minute, and with an execution of intent that was almost admirable, MacAllister had homed in, uprooted Iona and was off showing her round the video room.

Impressive.

Equally impressive was MacAllister's way, this unique approach, he had with women he fancied. When he met 'new booty' for the first time, what he did was to stare them in the eye, ask them really obvious questions, and then proceed to disagree with everything they said.

To be sure, a singular approach, but an approach which was

noted not only for its blatant unpleasantness, but also for its remarkably high success rate.

Over the years, many folk, in the interests of research, and to satisfy, among many things, a sense of blatant envy, had gone and tried to copy this technique. It wasn't easy. Disagreement, by definition, necessitated repeated shakings of the head, which, as you can well imagine, tended to confuse, if not totally terminate, the essential eye contact.

MacAllister, mind you, was the undoubted master.

'So,' he said, 'you're up for the post then, eh?'

'Yeah,' said Iona. 'It seems really nice round here. A nice, friendly bunch.'

'Nice? Friendly? You joking or something?' MacAllister laughed. 'Most days, about as nice and friendly as a pair of barbed wire kecks. Nine times out of ten, there's enough aggro in here to call in a UN peace force.' MacAllister stopped for a second, intensified his eye contact, then added, 'So, d'you like being a girl then, eh?'

'What?'

'A girl, d'you like being a girl?'

'Well,' said Iona, 'yeah, suppose so.'

'Never wish you were a man, no?'

'No, not really.'

'Bet you do. Bet every morning you wish you never had to bother with bras and dresses and all of that carry-on, eh?'

Iona started to giggle. She turned her head away.

'High heels,' said MacAllister, straining to maintain the all-important eye contact, 'must be fucking hellish.'

'They're not so bad,' said Iona. 'Once you get used to them.'

'Rubbish. Trainers and sandals. You trying to tell me you wouldn't prefer to be wearing a pair of trainers?'

Iona giggled. 'Okay,' she said. 'I normally wear trainers.'

MacAllister liked trainers. Bare legs and big trainers. 'Listen,' he said, 'd'you fancy going out some time, doing something?'

'Okay,' said Iona. 'D'you have a pen and paper?'

'Yeah.' MacAllister dug into his pockets for pen and paper. Sometimes this was just all so easy.

'Well,' said Iona, 'once you've found them, your pen and paper, write down the number of that phone over there – see it? – and, as from Monday, give it a call and ask for Iona. Okay? Yeah?'

Marina, meanwhile, having been pointed in the direction of Moses and The Oracle, was busy working them. The Oracle, mind, was strictly easy-peasy. For all the poor old bugger was pretending to be busy doing that crossword* of his, Marina could tell he was well taken by her. All she'd had to do was look at him, gently rub her inner thigh and, well, that was that. An anchor-jawed Oracle.

Moses, mind you, the great crusader, the tireless campaigner, would be requiring more tact. He might have favoured black collar-buttoned polo shirts but, in real terms, Moses was about as straight as his biblical namesake. He was also, according to MacAllister, very shy. So sexy was out. Being a friend was more important. The sort of friend he'd never had. Like the popular girl at school who'd never got round to speaking to him. The popular girl who seemed to take an interest in everybody apart from Moses. The popular girl who,

---

* The top half, by the way, was still spartan but, if you're interested, 1 across (A, S) was now A blank blank blank R blank blank U blank and then blank I blank S.

so legend had it, had shagged just about everybody in fifth and sixth year. No, Moses would want reassurance that she hadn't shagged just about everybody in fifth and sixth year, that she was just a nice person.

That was the plan then. To take interest. To reassure. To be a nice person.

Marina stood over Moses, watching him, taking in everything, trying to look curious, looking for something to comment on. Thankfully, she didn't have to. In a moment that was almost romantic, she managed to catch his eye. Marina smiled shyly. Moses smiled back. Already, his ears were starting to go red.

Good.

Now to get going.

What did she want to do? She wanted to talk.

Okay then.

'Did you hear about the fat polar bear?'

'Sorry,' said Moses.

'The fat polar bear? D'you not hear about him?'

Moses shook his head. 'No.'

'Well,' said Marina, scrunching her shoulders. 'He broke the ice.' Marina extended her hand. 'Marina, Marina Wilson.'

Moses laughed, shook the hand, and gave his name.

'What you working on?' said Marina.

'Eh, doing a feature tonight on, eh, why players from the Highland League are never considered for selection for the national side.'

Marina nodded. It would be a bit daft to feign interest in the subject – she'd already forgotten what he'd said – but she could she supposed feign interest in the process.

'So, how long would you be working on something like this?'

'Eh,' said Moses, 'couple of weeks maybe. But there's always two or three stories on the go, and, of course, there's always piles of new stuff coming in.'

'And you write your own scripts, and present them yourself?'

'Oh, aye. Yeah.'

'Must be great,' said Marina, 'to see something through, all the way from start to finish.'

'It is, yeah. Very satisfying.'

Marina nodded. And kept nodding. Moses, bless him, was now blushing all over. Trouble was Marina couldn't think of anything else to say. Normally, around this time, she'd start sending out signals. She had to remind herself not to.

'You never fancied doing something like this yourself,' said Moses. 'Some reporting.'

'Yeah,' said Marina. 'What I was thinking was maybe, see how it goes – if it goes, fingers crossed – then maybe take it from there. I'm not really the type to be tied to an office. Like to get stuck in, you know, like to get my hands dirty. Yeah, I'm quite single-minded when I get going.' Marina tapped the screen. 'Field work. Research. Writing it up. That's more what I'm into.' This was getting a bit awkward. Time to change the subject. What else had MacAllister said? Something about Moses being into – what was it again? Oh yeah, civil rights, all that kind of palaver.

'You're quite political yourself, aren't you?'

Moses sat back. He put his hands behind his head, like he was going to give a long speech – a long speech he was in the habit of giving.

'No, I wouldn't say political exactly. That gives you the visions of the men in grey suits. I just see myself as being the guy who covers the issues that nobody else bothers to 'cause

a) there's too much unrewarding work involved, or b) there's an off-chance you'd maybe ruffle a few moneyed feathers.'

Moses sat forward again, tapping his pencil on his keyboard.

He wasn't finished. Marina knew he wasn't finished. Surprisingly, for such a dweeb, he was an arrogant sod.

'Like this Highland League thing, there's a lot more to this than meets the eye, you know. The piece is going out tonight, so, for the time being, it's finished, in the can, but, don't you worry, I'll come back to it. Yeah, I'll be back.'

'I'll keep a close watch,' said Marina. 'Anyway, talking of getting back, I better see what's happening.'

'Okay. Yeah. Nice meeting you. Best of luck and all that.'

'Thanks. Fingers crossed.' Marina crossed her fingers, then raised her eyebrows. She thought she could get away with that.

'Yeah,' said Moses. 'Fingers crossed.' Moses crossed his fingers. Then he, too, tried raising his eyebrows.

He was looking at her. He was enjoying looking at her. This girl was wonderful. Really pretty. Just the kind of girl he'd always wanted. Asking him all these questions. Yeah, she was interested, interested in him, interested in what he did. Yeah, Moses liked her. He definitely liked her.

In fact, she reminded him of someone – the only lass he'd ever loved – that lassie, that lassie from fifth and sixth year.

Moses' heart skipped a beat. To this day, she still had that effect on him.

'You not think it's about time you took those ridiculous ties off, eh?'

Sinclair shrugged.

'Look, I know what you're playing at; and no, you're not

going to wear them for the photos. This is the weather's big day, and for once, you're not taking over. Come on. Enough's enough.'

Problem No. 3 in the management training video was *How to Deal with Petulance*. And the way you dealt with petulance – otherwise known as utter stupidity – was to be serious, utterly serious.

'I'm being serious,' said Station Controller Bob Sutherland. 'I'm being utterly serious.'

'Look,' said Sinclair, 'have you seen it, have you seen the tape?'

'Yes, I've seen your tape.' It was still in the machine when, earlier on, after the Lindy débâcle, Bob'd been through, brushing up on his sloppy delivery. 'Yes, it's impressive. Yes, we'll maybe – maybe – leak it to the press. Maybe get you a mention in Moses' column or something. But no, you're not getting to wear them. This is just stupid. And another thing, while we're at it, what've you been saying to all these lassies?'

'What?'

'You know. Don't come it. You've been meeting them off the lift. The big handshakes. The big welcome. That's fine. Setting them at ease. Grand. But then – wham bam – next thing they know you're ripping the piss out of them for having famous dads.'

'Well, they've all got famous dads!'

'I know they've all got famous dads. That's why they're here.'

'What, they're here cause they've got famous dads? Funny, but I thought they were here cause they were up for the weather.'

'True. And it just so happens that, in this day and age, the god that is market research has shown that to be a weather, all you need is a pleasant personality, an O level in geography and a famous dad. Hence, our six candidates. Okay?'

'Jesus,' said Sinclair, 'what about star quality? What about talent, eh? You know if you were to trawl round every chip shop in this town I guarantee you, I promise you, you'd find a dozen, at least a dozen, with more star quality than this lot could muster between them.'

Bob shook his head. 'You have a problem with this, don't you?'

'No, funnily enough, I don't think *I've* got a problem with this. I think *you've* got a problem with this. And why are they all women? Is that not against some sort of trade descriptions act or something?'

'Sex equality act – and, no, it's not. Now, those ties, off.'

Sinclair shook his head. 'You don't understand. I had the six, I had the big six. And you just don't care. You just don't care, do you?'

Bob Sutherland thought for a second. There was an answer to that, an answer to 'you don't care'. And the answer was to be found on the ever-reliable training video. Problem No 4: *What to Do When Somebody Says You Don't Care. Give Them the Big Speech!*

So Bob gave the big speech.

'You're saying I don't care, that I don't care. Who's first in here every morning, eh – and I don't care? Who's last to leave here every night – and I don't care? I take home work all the time. Every single night. Weekends and all. You know this, I've not had so much as a whole weekend off to myself this past month. Since I've started here I've not had one proper holiday. Not one. I get calls morning, noon and night. Every morning, every noon and every night. "Could you come down for this seminar?" "Could you come and give a wee talk to the folks in Birmingham?" As if I would want to, eh, as if anyone would want to. But, oh no, I've to go, I've got to go. All for the sake of the station, all for the sake of caring. See that's one of the things about success, I mean real success, not your Mickey Mouse success, real success, it just gives you more work. More and more work. Guaranteed, I'll be here late the night. Guaranteed, I'll get called late the night. And what for, eh? For getting it in the neck all the time, that's what for: from advertisers, from backers, from watchdogs, from the likes of you lot. Anything goes wrong, anybody fucks up, it's me that's to carry the can, me that's to take the flak.

'Oh aye, and how could I forget, another thing, Jesus, how could I forget – we've got all our resident nutters out there. How could I forget the nutters? And who d'you think they go for, eh? Me. All them Clyde and Forth bampots. Clyde and Forth. Clyde and Forth. Clyde and Forth. "Oh no, you should be called Clyde and Forth. Clyde and Forth, that's what you should be called." And whose windows do they decide to go and put in, eh? And who do they go and send the letter bombs to? And who gets the shite shoved through his door? The bloody nuisance phone calls? You want to know who? I'll give you a clue, it's not the bloody prima donna who's been wandering about here all morning wearing six horizontal stripeys, that's for sure. Get real, pal. Come on.'

That was the big speech. For the most part, a word-for-word reproduction of the example shown on the training video, with emphasis, as instructed, on repetition, stress and accent – not facts and figures. There, on the training video, the big speech was delivered by none other than the accomplished and versatile board-treader Ben Kingsley, slightly more famous for his Oscar-winning portrayal in the title role of Sir Richard Attenborough's *Ghandi*.

Nevertheless, given such an esteemed role model, Bob thought he'd done mighty fine.

The sarcy Sinclair, mind you, contented himself with a slow hand-clap.

Kenny the cameraman and Stevie the soundman were busy setting up the studio for the auditions.

All that was to happen was that, just like the real thing, the girls were to stand in front of a big, empty blue screen. The text would be on autocue. Adjacent to the autocue would be the big-screen telly, wheeled through especially for the occasion from the video room. Through some elaborate technology, on the television's big blue screen, would, at any given time, be superimposed one of three maps of the region. The autocued text would indicate a change of maps by displaying a circled A, B or C, corresponding with the three buttons at the top of the remote control. While, secured over the television screen was a net grid, split into six sections. Again, the autocued text would contain instructions on where to point. When the numbers were in red, the girls were to point to the appropriate section and continue looking at the camera. When the numbers were in green, the girls had to turn and point at the big, empty blue screen. Two numbers indicated a sweeping motion.

The interview panel, the football reporters and Bob Sutherland, would sit in on the auditions then wheel the big-screen telly back through to the video room and study the recordings. A decision was to be reached today. A press conference and photo session had already been called for half-five. The champagne was on ice.

Kenny the cameraman and Stevie the soundman were fair looking forward to all this. Unfortunately, they weren't going to have a say, but they were going to get to sit in, to observe the process. The process of selecting someone who would, and this was the really interesting bit, be catapulted to instant, overnight stardom. You see this wasn't like winning some ten-a-penny Saturday night talent show, where part of the prize was landing a bottom of the bill slot for a summer season at the Winter Gardens; no, this was fame and fortune guaranteed. Broadcasting to the central belt, millions of folk, five nights a week – only assassins could get to be that famous that quick.

Then, of course, there was the other angle to be considered – they would get to see the ones who were simply crap.

So, bearing all this in mind, you can understand as how Kenny the cameraman and Stevie the soundman were mighty miffed when The Oracle, complete with crossword, came hobbling through; bandy-legged, like he'd just spent the last week on a particularly gruelling cattle drive.

The poor old bugger seemed to be in some kind of pain.

Some kind of excruciating pain.

A pain that could only mean one thing.

Big Joe.

Marina went to the toilet, gasping for a last quick fag before the auditions started.

And who should she encounter there, sitting on the marble-effect sink surround, swinging her legs back and forth, but Iona, she of the sliced tooth.

Iona, too, was smoking.

'Showing, dear,' said Iona. 'They're showing.'

'What?'

'They're showing. Your breasts, girl. Your breasts.' Iona pronounced breasts to rhyme with beasts.

Marina looked down.

'Not the flesh, dumbwit, the shape.' Iona took a drag. 'You're not allowed them, you know. Lose brownie points for that. Might as well go home now, eh? See ya. Wouldn't want to be ya.'

Marina panicked. She looked at herself in the mirror and straightened her jacket.

Iona continued to swing her legs. 'They look nice, too. Shame, eh. Wish I had nice ones.'

Marina put her hands to her breasts.

Iona laughed. 'Christ, girlfriend, pushing them in isn't going to help. Telling you, once you're in profile, the whole of bloody Ayrshire's going to be in shadow. Poor sods'll be forever thinking there's a thunderstorm on the way.'

'You're lying,' said Marina. 'Just trying to get me anxious, that's all. I know your sort.'

'Hey, you trying to tell me, with a figure like yours, those legs, that arse, those shoulders, that you don't have nice ones, nice juicy ones. 'Bout a, eh, let's guess, let's hazard a guess, what, 34C. Am I right? Course you have. How else would I know then, eh? You can tell. You can always tell.'

'Doesn't matter, anyway,' said Marina, snootily, casually teasing her hair, 'the gig's as good as mine.'

Iona extinguished her fag under the tap. 'Not according to MacAllister it's not.'

'What? What d'you mean?'

'No, he's voting for me. He wants me; it's the only way he'll get me. The old guy's voting for me' – Iona laughed – 'and there was you flaunting yourself, touching yourself. I seen you. I just had to look at him. And, by the way,

Sinclair hates you, hates the likes of you. Hates spoilt little rich kids.'

This was starting to get to Marina. It couldn't be true, could it? MacAllister? No. No way.

'I don't believe you. What about Sutherland then? What about Moses?'

'Sutherland? He'll only veto. He won't vote. Moses? Can't believe you wasted your time on *that*. Anyway, who'd want the support of a jerk who only ever champions losers? Haven't you done your homework, girl?'

Marina decided to fight back.

'No,' she said, 'you won't get in. Not with that tooth. See, what they want is good-looking, they don't want sexy. They want the girl next door, not the slag behind the bike sheds. That's the trouble with you – what is it you call yourselves again, proles? – just don't look after your gnashers, do you? Always the give-away. Always show yourselves up, eh? Your mam wears her slippers to the chip shop and you never brush your teeth. Shame, though, eh? Mean really sexy. Yeah, you're really sexy, Iona.'

'Want a bet?'

'What?'

'Want a bet I don't get the gig? Come on. I like a bet. Put your money where your mouth is.'

'No,' said Marina. 'I wouldn't take your money. Wouldn't know where it's been.'

Iona shrugged.

Then she did something really strange. She leaned her head forward, right forward, then stuck her fingers into her mouth, and proceeded to bring out a a single-molared plate.

Like the wicked witch of the north, Iona grinned.

Then she put the plate back in.

But this time, horror of horrors, the tooth was straight, perfect.

Iona smiled, just like the girl next door.

'Sometimes,' said Iona, 'you need to attract attention. While, at other times, you just need to attend to your attractions.'

'Bastard,' said Marina.

'Loser,' said Iona.

Now Big Joe was a long-serving first division manager, whose continued employment owed far more to his media-friendly status than any talent he had for organizing and motivating his players. See first division chairmen, having penny-pinched their way to their millions by turning small companies into medium-sized companies, with big turnovers and limited over-heads, liked the cost-effectiveness of media-friendly managers. Media-friendly managers were always on the telly, always on the radio, always in the news. And if, as was popularly believed, public awareness of a product was the most important part of advertising, then Big Joe was worth his weight in column inches and screen time.

Back during the Seventies, Big Joe the player had made his name as a seriously hard bastard in a succession of fairly unfashionable sides. Failing to collect honours of any kind, his was never the most distinguished of careers. Where Big Joe did distinguish himself, however, was in his financial affairs. Whereas his contemporaries chose to fritter away their hard-earned pounds and pennies on fast cars, loose women and good times, Big Joe – who, being the son of a well-known gangster, had been brought up to accept such perks only if they were gratis – decided instead to invest his precious income. And what did Big Joe choose to invest in? Why, Bubbles Playtime Sauna and Sexy Sadie's Massage Parlour. To name but two.

'I need,' said The Oracle.

'No problem,' said Big Joe. 'Anything specific?'

'Young, boyish-looking, with a squint tooth. Squinting out the way, like that.' The Oracle demonstrated. Just like Iona's!

Big Joe said, 'Now that could be a problem. Got plenty missing teeth, but squint. Got to be squint, eh? Out the way? That one?'

'Yeah,' said The Oracle, 'left-hand side big one.'

'Okay, c'mon with me. We'll have a look. See what's happening.'

Big Joe went through the room, switched on his trusty Apple Mac, and keyed in the word 'Teeth'.

Meanwhile, out in the van, the Forth and Clyde mobile – nicknamed Finda, from FACt Finder – waited Kenny the cameraman and Stevie the soundman. Kenny listening to a Carl Craig mix on his personal stereo, Stevie stirring his cream of mushroom cup-a-soup.

Lindy Anderson was going round being a pure pain. Basically, FAC TV's head of arts and entertainment was trying to if not quite sabotage proceedings, then certainly put a dampener on them. Station Controller Bob Sutherland, great leader and facilitator that he thought he was, decided something had to be done about this.

And the word that came to mind, courtesy of Problem No. 5 in the management training video – *What to Do When One of Your Minions is Being Disruptive* – was 'involve'. Yeah, Lindy had to be involved.

So Bob put it to Lindy that she should, for the duration

of the auditions, take the place of The Oracle; she would then, stressed Bob, become *a major player in a decision-making process.*

Bob explained as how it would be necessary, later on, for The Oracle, once he returned, to take his place, as planned, in the publicity photos.

Bob asked Lindy what she thought of the idea.

Lindy smiled. 'D'you know what I like about you, Bob Sutherland? No? Well let me tell you then. Absolutely fuck all. Bugger all. Zero. D'you know what this is like? This is like me being in charge of a football team and just picking the players I fancy. Wonder what all your viewers – sorry, all your *millions* of viewers – would say to that then, eh? Honestly, just the bloody same. Just a meat market.'

'Now not,' stressed Bob, 'if you choose to become part of the decision-making process.'

Lindy shook her head.

'Please,' begged Bob, 'look, I'm sitting in, I've got a right of veto. You can choose. I'll let you choose. Promise, I'll ignore what the others say. Okay? I want you to be involved, Lindy. Think about it. Just for a few seconds, give your tongue a rest and think about it. A few seconds. Please. A few seconds. That's all I'm asking.'

Lindy stopped. A few seconds. Okay, she'd give him a few seconds – but she wasn't going to think about it. No way was she going to give in. No fucking way.

Not unless . . .

Unless . . .

'Okay,' said Lindy. 'I'll do it. But on one condition, and one condition only, that you either tell me, or find out for me, who grassed us off to *The Late Show.*'

Bob sucked air.

'Well?' said Lindy. 'I know it was one of them. MacAllister? Sinclair? Had to be. Had to be one of them. Which one? Come on. Tell me.'

Bob shook his head.

'Is that a no, you won't tell me, or a no, it wasn't one of them?'

'Eh, a no, it wasn't one of them.'

Lindy looked to Bob.

'Who then?' she said.

Of all people, Bob pointed to Moses.

This time, it was Lindy's turn to suck air.

'Dead meat,' she said. 'Fucking dead meat.'

Following on from the verbals with Iona, Marina'd had a panic attack and locked herself in one of the cubicles. Then, with a speed and determination of purpose any secret agent would've been proud of, she promptly stripped off her top half, examined her cleavage and decided to apply some more strips of double-sided tape. After a while, she dispensed with strips and just went all the way round. Tighter and tighter she went. Till the tape was all used up. Near enough a whole roll.

It was only when she was finished, and trying – and failing – to put her sports bra back on, that Marina realized she could've, and probably should've, put the tape on over her bra.

Wild at herself, Marina tried to calm down. That fucking bitch! It was that fucking bitch's fault! She would pay for this. Oh, how she would pay for it all right.

Marina looked at her watch. It was near enough time to go through to make-up and styling.

Still keyed up, Marina put her bra in her bag, dressed then checked her angles in the mirror. Everything was fine, she told herself. It was all going to work out okay.

After a quick going-over in make-up and styling, it was time to perform.

They'd drawn lots. Marina was last to go.

Waiting her turn, Marina sat in the waiting room, reading through the instructions.

You were to do this cold. You never got to see any of the others perform. No run-throughs. Very little explanation. Just your basic instructions, typed out, double-spaced, with the odd yellow highlight, on a sheet of A4.

It was Bob Sutherland who came to get her. 'Okay,' he said. 'Last but not least, eh? Best of luck, pal.'

They went through.

Bob Sutherland himself was the master of ceremonies. He handed Marina a remote control. Pressing the remote control would activate the autocue. It could go forward, it could go back. Bob demonstrated. The three buttons at the top were for the three maps. Again, Bob demonstrated. It was, said Bob, once you got going, all very straightforward.

'Good luck,' he said. 'We'll give you a minute to get your bearings, then you're on your own, okay? Play about with the remote. Get used to the surroundings. Take your time. Mind, you decide when you want to start.'

Bob returned to his seat.

Alongside him were the bastard MacAllister, the doe-eyed Moses, the still multi-tied Sinclair and some daft woman who'd been storming about earlier. The Oracle was nowhere to be seen.

Marina walked over, centre-stage, in front of the big blue empty screen.

This was it then. This was for real.

Marina tried to concentrate on the autocue. It wasn't easy. The words were writ so large she could make out the individual dots that made up the letters. It was like looking into a microscope. Any second you half-expected them to move.

And if that wasn't bad enough, there was the telly, the telly with the map, with the net-grid, with Marina.

Marina was putting off looking over. She'd never seen herself on telly before. Like most folk, she couldn't even stand to see photos of herself. Of all the hundreds she'd had taken over the years, there was only the one she really liked. One of her and mummy, from just last summer, out in the back garden. Marina liked that photo.

With eyes closed and fingers crossed, Marina made a final wish – that when she opened her eyes and looked over at the telly, then that's how she would look, like the photo in the garden.

Marina uncrossed her fingers. She opened her eyes. She looked over at the screen.

And there she was.

Marina could hardly believe it.

It was just like the photo in the back garden.

Her face was just the same. Fresh. Happy. Relaxed. Pretty.

There was nothing wrong. It was all just nerves, she told herself, just nerves. You couldn't do something like this unless you were nervous. Of course you couldn't. Of course she liked photos of herself, other photos. She loved herself. There was absolutely nothing wrong with her.

'Right,' said Bob, 'few seconds. Then let's go, okay?'

And, to think, this was how she was going to look all the time. In the eyes of millions!

Marina swivelled. There was nothing wrong with her shape. There was no movement at all. Her hair looked great. Her suit looked great.

No problem.

This was all going to be no problem.

Marina read through the words on the autocue. This time they shone. *It's going to be a bright, sunshiney day, with temperatures reaching a high of . . .*

Marina nodded at Bob.

She was ready. She clapped her hands on her hips, took a deep breath, a really deep breath, and got ready to press the button on the remote.

Mind you, with hindsight, about a millisecond or so, the deep breath, the really deep breath, was probably a bad idea, a really bad idea.

Following the performances, the adjudicators wheeled the big-screen TV through to the video room, and sat themselves down on the big, comfy sofa to study the recordings and consider their verdict.

But Lindy couldn't concentrate. She was too busy thinking about Moses, about how she was going to destroy the sanctimonious, grassing little git. Violence. Yeah, violence seemed like a good idea. Why not?

Lindy voted for Iona. She was easily the best.

After the disaster, Moses had made a half-hearted attempt to get Marina a second chance. Could've happened to anybody. It was a shame. Would've been nice to've had her as a friend, somebody like that, somebody popular. Just imagine, the popular girl from fifth and sixth year – finding out what she was really like. Moses' heart skipped another beat.

But, alas, Moses would never know. It was one of the rules, one of the written-down rules – you weren't allowed a second chance. This was an audition for live telly. You weren't allowed second chances on live telly.

In deference to being obvious, Moses had then put forward the case of Curly, the one off *AA Roadwatch*. It occurred to him how you never seen lassies with really curly hair on telly. But Lindy, who, for some reason, seemed to be in charge, and seemed to be even more obstreperous than usual, told Moses to shut up or die.

Given such clear and contrasting options, Moses, not surprisingly, chose to shut up.

Moses ended up voting for Iona. For all that it mattered, she was probably the best.

Early on in his career, just as he was beginning to get famous, MacAllister had decided to align himself with one cause and one cause only.

MacAllister's choice of cause had been, and still was, the evils of gambling. These days, his main bugbear was the national lottery. A tax, said MacAllister, which, because it was the same for the poor as it was the rich, was about as wrong as wrong could be.

As much as all this was true, MacAllister indeed was anti-gambling, there remained, however, a slightly more slanted reasoning behind FAC TV's resident Lothario having such a strong opposition to the occasional flutter. Born of superstition, it was an opposition that had more to do with fear. MacAllister, you see, was petrified. All his life he'd been the luckiest, jammiest sod around. He was terrified that one day all this would, like the proverbial bubble, just burst, never to return again. In fact, MacAllister knew, knew for certain, that if he ever bought a lottery ticket, or attempted the pools, trying to exploit his run of good luck for financial gain, then that would be that. The way he seen it, he would win shit-loads of money, millions, and from that moment on he'd be the most miserable sod alive.

No, MacAllister's good fortune was never to be risked in the pursuit of mere materialism. Never.

And, all being well, the blessed MacAllister would continue to enjoy the life to which he'd become accustomed.

Like, take today. Nobody could've been that lucky. Nobody. To think, the lassie he'd effectively guaranteed the job to last night, had went and blown it. Whereas the lassie he'd effectively guaranteed the job to this afternoon, had easily been the best.

Somebody up there liked MacAllister. Had to be.

MacAllister voted for Iona. Really, it was that easy.

Despite another impassioned request from Station Controller Bob Sutherland, Sinclair still wasn't taking his ties off. Not for the photo shoot. Not even for tonight's programme.

And as for the candidates? Shite. All of them. Shite.

Sinclair voted for Duane Doberman. Now there was a star.

Throughout the post-performance analysis, Bob Sutherland had kept a constant eye on the auditions video, the actual tape. The idea of it, this tape, falling into the wrong hands – Sinclair's, say, or, even worse, MacAllister's – was almost too painful to contemplate.

The last of them, the Chancellor of the Exchequer's daughter, for God's sake, had just been a disaster. She'd taken this deep breath, this really deep breath, then stalled, like she just couldn't breathe out again. And she couldn't. She just couldn't breathe. To make matters worse, she'd then fumbled her way through the script for a few agonized seconds – which, to the onlooking judging panel, seemed more like tortured hours – before finally seeing sense, pulling herself together and doing the right and proper thing, i.e. bursting into tears and running off-stage.

To think, too, the Chancellor of the Exchequer's daughter, the newly-appointed Chancellor of the Exchequer aka the Honourable Member for Thuglands Central aka a one-party state if ever there was one with enough (alleged) corruption and gangland activity to fuel a generation of Ed McBains.

Yeah, Bob was keeping his eye on the video. Once all this was over, it was going straight in the safe. Like the tape with Kirsty Young and the mini skirt, this was never going to be seen by anybody.

It was like the aftermath of a beauty pageant. The tension of performance over, the previously silent girls were all through in the visitors' room, yapping away, and getting stuck into the laid-on champagne and nibbles. Yet while the other candidates – Curly, Dodgy, Podgy and Tar-head – were all busy making great play of congratulating Iona, loads of hugs and air kisses, Marina was biding her time. Surprise, as they said, was always the strongest weapon.

Then, just as Curly was finishing up with her best wishes and Podgy was about to take over, Marina made her move.

And what a move. In a split second, she grabbed a hold of Iona's shoulders and stuck her leading leg out behind. With an almighty, walloping thud, Iona was spun to the deck.

Marina wasn't finished.

Quick as a flash, she hitched up her skirt and was down, pinning Iona's flailing arms with her knees.

'Right,' she sneered. 'Let's have a look, shall we. Now, open wide.'

Sacrificing the knuckles of her left hand, Marina prised and kept open Iona's mouth. With the fingers of her right hand, Marina excavated.

Now all this had happened so fast, and was so unexpected, that Curly, Dodgy, Podgy and Tar-head — who, despite their failings, were basically decent sorts — were caught unawares, and appeared slow in their efforts to do the decent thing and untangle the two combatants.

Yet, what they initially lacked in urgency, they duly made up for in effort, and somehow managed to haul off the surprisingly strong Marina.

But, alas, too late to stop the dentistry.

Iona was now the one needing to be restrained.

'Bathtard!' she lisped. 'Ya fucking bathtard!'

There was blood coming from Marina's left-hand fingers, her prising fingers — as expected, typical of the breed, the scheming schemey bitch had bit into her — but Marina's right-hand fingers, the extractors, now held what she wanted.

'Pleath! Give it back! I'll fucking kill ya, ya thlut.'

Marina clenched her fist. There was no way she was giving it back. The all-important squint tooth.

'Let's see how you look in your photos now then, Bozo.'

Understandably taken aback by this turn of events — that lassie's got a false tooth! The lassie that won's got a false tooth — Curly, Dodgy, Podgy and Tar-head had, through really no fault of their own, lessened their restraining grip on the now lesser-toothed Iona.

Iona seized the moment. In an instant, she freed herself and leapt forward, barging Marina to the deck.

'Bathtard!' she screamed. 'Bathtard!'

Iona was a less cultivated assailant than Marina. More of an impassioned scrapper really. Her efforts to unclench Marina's fist, the one that held the dingied denture, though animated and worthy of ten out of ten for aggression, were as doomed as they were desperate.

So Iona, a devious wee soul, decided instead on a trade-off. She made a grab for Marina's top: her blouse and jacket.

Curly, Dodgy, Podgy and Tar-head, meanwhile, having been once again called upon to do the decent thing and demonstrate their break-up routine, soon had a hold of Iona by the arms; Tar-head and Curly on one arm, Dodgy and Podgy on the other. On the count of three, they'd go for it.

'One.'

'Two.'

'Three.'

'Go for it!'

And on 'Go for it!', there was this awfy ripping and tearing sound.

Iona hadn't let go of the garments. The garments, however, rather shockingly, when you took into consideration the small fortune which had just been spent on them, had indeed come adrift from their precious stitching.

Iona was now in possession of the front of a designer dress jacket, and most of a sticky designer blouse.

Marina was lying there – much to the shock of Curly, Dodgy, Podgy and Tar-head – effectively topless, apart from a few rags of clothes and what amounted to near enough a roll of now fluff covered, double-sided tape.

'Thwap,' said Iona. 'Give me the tooth, I'll give you my jacket. Fair thwap.'

'Never,' said Marina, getting up. 'Never.'

Iona launched another attack. But this time the combined forces of Curly, Dodgy, Podgy and Tar-head were ready for her. Prevention, they now realized, was probably the best course of action in such circumstances.

'Let me go,' screamed Iona, 'ya bunch of loothers.'

Marina saw her chance. She rushed out the waiting room and through to the adjacent toilet.

'Bathtard,' screamed Iona. 'Quick! Thtop her! Thee's going to kill it.'

Curly, Dodgy, Podgy, Tar-head and Iona promptly raced through to the toilet after Marina.

But it was too late. By the time they got there all they could hear was the sound of a flushed cistern, with Marina's ghoulish laughter taunting them from behind the door of the locked cubicle.

'Bathtard!' screamed Iona. 'Bathtard. You'll pay for thith.'

They were just back, too, barely in the door, barely time to put their feet up, when who should come over but . . .

'You got a minute, yeah? It's just I want to go out and interview somebody. Stays in the town, like. Just half an hour, that's all. An hour tops. No problem. Back well before then. I've been on the phone to him. It's all set up, all arranged. Just a couple of questions, that's all. He knows his answers, knows what he's going to say. He's going out, anyway, he's got to go out and see somebody. Come on. Won't be long. Please? It's all to do with this feature I'm doing, about how players from the Highland League are never considered for the national side. It's quite interesting really, sort of hidden agenda kind of angle. It all started years ago with . . .'

Kenny the cameraman put his (vegetarian) cheese and pickle sandwich back in the drawer. Stevie the soundman marked his place with a napkin, then put his copy of the new edition of *The Face* to one side.

The crew started getting its gear together.

'Listen,' said Moses, 'promise, honest, we won't be long.

Look, sorry, I know I'm running a bit late. It was all that carry-on with the auditions for the weather. Anyway, I've got to get back for this stupid photo shoot. We'll be back. No problem. Plenty of time for you to do your editing. Plenty of time.'

Kenny went into his drawer. He pulled out his stopwatch, set it, then handed it over to Moses. The stopwatch was set for an hour.

'Yeah,' said Moses, 'an hour. No problem. Back well before then. Plenty of time. Right, got everything? Ready? Aye?'

Kenny the cameraman smiled. Yeah, he was ready. But was Moses? There was something to be seen over behind Moses' shoulder.

Moses turned and looked.

Lindy Anderson was putting her coat on. Lindy Anderson was smiling.

'Yeah?' said Moses.

'Yeah,' said Lindy. 'See today you've got a special guest; I'm coming along. Lucky you, eh? Yeah, for once, I want to see a true professional at work.'

Having relieved the excruciation in his nether regions, and having completed a wee piece with Big Joe – re. the terrible pressures put upon the modern-day referee, what with TV evidence etc., always a good standby that one – The Oracle was back at his desk and back at his crossword.

There was only the one to go. That blasted 1 across. A,S (9,4). A blank P blank R blank blank U blank then blank I blank S.

What the fuck was it?

He'd got the rest of them in the van on the way back. The bit of intrigue, as Big Joe had a habit of calling them – her name was Mandy, her teeth were awful, it was the best as could be managed at such short notice — had, like they said about exercise, certainly helped clear the mind. But this 1 across.

For the moment, The Oracle was beat.

And, it has to be said, the commotion going on didn't help.

The raised voices.

Then running.

Six girls running.

Girls, eh.

Clowning around.

Next thing, four of the weather girls were through talking to MacAllister.

The Oracle tried not to listen.

He failed.

Apparently, there was a problem. Apparently, a couple of the girls had been — and maybe still were? — fighting.

The Oracle edged about in his seat. Fighting, girls fighting. He normally paid good money to see that kind of thing.

Jesus, no!

The Oracle tried to concentrate on his crossword.

A – P – R – – U – – I – S.

He failed.

Apparently, one of them was topless. Apart from a roll of double-sided tape covering her breasts one of them was topless!

The Oracle nearly choked.

Jesus Christ, no!

Double-sided tape.

Imagine it. Your hands! You're tongue! Everything! Stuck! Forever!

The Oracle didn't want to think about that. He tried instead to concentrate on his crossword.

A blank P blank R blank blank . . .

It was no good.

Apparently, the one with the tooth, the squint tooth, the sliced tooth, had had her tooth knocked out.

Apparently, there was blood, blood everywhere.

This was too much.

The tooth. The face. The boyish good looks.

Not to mention sticky breasts.

Sticky fucking breasts!

Nah, The Oracle would have to go and see what was going on. He had to.

Not for the first time, MacAllister found himself having problems in a female toilet.

Mind you, on this occasion, at least he'd been summoned.

Decent as they undoubtedly were, Curly, Dodgy, Podgy and Tar-head had had enough. They'd went through, explained the situation to MacAllister, and said that they were off home. They had, they reasoned, tried their best.

From here on in, MacAllister could sort it out.

So, MacAllister was in the female toilet, with Marina, locked inside the cubicle, crying her eyes out, and Iona, outside the cubicle, going, 'Bathtard! Thlut! Thitebag!'

MacAllister wasn't really getting anywhere. He tried for what seemed like ages, but Marina wasn't saying a thing, she just cried and cried. As to whether she really had flushed the tooth away; well, for the time being, you had to suppose she had.

'Listen,' whispered MacAllister to Iona, 'have you a spare?'

'A thwat?'

'A thpare. Sorry, a spare, a spare tooth. Another denture.'

Iona thought. 'There'th another one back at the houthe. An old one. It never fitted properly.'

'Yeah, but is it okay, though? Mean, can you wear it for the photos?'

'Thuppothe tho.'

'Good.' MacAllister spoke loudly again. 'Marina? Marina, love? Are you listening to me? Marina, look, if you don't open the door, sorry but I'm going to have to smash it. I'll count to three.'

MacAllister handed paper and a pencil over to Iona. 'Quick,' he whispered, 'write down your address, tell me where the tooth is and give me your keys.'

MacAllister waited a second then shouted, 'One!'

Iona wrote down the address. She told MacAllister that the tooth was in the toilet cabinet and gave him her keys.

Just as MacAllister was about to say 'Two', the cubicle door opened and out stepped Marina.

And what a sight she was.

She'd obviously been trying to take the tape off, but hadn't met with any great success. She'd got some of it, but those strips that came in contact with the skin had just been sticky and painful. Consequently, she was covered in the stuff. Her top half, her hair, skirt, hands and arms were all streaked with ribbons of double-sided tape.

Not that Iona was concerned. She just screamed 'BATH-TARD!' and launched herself on another attack.

It was as much as MacAllister could do, using all his might and ingenuity, to keep the two apart.

Then the door opened, the door into the toilet.

'Coo-ee, is anybody in?'

'Quick,' said MacAllister, 'help. For God's sake, help me.'

But The Oracle couldn't help. He just stood there, slavering. The topless versus the toothless. This was the stuff of dreams.

Riddled with guilt, The Oracle tried to concentrate on his crossword.

'A blank P blank R . . .'

'What?' said MacAllister. 'For God's sake, no time for that. Help me, man, help me.'

No, it was no good. The Oracle had to touch. He had to have his feel.

But as he edged closer, the sense of relief from making the decision, from surrendering himself to the quest for flesh, didn't seem to stop, instead it just seemed to overwhelm him and make him dizzy. And then, as though suddenly knee-deep in the devil's very own treacle, he just couldn't make himself move.

And then there was pain.

Anxious, MacAllister said, 'Are you all right?'

No, The Oracle wasn't all right.

MacAllister untangled himself from the two girls and rushed over.

But it was too late. The legs gave way and The Oracle crumpled to the deck.

Supporting The Oracle's head on his lap, MacAllister said, 'God, man. What happened?'

There was blood trickling from The Oracle's mouth.

Then, of all the things to do, The Oracle started grinning.

'Listen,' he said, his voice barely a whisper. 'I got it. I got it.'

'What?' said MacAllister. 'You got what?'

'Tits,' said The Oracle. 'Tits.'

'"Tits"?' said MacAllister. '"Tits"? What you on about "Tits"?'

This time, The Oracle laughed.

'No,' he said. 'Not tits, tips. A comma S, nine and four, asparagus tips.'

As advised by the management training video (Problem No. 6: *Anticipating Aggro*), Station Controller Bob Sutherland always avoided folk between the hours of three and four-thirty. Always a bad time, they said, three till four-thirty, for folk coming up to you and hassling you with their pent-up problems. So, between those hours, Bob took himself off for a really long wander round The Totem, seeking out somebody he hadn't seen for a while, usually somebody that was just setting off on holiday – they were always the least likely to be concerned with work – for a cup of tea and a blether.

Mind you, today, when he returned from walkabout, as Bob liked to call it, he couldn't help but be curious as to where all the minions had buggered off to.

Normally, at this time, the place was as close as it ever got to being a hive of activity, but only one of them was to be seen, feet up on his desk, playing with his six horizontal stripeys.

'Where is everybody?' said Bob.

'Well,' said Sinclair, 'Moses is away out interviewing.'

'*What?* He's supposed to be here for a photo shoot. I'll kill him.'

'Correct,' said Sinclair. 'And, guess what, Lindy's away with him.'

'Oh God, no!'

'She was most insistent.'

'Jesus. She *will* kill him.'

'Sorry?'

'Nothing,' said Bob. 'Nothing. What about MacAllister? The Oracle? That Lassie? All the other lassies?'

'Ah,' said Sinclair, and gave a brief résumé of everything that had happened. 'MacAllister is presently trying to resolve the situation. And, I believe, The Oracle's in there as well.'

It was time to make a decision, an important decision, an executive decision – Bob decided he didn't want anything to do with this. Nah, if you weren't aware of a problem, then you weren't part of a problem. That was No. 7 in the training video. Huge, big letters. Bold as fuck. Flashed it up between Nos. 6 and 8. *Remember, if you're not aware of a problem, then you're not part of a problem.* Yeah, let MacAllister sort it out. MacAllister was good at things like that.

Bob tried to be positive. 'Well, at least they're here, anyway.'

Sinclair smiled. 'And, of course, so am I.'

'But,' said Bob 'you're still wearing those stupid ties. Many times do I have to tell you? Enough's enough. You've had your wee joke. We've all had a laugh. Come on. You're supposed to be getting your photo taken. We're supposed to be showing a united front.'

Sinclair shook his head. 'They're not coming off. I want everybody to know about this. Nobody's taken a blind bit of notice of me all day. If you don't go to the press, I'm going to the press. You'll be laughing on the other side of your face, Bob Sutherland.'

'What? You must be joking. 'Cause a bunch of newsreaders are wearing ties you were wearing months ago? You never think that maybe all this is just coincidence?'

'Weeks ago,' corrected Sinclair. 'And no it's not coincidence, it's important.'

Bob had had enough. It was time for Problem No. 8: *What to Do When Folks are Getting Too Big for Their Boots*.

'Come here,' he said, 'step into my office, will you. There's something I've been meaning to show you.'

To say the least, Moses was somewhat nervous. Nobody'd ever been out on a job with him before. Least of all somebody with a well-known dislike, bordering on clinical hatred, of football, and football reporters in particular. Not only that, but since this afternoon, that hatred had been quite particular, quite specifically directed at poor Moses himself.

Consequently, the piece had been a bit flat. The interviewee, Duncan Gray, a minor legend in his time in the Highland League, but a total nonentity as far as the Central Belt was concerned, had been informative, passionate and thoroughly appropriate. He'd gave good quote, the viewers would be interested in what he had to say, and thereby swayed by Moses' original conjecture; but see, well, Moses himself hadn't risen to the occasion. There was no stimulation, no spark. His mind was on other things.

Like, just why exactly was Lindy around? What could she be up to?

Then, just as Moses was doing his final piece to camera, outside the tenement entrance to Duncan Gray's southside flat, Lindy stepped over to Stevie the soundman.

After a brief discussion, Stevie the soundman handed Lindy his boom microphone.

Ever the professional, Moses kept talking.

Ever the professional, Kenny the cameraman kept filming.

Lindy, meanwhile, proceeded to remove the fur cover from the boom microphone.

Then, with both hands, she raised the boom microphone, like an axe, above her head.

Bob Sutherland invited Sinclair to take a seat, then put his famous 'Do not – under any circumstances – disturb' sign on the outside doorknob.

Bob closed the door then walked over to a filing cabinet marked 'Personnel'.

After flicking through the files for a minute, he found the one he was looking for, then flung it on the desk, in front of Sinclair.

(By the way, the answer to Problem No. 8 was *Destroy*!)

'So,' said Sinclair, 'my file. So what?'

'You're a funny bugger you, eh,' said Bob. 'You come over as being, well, camp. Faintly, mind. No raging or nothing, just faintly. Not that it matters, but nobody knows one way or the other. Clever. Wee bit of mystery now and again never does you any harm. Then there's your background. At times, you come over as being nothing less than a typically spoilt, middle-class – upper-class? – twat. Yet, in the same breath – and this is clever, this is really clever – you make it perfectly clear you've not the slightest bit of time for the likes of the middle classes, let alone the upper classes. The viewers like that. They like it cause they think it's real. See they want their stars to be different, yet at the same time real. They don't like the idea that folk change off-screen. Never have done. They like consistency.

'Now all this is fascinating, cause it's not contrived, it's natural. You're just a natural man of mystery. The viewers love it. And there's another thing you are, you're ambitious. And there's nothing that's going to hold you back, eh? Unless,' Bob tapped the file then laughed. 'You see, Sinclair, to cut a long story short, I know about you. For a start, I know that's not your real name. Well, it is, but – it's the other way round, eh? See you're not Sinclair Stevens, you're Stephen Sinclair. And you weren't' – Bob consulted the file – '"brought up somewhere in Fife that you've long since forgotten the name of before at the age of fourteen moving to glorious Glasgow"; were you, Stephen?'

Sinclair – Stephen – was shitting himself.

'No, Sinclair, you were brought up in the beautiful western isle of Barra. In other words, and this is where it gets really interesting, where it really starts to make a lot of sense, your native tongue is therefore not English, is it? Co's fhearr do chrochadh no do dnicheannadh, Steafan.'

Sinclair – Steafan – sat there, for the moment, saying nothing, thinking about everything.

'Who told you?' he said. 'How did you find out?'

'Oh,' said Bob, 'that doesn't matter. You'd be amazed at how much I know about what goes on round here. So, anyway, what I'm trying to say is, there's an area of television that we here at FAC TV, at the government's request, are currently ploughing a fair bit of money into.'

'No,' said Sinclair. 'Don't you fucking threaten me with that.'

'The viewing figures for Gael TV, it has to be said, are not what you're used to, consequently the money'll obviously be a bit less as well, and it'll mostly be graveyard slots I'm afraid – live though, you like being live, don't you, Sinclair; sorry, Steafan?'

'No way. No way am I doing Sheep TV. Never. You wouldn't do this to me. It'd ruin me.'

'Well,' said Bob, 'there's an alternative; and you can start by taking off – well, guess what – and putting on your best, big smile and going out and rounding up the rest of your colleagues, and making sure they're smart and presentable for the photo session. How does that sound? Tha gaidhlig beo, Steafan. Tha gaidhlig beo.'

Conveniently, in the convenience, Marina had fainted.

What had happened was: Iona had said, 'Ith he dead?'

MacAllister had said, 'Aye. I think so.'

Then Marina had fainted.

On his mobile, MacAllister phoned 999 and explained the situation. He then went out to tell Bob Sutherland what had happened. But Bob Sutherland had his famous 'Do not – under any circumstances – disturb' notice outside the door. For the time being, it would have to wait.

Iona seemed heartbroken. 'Doth thith mean the phototh'll be canthelled?'

'No.' MacAllister quickly worked it all out, what he was going to do. 'Listen,' he said, 'here's what's going to happen, okay. We're going to move him through to the male toilet, then I'm going to take her home, then I'm going to go and collect your tooth, then I'm going to go and see his wife, then I'm coming back, and then we're going to do the photos. In the meantime, you're to stay and watch the body. Okay?'

'Okay,' said Iona.

It was more than likely the police would turn up. The last thing MacAllister wanted – and definitely, absolutely definitely, the last thing Bob Sutherland would be wanting – would be for word getting out of a dead reporter being found in the female toilet of a television studio, with, thrown in for good measure, a comatose and half-naked daughter of the newly-appointed Chancellor of the Exchequer. Half-naked, of course, apart from all that double-sided tape.

Jesus.

Iona gave MacAllister a hand to drag The Oracle through to the male toilet.

'Okay,' said MacAllister. 'Right, you stay here. I'll be back in about forty minutes. Mind, anybody asks, I discovered the body. Anybody asks where I am, say I'm away seeing his wife. Whatever you do, don't mention her.' MacAllister pointed through the wall. 'Got that? Anybody mentions Marina. She left ages ago. Okay?'

'Okay.'

MacAllister went back through to get Marina.

Thankfully, she was still out of it. MacAllister took off his jacket, put it over Marina, then slung her over his shoulder.

He made his way to the lift, pressed the call button and waited.

'Come on,' he said. 'Come on.'

A few seconds later, the lift doors opened.

And there, next to the tropical pot plant, with the cheesy children's choir belting out 'Betcha By Golly Wow', stood Kenny the cameraman, Stevie the soundman, a smug-to-bursting Lindy, and a mixed grill of a Moses – with two black eyes coming up the size of burgers, a burst tomato for a mouth and a nose that, well, called to mind nothing so much as a crumbling tattie scone.

By return of lift, came the ambulance folk. They asked for the male toilet.

That got them some queer looks – in his haste, MacAllister hadn't bothered to explain anything – so they added a wee bit more information.

'We've come to collect a body,' they said.

'A body?' said the anxious Moses. 'What d'you mean "a body"?'

'A body,' said the paramedics. 'A corpse. Some deid cunt.'

While Moses, who, it has to be said, had had a hard half hour of it, proceeded to go and faint, Lindy showed the paramedics through to the male toilet.

Wherein they encountered a grief-stricken Iona – merely her way of hiding her toothless state, not a reflection of any genuine concern – and what appeared to be a dead Oracle.

The paramedics confirmed that, yes, despite the look of contented achievement on his face, The Oracle was indeed dead. Probably a heart attack.

Iona passed on to Lindy what MacAllister had told her.

Lindy promptly went through and told Station Controller Bob Sutherland that one of his pride and joys had snuffed it.

'What?' said Bob. 'Shit.' Oh God, that meant he was going to have to release a press statement. It was usually The Oracle who took care of all that morbid stuff. The Oracle could rattle off twelve obituaries a day. In his sleep. Probably not when he was dead, mind. Bob tried to calm down. He remembered the training video. Problem No. 9: *When Something Goes Wrong – Make Sure You've Got a Scapegoat.*

'Where's Moses?' said Bob. 'Get me Moses.'

'Out of it,' said Lindy.

'What?'

Lindy explained.

'Where's MacAllister then?' said Bob. 'Get me MacAllister.'

'Absent,' said Lindy.

'"Absent"? What d'you mean "absent"?'

Lindy relayed what the grief-stricken Iona had told her.

Bob was getting desperate.

'Where's Sinclair?' said Bob. 'Where the fuck is Sinclair? Christ, he was here just a minute ago.'

And just then, cometh the hour, cometh the man, the

lift doors opened, and out stepped the sought-after Sinclair; wearing only one tie, and carrying a big bunch of flowers and an even bigger box of chocolates.

The Oracle's body was being stretchered away by the paramedics. Iona was howling. Moses was flat out with his steam-rollered face. And Station Controller Bob Sutherland was approaching hysteria.

Utterly oblivious to any let alone all of this, Sinclair meekly shuffled forward.

'These are for you,' he said, handing the flowers and chocolates over to Bob. 'I want to apologise for all the trouble I've caused. See I've been under a lot of pressure of late. I'm really sorry. You'll see a new me from now on, a new Sinclair. Promise.'

Just as Bob was about to land one, a really good one, on Sinclair Stevens's perfect chin, (Problem No. 10 in the management training video, the final problem: *Things You Can Normally Get Away With When You've Reached the End of Your Tether*), the lift doors opened again, dramatically causing Bob's fist to stop, like a freeze-frame, in mid-air. This time it was the police – and, with a turn of thought the likes of which only shock and total panic can induce, Bob couldn't help but wonder where the newly-appointed Chancellor of the Exchequer's daughter had got to. Station Controller Bob Sutherland gulped.

It was a click then a constant hiss that woke Marina. She was lying on her sofa, her Jesus draped over the top of her. Then she remembered. She'd set the video to record tonight's edition of *Forth and Clyde Today*, anticipating a feature on the new weather girl.

And it all came flooding back. The whole, horrid shebang.

Marina made to get up, to switch the machine off, but she couldn't, couldn't move at all. She was stuck to the sofa. Then she tried to remove her Jesus, so's she could fling it at the telly, but that was stuck as well.

Marina was beeling. Somebody was going to have to pay for all this. Yeah, somebody was going to get it. Then she remembered – she knew where they would be. Marina reached for the phone. She dialled daddy's number.

'And, later on, we'll be having a tribute to the man they called The Oracle, Jim Galbraith, who died today, aged sixty-three.'

Once he'd got the headlines, Kenny the cameraman fast-forwarded to get to their stuff. Stevie the soundman was busy making the tea, pasta with bits in it. After all the hassle, it was the back of eight when they'd finally got home to their cramped yet comfy Morgan Street studio flat.

First up, Sinclair paid tribute to The Oracle. Hastily written by a groggy Moses, with some archive footage and tele-phoned messages from Big Joe and a couple of other rent-a-quotes, it was genuinely touching. They showed the film of The Oracle's body being taken away, with a few of them standing about outside looking suitably shaken. By far, the most shaken was Sinclair. As pale as tropical sand, if you didn't know any better, you'd have thought he'd just had the most serious of threats to his financial and occupational livelihood.

And, of course, he had. Kenny and Stevie could tell that Sinclair had just received the threat.

They looked at each other and smiled.

For it was them who'd told Bob Sutherland about Sinclair's true origins. They'd found out while they were over on a shoot for a holiday programme in the Western Isles. Due to bad weather their boat had had to stop off at Barra. There, they'd gone to the local bothy, only to discover it was plastered with all these signed pictures of Sinclair. Sure, said the locals, all seven of them, everybody could mind of wee Stevie Sinclair. An awfy nice laddie. Nice to see him doing so well for himself.

Next up was Moses' piece. Only it wasn't Moses who delivered it. What with him being smashed of face, The Oracle being dead and the latecomer MacAllister being tied up with Bob Sutherland – trying to get his story straight, assuring Bob that Marina had nothing at all to do with The Oracle's untimely demise – it was left to a somewhat reluctant Lindy to do the honours. She voiced-over the questions and did the studio presentation. Admirably, it had to be said. In fact, she was so good, when he watched the run-through, Bob Sutherland decided it might've been an idea to give her the highly paid job of sports anchor, ditch the increasingly unhinged Sinclair and transfer the oversensitive Moses to arts and entertainment. Maybe get in a couple of new sports reporters. Somebody like the ever-popular Big Joe. Yeah, honest to goodness ex-players. That was the way forward. And, funnily enough, there you go, that's exactly what the latest round of market research was saying.

Kenny the cameraman and Stevie the soundman looked at each other and smiled.

Not only had they clyped on Sinclair, but it was them who'd grassed off Lindy to the BBC. They maybe couldn't destroy her career, but, boy, they could certainly destroy her prospects.

And why had they gone and blamed the hapless Moses? Cause, when all was said and done, they liked Moses. The guy's heart was in the right place. But the more he got into this, and cornered himself into the cult of personality, with its attendant endless self-justification, the more his pieces, his concerns, would end up being secondary. Kenny and Stevie didn't want that to happen. They wanted to save Moses. And if that meant destroying him, then so be it.

MacAllister's piece on Reinaldo was next. You couldn't deny it, for what it was it was funny. MacAllister, to give him his due, knew how to work his audience.

That was the thing. Corrupt as he was, crap as he was, you just couldn't get one over on MacAllister. Every bit of scandal, and there was plenty of scandal, just seemed to make him more famous. He was adored by the public, best buddies with his subjects and respected by his colleagues. Even so, this morning, back at the airport, Kenny and Stevie gave it their usual try.

Reinaldo had been trying to coax MacAllister into staying on after tonight's meal, the celebration meal, for a game of poker, with Luigi and a few colleagues from the catering world. Of course, MacAllister, Mr Anti-gambling, had said no.

But when MacAllister went out to make his call to Marina, Kenny and Stevie – who knew fear was the real reason behind MacAllister's aversion to gambling – had pressed the point, urging Reinaldo and Luigi to keep on at him. MacAllister, they said, once he had a few drinks down him, really did like a hand of cards. In fact, he was well into it. Liked to play for really big stakes.

It was a pathetic effort, a desperate effort. Really, they should've been ashamed of themselves.

Christ, MacAllister didn't even play cards.

But what they didn't know was, Iona did.

Yeah, Iona liked a hand of cards.

And when, over at Luigi's, during the big celebration meal, Reinaldo had once again broached the subject, Iona, buoyed up by seeing her photo in all the first editions of the papers — an umbrella in one hand, a glass of champagne in the other — jumped at the chance. As if she could lose on a day like this.

MacAllister had said no. No way was he gambling.

But Iona was in.

Absolutely jiggered after his day — stopping fights, dragging bodies, carrying bodies, comforting distraught widows — MacAllister was in no mood to argue. He just wanted to get home, cuddle up to Iona and crash out. Anyway, it would be okay. After all, it wasn't as if he was taking part, it was Iona.

Best of luck to her.

So they went through the back and played their cards. Iona was good. She won hand after hand. Soon, there were thousands of pounds lying in front of her.

The restaurateurs — Reinaldo, Luigi, a few of their friends — could see she was on a serious winning streak and called it a night.

MacAllister was relieved when it was all over. He phoned for a taxi.

By the time they got their coats on and said their goodnights, Luigi came through to tell them their taxi was waiting out front.

It was a funny taxi, mind. It was a normal fast black, but there was something distinctly odd about it, something sinister. MacAllister couldn't quite put his finger on it.

There were no seat-belts.

There was this funny smell.

It seemed awfy spartan.

In the back of the taxi, once they were under way, Iona handed a bundle of bills over to MacAllister.

'What's this for?' said MacAllister.

'The stake.'

'The what?'

Iona looked sheepish. 'Sorry,' she said. 'I've been naughty. Maybe I should explain.'

Iona said that when Reinaldo had first mentioned the card game, she realized she hadn't had a decent stake on her. You needed a decent stake to get into one of these kinds of games. Knowing MacAllister's aversion to gambling, she hadn't asked him for it. So, during their lengthy and passionate pre-pudding snog, she'd made a point of fingering MacAllister's mighty wad, the wad that would choke a spin drier, and helping herself to a few bills in the process. She hoped he didn't mind. Just a couple of hundred.

'*What?*'

MacAllister was sweating. If his money had been used to gamble, then – God! NO! NO! NO! – he'd been gambling! He'd been gambling!

'Are you all right?' said Iona. 'Look, it's okay, we won. We won thousands. See?'

Iona took the bundle of notes, fanned them out, flailed out her arms, and sprayed the winnings, like so much confetti, all over the back of the cab.

'Stop!' said MacAllister. 'Stop the cab! I need to get out!'

But, trouble was, there was never any intention of stopping. The driver had his instructions. They weren't to stop until they reached the prescribed destination, a deserted warehouse, somewhere in the darkest heart of the notorious Thuglands Central.

Smoked

JAMES MEEK

I DRANK AND slept and dreamed I was a poisoned angel, with feet like a bird's, standing on the edge of a crater looking down at an ocean of clouds boiling with bruise-coloured folds. I was poisoned by the thought that in one of the alternative moments the angels lived through, God had made a world other than the one we knew, our existence where the only tendency was towards an infinite complication in artefacts and deeds. I asked him, he was everywhere, but he didn't pay attention, he wasn't even aware of the nature of the question. I watched the lightning shooting upwards into the firmament from the clouds, and other angels darting like gnats around the flashes. I'd shoulder-charged the ends of time and broken through to the circularity of it, meeting myself each way, and still there was no trace of the world, no clue God had ever made it, only a memory planted inextractably, like the traces of poison, of a blue and white sphere of seas and mountains and beings. I pushed myself off the rock with the sound of claws scratching against it and dived towards the clouds. I wanted to be the first angel to commit suicide.

I woke up. I lay in bed petting my grief that something had been lost, something which could only be the world I suspected God of having made – in an alternative course the angels had been forced to pass by without looking back. I felt as bad as if a woman I loved without her noticing had told me about another man. A better man.

Outside the window was the world I was mourning the loss of. The mountains were to the west side and the sea was to the east, the green fields to the north and the river to the south.

There were two things I admired Helmet for: wearing a fox-fur hat in bed, and teaching his dog to fetch his newspaper from the shop. I thought the hat was a pose before I found out how cold it could be where he lived. He lived in an old fisherman's cottage near the stony beach. I could see it from my window on the hill. With some people the hat would still be a pose, even if they were cold, but he wore it because it was what he had. It wasn't like he'd killed the fox himself, either. As for the dog, there must have been a lot of training involved. And if I'd seen him doing the training, I would've thought he was a right wanker. But I hadn't. That's the secret. Never let anyone see you practising. One day I was round and the dog burst through a flap in the door, trotted in, bounded up on the bed and laid a neatly folded copy of the *Courier* on Helmet's lap. And it was like with the hat. Helmet didn't make an issue of it. He put on a pair of reading glasses and offered to split the paper with me. He turned to the death notices first, hoping to find the old fisherman's name there.

He wanted the old fisherman to die and leave him the house. Helmet had been paying him ten pounds a week in rent for five years and they split the two-room effort down the middle but Helmet wanted more space for his records. Sometimes he left a few albums on the fisherman's table by way of a hint but the fisherman would always find something in them that interfered with his sense of taboos and would throw them out the window, where they could carry a fair way if the wind was right. I once came across an astounding LP wrapped up in the dried kelp and bladderwrack on the beach. The cover was shot but the vinyl was fine. I kept it. All items washed up on the beach are the property of the Queen. If she ever comes round to pick it up, she can have it.

The fisherman was in his seventies but didn't seem to be about to die. Helmet claimed he had no relatives but I told him there was no law that property passed to a tenant on the owner's death. I said he'd have to be nice to him. Helmet didn't say anything to that, he folded his arms across his chest and looked through the window at the sea.

He never even helped the old boy build his smoking shed. The fisherman had decided he would supplement his pension by making smokies on his back green like they did in Arbroath. He did build the shed, about the size of an outside toilet, but he never organized a proper fish supply and used to go to the fishmonger for packets of filleted haddock and fix them to racks with clothes pegs. Then he'd start faffing round with firelighters and bundles of firewood from the filling station. We came into the kitchenette once and found him trying to eat one of his smokies. It looked like a lung cancer autopsy. And Broughty Ferry wasn't about fish. It was about gardening, retail and sheltered housing. The old fisherman was as popular with the neighbours as a naked aborigine walking onto the stage of Sydney Opera House during a performance of *Götterdämmerung* and asking the audience to leave so he could re-establish the site of the Kookaburra Dreaming.

My work as a seal counter left me with time on my hands. I was supposed to bike over to Tentsmuir every day at dawn and count heads but I found it easier, after a few hours' research in the library, to work out a likely population curve and fabricate the figures on a daily basis. When I went down the Ferry I'd use the people I passed to incorporate a random element. A young child meant fecundity among the seals. Two white-haired pensioners together meant a low death rate. A good-looking boy or girl meant a population explosion or a deadly epidemic. If I fell stricken in love on the street I intended to create billions of seals. I was waiting to be stricken. I was expecting it. If she wasn't interested, I could always kill them later.

The morning after the dream Helmet called to see if I was coming over. He asked me to buy some pies on the way, and a couple of strawberry tarts. At the counter in Goodfellow & Steven the girl handed me the bags, I paid and left the shop. A gull sprang off the edge of the pavement, perfectly white, and stroked my jacket with the edge of its wing when it spun up towards the cloud. I stopped and looked in the bags. The baked goods nestled in unchanging twos. I went back inside.

I didn't ask for these, I said.

The girl put her hands on the counter and stood on tiptoe, peering into the mouths of the bags.

I made them up for you, she said. Did you want something different?

It's what I wanted but I didn't ask for them.

The girl settled back on her heels with a squeak of shoe-leather and a rustle of her smock and we looked at each other. These seconds would be the best of the day. The seals were to have a hard going of it later.

You come in here every morning and ask for exactly the same thing, she said. Two pies and two tarts.

I looked at her.

I was trying to save time, she said.

Everyone does that here. You can't, though. It loses its value.

That was how I found out that Helmet never left the house.

He lived off a pie and a tart and tap-water six days a week. I was keeping him alive.

He came to the door bare-chested, wearing the grey leggings and the fur hat. We went through and lay side by side on the bed in his room. He'd been in it. He had a beautiful narrow chest, and a flat stomach, not by exercise, but by luck. He had tiny hard nipples sticking up like the backsides of buttons. I often felt like laying the flat of my hand on them, to see what it felt like, but I never did, not because I was afraid he'd think I was a poof, or'd scream or SAS my windpipe, but cause I was afraid of my bigoted future self giving me a good kicking for it ten years down the road.

I arranged the baked items between us on the bedcover and we lay on our sides on one elbow.

I dreamed about God last night, I said.

Did he tell you to kill a fisherman? said Helmet.

No.

Helmet hooded his eyes and tore off a piece of pie with his teeth. There was a thunder of jet engines over town as the fighters from over the river headed out to sea.

Helmet's dog came in with the *Courier* and we divvied it up. The room had two windows, one looking onto the shore and the other into the back green. The old fisherman was to be seen pottering about so it was pointless for Helmet to be checking the deaths.

It's pointless for you to be checking the deaths, I said. He's out there. He's alive.

Helmet levelled his heavy black-framed glasses at me over the top of the paper. If it says in here he's died, he's died. There's nothing he can do about it.

Does it say he's died?

Yes.

There were two things I admired Helmet for: the hat and the dog. It wasn't much. Everything else about him was repulsive. I looked in the paper. Sure enough, there was the old boy's name, George Brynie. Peacefully, on 10 October, and a poem. We think of you most every day/ But now that you are gone/ There's really not much else to say/ We must be moving on.

I got up and went to the back window. The door of the shed opened and the fisherman came out, coughing in waves of smoke. He caught my eye and raised his hand. I waved back. I looked at my watch. It was the tenth of the month.

If you can pay for a death notice, I said, how about paying me back for the food?

Helmet lifted his finger and held it still in the air for a second, his way of smiling, went over to a box on top of one of the shelves of records, took out a fifty-pound note and gave it to me. I'd never seen one before, but that wasn't going to stop me pocketing it.

I wonder how this death notice is going to be enacted, I said.

There's a good sharp kitchen knife, said Helmet, taking off his glasses.

I looked into Helmet's eyes. We were standing in the narrow space on opposite sides of the bed. He'd always been calm, certain and determined, but nothing had ever seemed to come of it. It'd never been possible to believe that the only goal towards which his self-conviction was taking him was finding more space for his records, even in the days when he'd still lived with his parents and he'd only had a few hundred. I tried to remember all the trivial things we'd talked about. They were trivial. And if I'd known they were trivial even then it meant I'd always known there was something not trivial which was not being spoken of. If the trivial things had been about money and entertainment, the thing not spoken of was a man's life. Helmet was sober and calculating now in his record-lined room which was more to him than the world he didn't enter any more and so it was the man's life, perhaps, that was trivial now. I feared for the fisherman. But I was wondering about the money too.

I opened my mouth to speak about the law and understood for Helmet it would be necessary to go deeper.

He hasn't done you any harm, I said. You can't do it.

I won't get found out.

That's not what I mean. I mean it's wrong.

Why? Is this something to do with your dream?

It's to do with thousands of years of human civilization.

I haven't been around for thousands of years. I'm only twenty-seven. He's lived long enough. He takes up too much space. He stinks of smoke and fish.

You're exaggerating. He doesn't get in your way. Killing him is too extreme.

You're only saying that because you think I'll get found out.

No! I'm not!

I was trying to convince myself, and trying not to think about Helmet with a kitchen knife in his hand, coming up behind old Brynie in the kitchen while he was frying his supper that evening. It's wrong, I said. It's immoral, murder is wrong.

Why?

I looked out of the window at the sea. The edges of the waves slid up sharp and solid as the jags of a broken bottle. I tried to think of reasons for things we don't usually seek reasons for because if we did we'd realize how badly we needed them at the same time as we realized how hard they were to find, as if you'd become addicted to a drug in your sleep and woken up to find it hadn't been invented, as if you suspected a better world had been made and unmade behind your back before you'd had a chance to savour it.

He's a human being like you, I said. What if everyone killed anyone who got in their way?

They won't, said Helmet. Everyone's afraid of getting caught. And the rest are afraid of having to clear up the mess.

Jesus, I said.

Is that your dream again? Is it religion, is that it?

No! You know I don't believe in that. Listen, Helmet, you're a human being, it's what you are, you can't help it, and it's in your nature to be angry, but it's also in your nature to be merciful and feel pity.

He doesn't deserve any mercy.

But he hasn't done anything wrong!

He has, he's stopped me taking his room for my records.

The whole house belongs to him!

Exactly, said Helmet. That's why I can't go on like this.

I sat down on the edge of the bed. I felt as if the blood bank'd just tapped me for all I had.

When are you thinking of doing this? I said.

After tea, said Helmet.

All the blood came flooding back, with interest on the loan, and if the knife'd been there on the bed I would have filleted the boy on the spot.

You're fucking ill, you are, I said.

Easy, said Helmet.

You don't see the seals killing each other.

I'm not a seal. They don't collect records. I could see his

brain working in the flexing of the flesh of his forehead. And if they did, they'd have more room for them out there.

The phone rang. It was out in the hall. The fisherman answered it. He knocked and put his head round the door. Phone, he said flatly and disappeared.

He was a small man, bony. Getting the point of the knife through his dungarees and sweater and on between the ribs would be hard. The worst moment would be halfway when Brynie was still alive but the blade was half in and it was too late to change your mind and say: God, sorry George, didn't mean it. Especially if there'd been no row beforehand.

Forget it, Helmet, I said. They'll catch you anyway.

Oh! he said, pointing at me as he went out. Like I said. And they won't.

I picked up the *Courier* again and leafed through. I shivered. Someone had draped my chest in a soaked bedsheet. The text blurred on the white. Scientists shocked by latest seal numbers, said a headline on a single column story. The rest of it was punched through by canine teeth and smeared with dog saliva. The worst thing was his trust in me. No, the worst thing was that his trust might be justified. That I'd wait until he did it, because surely he wouldn't, and afterwards it'd be done, and Brynie would be dead, and there'd be no bringing him back, so what would the point be in destroying Helmet, let his conscience be his executioner? Not that he had one. And where did you go to denounce your friend for planning to murder a stranger? The victim? The police? His mother?

Helmet came back. I could tell there was someone still on the line from the way he stood in the doorway.

It's the man, he said. D'you want to put something on the 1979?

Tell him to call back. Let's talk more about your plans for tonight.

I'm putting a tenner on Callaghan.

I got up and went out into the hall where the receiver hung bobbing on the end of its wire, stotting gently against the woodchip. Helmet watched without saying anything while I picked it up.

Could you call back, I said.

Minimum stake's a fiver, said a voice like stones grinding together. Callaghan 5–1, Thatcher 3–2, Steel 100–1, Wilson 100–1. Ten minutes to the off so make up your mind, eh. Your pal took me for fifty quid last week.

Fifty, eh?

Backed Reagan in the 1980 at Washington on 2–1. The old guy was ahead by three furlongs. So're you in or what? The voice went into a coughing fit. It sounded like someone was stirring his guts with a poker.

I asked Helmet what the year was. He said 1997. I asked him what we were betting on.

1979 general election results, he said.

It was Thatcher, I said. Thatcher won it. You remember. You were already born then.

Was he born? You couldn't imagine him with an umbilical cord. With some people you could. With some people you didn't have to imagine, they still had it, they were sitting in the pub and you looked down and you noticed this long, manky, trodden-in bit of fleshy string leading to the door, and you'd see it twitch a couple of times, and your drinking companion'd drain his pint and say, Must be getting back, they'll be starting to worry. And off he'd go, coiling it in his hands as he went.

How d'you know she won it? said Helmet.

I remember, I said. It happened nineteen years ago. It happened. It occurred. Callaghan lost. He did. He wasn't prime minister any more. You can't go back. It's already been. You know what your trouble is? You don't go out enough. You sit in here with your records and you think it's acceptable to murder people and time loses its meaning for you, you can't tell the difference any more between good and bad and right and wrong and past and future. Don't think you'll convince me there's money to be made betting on Callaghan to win the 1979 general election because these things happen only once, they've been already. D'you think it's going to get to me because I sit here with you inside your four walls, inside your record collection, for an hour or two? It's not, because I go outside and I see that what's broken stays broken, and what's dead stays dead, and what gets old doesn't turn young, and that people live with that, they get so used to it they don't even think about it, and they get by without killing each other and without trying to cheat the past. It can't be done. And you will get caught if you kill the fisherman. Come out for a drink tonight.

Helmet covered his upper lip with his lower one and looked down at the floor. He went over to the phone and told the guy to call back when he was ready to start. He stepped back onto the bed, scratching his stomach, and lay down. I sat down on the edge, facing away from him. Neither of us said anything for a while. From where I sat I could see a long red freighter gliding at speed upriver, powering flatly through the waves behind the delving pilot boat.

So who d'you reckon's going to win? said Helmet.

Thatcher, I said. She wins the 1979 general election every time.

Why don't you put money on it if you're so sure?

Who's the bookie?

Don't know. Just started ringing up. He sends a young lad round to collect the stake or give you your winnings. I'm ahead so far. He got skinned on the 1966 World Cup.

You had your money on England, eh?

There was a tip. What about the 1979?

The phone rang.

Go on then, I said.

How much?

Fifty.

Fifty.

We went together to the phone. Helmet placed the bet and held the receiver between our heads so we could both make out the commentary.

There was a sound like a pistol shot down the line and they were off with the old guy doing the live commentary bit. And it's Thatcher in the lead followed by Callaghan then Steel from Wilson and Callaghan going strongly and Steel and Wilson fighting for third and fourth place and Callaghan's pulled level with Thatcher and they're neck and neck and Wilson now, Wilson coming strongly into third but Steel's coming up on the outside, now it's Callaghan from Thatcher and Steel with Wilson trailing, and as they come into the final furlong Thatcher's out in front and she's opening up the gap, it's Thatcher from Callaghan with Steel and Steel's fallen! Steel's fallen, and Callaghan's putting on a sudden burst and he's pulled ahead of Thatcher, Callaghan's in front, he's ahead as they cross the line and it's Callaghan first, Thatcher in second, Wilson coming in a long way behind in third and the vets now moving swiftly over to David Steel, I'm afraid he'll have to be shot, but what a superb finish from Jim Callaghan, beating the favourite Margaret Thatcher in a magnificent race which will yet again have the punters tearing up their form books in despair. Give Helmet the cash.

Eh? I said.

Just give Helmet the stake, the voice said. I'll pick it up later.

That was the 1979 general election.

Plus five quid tax, that'll be 55 pounds.

That's not on, I said. Thatcher won.

Fine. You're barred. D'you understand me? Barred. You heard the result, if you'd like to hand over the money to Helmet there we won't have any further problems.

I want to know who gave you permission to fuck around with history like that.

If it's history you want go to the library. This is the past we deal with here, and we can do what we like with it. It hasn't been nationalized.

I'll give Helmet the money. But admit she won. I remember.

That's your business, sir. No-one's trying to tell you what to put in your memory.

Eighteen years of Tory rule!

It could've been a dream. It's your private business. All we ask is that you don't try to spoil other people's free use of the common past by dumping your memories all over it. The bookie hung up.

I fancied Thatcher myself, said Helmet, taking the cash and sticking the notes into his waistband. He went back into his room, put a copy of *Super Trouper* on the turntable and lay down on the bed with his hands behind his head, looking at the ceiling. I expected to see fox fur under his armpits but the hairs were black, flat and separate.

Come out for a bit, I said.

No, said Helmet.

If you came out you'd see what I mean about the way things are. It'd all fall into place. You'd see that time only goes one way, the past only happens once, and that killing people is too complicated.

You're saying I shouldn't kill him because it's too complicated? said Helmet, frowning at the ceiling.

Yes, I said. That's one reason. The sweat was over me again, hot this time. If you came out with me you'd remember there's more than just you and me and the fisherman. There are so many people, and they're all connected, and if you kill one of them, others are bound to get dragged in.

I can put your mind to rest on that. It's not complicated at all. It's very simple. There's me, and the fisherman, and I kill him, and then there's just me. That's it. It's not a problem.

Are you coming out?

No.

Don't do anything, I said. It's not like taking a record off. You can't put it on again. It's not like the ships that come up the river and always go back out. It's not like Thatcher. True enough, we never saw her in the flesh. Maybe she never did win. Maybe she doesn't exist. But the fisherman does.

Not for long, said Helmet.

I went to the turntable, flicked the arm aside, took off the Abba album and snapped it in two.

That's what happens, I said.

No it isn't, said Helmet. I've got a couple more of them. That's a fiver you owe me.

What if I broke them all? I said.

Helmet said nothing but I saw his lips press together and a dark tongue-tip zip them up moist.

I'm going out, I said. I'll come round again before tea.

Helmet was silent.

Brynie was working on fish in the kitchen. I saw the big knife hanging flat vertical on a magnet.

Hi, I said. How's it going?

All right, said the fisherman.

Helmet said it'd be OK if I borrowed a knife for a couple of hours.

Help yourself.

I took the knife off the magnet. It was shiny stainless steel with a black plastic handle and a broad ten-inch blade. I held it suspended, holding the handle between thumb and one finger.

Take care, then, I said.

Brynie looked at me over his shoulder with his eyebrows arrowed into his nose and went back to his fish. I went out into the street.

The sun had come out. There weren't so many folk down where I was near the old lifeboat shed. I saw a rapid movement across the wall of a tenement opposite, like a cursor fleeing across a screen. It was the light reflecting off the blade of the knife swinging in my hand. I was wearing a red woollen jumper and black jeans. I lifted the hem of the jumper and started pushing the blade down the front of my jeans, blade turned out. The thigh cringed from the cold of the metal as it went down. The point pricked me and I drew in breath. A white-haired couple went past looking at me and wondering out loud what the lad was doing. I pulled the jumper over the knife handle and set off for Visocchi's. It was hard to walk without stabbing myself in the leg. It felt as if I already had. I limped along slowly, looking down every second to see if blood was blooming on my jeans. There was no sign but what an idea for a product: tampons for soccer casuals. I used to be afraid to wear white jeans to the game but now with super-absorbent wound-strength Tampax I can go out tooled up with absolute confidence.

I went into the café. I saw the girl from the baker's on her own in the corner with a pot of tea and a mini-pizza and asked if I could join her. She looked up from under eyelashes lumpy with kohl, like charred fishbones floating on a rockpool. She managed not to smile. She waved with her hand to the seat opposite. I sat down. The girl screamed and her knees snapped up to crash into the underneath of the table as she recoiled.

I held up my hands. It's OK, I said. There are things which can't be explained but this isn't one of them. I snatched a napkin off the table, opened it and spread it over my lap, covering the two inches of knife blade which had pierced the jeans and poked out into the open air from the top of my knee. I'll tell you about it once everyone's stopped looking.

I need to be getting back, said the girl, pale.

I turned my head. One by one folk went back to their food as they met my eye.

It's not mine, I said, picking up a menu and leaning forward. I just happen to have it on me this one time. And I thought if I walked through the streets of Broughty Ferry with a ten-inch kitchen knife in my hands I might cause anxiety.

You could have put it in a bag, said the girl.

I didn't have time. Listen, I'm going to take it out now, and put it on the table. OK?

I need to be getting back.

Just be calm. I don't like it either. That's why I want to take it out of my trousers right now, and put it on the table.

Can't you wait till I've gone?

If I wait any longer I'm going to turn my leg into fajitas. Just be calm.

How should I be calm?

You see me coming into the bakery every morning, don't you?

That's what they do! They keep telling you! It could be someone you know!

Wait, I said. I screened my lap with the menu, slid the knife out and laid it on the table.

D'you have to go back right now? I asked.

No. What is it you do?

I'm a seal counter. I count seals.

The girl picked a splinter of once-frozen cheese off the mini-pizza and nipped it with her teeth. Her nails were pink. So how many are there? she said.

Enough.

How many seals is enough?

I don't know. How many people is enough?

Four, said the girl seriously, looking at me and twiddling another bit of cheese between her pink nails. A strand of hair swung in and hooked her lips. She flicked it back behind her ear and put the splinter on her tongue.

A waitress came. I ordered a steak and a pot of tea.

There's one! said the girl, pointing over my shoulder.

I looked round. What? I said.

You missed it, said the girl. There was a seal coming out the charity shop with a drip-dry brown nylon top. She grinned and looked pleased with herself.

The waitress came back and tried to lay down a steak knife at my place. I lifted the fisherman's blade. It's OK, I've got one, I said.

The waitress opened her mouth, closed it and walked away.

The girl was angry with me for not being good about her joke. She rested her chin on her hand and looked out the window. I asked her what her name was. She didn't pay any attention.

Listen, I said. I have this friend. He wears a fox-fur hat in bed and taught his dog to fetch the newspaper for him. He's been indoors for too long. He says he's going to kill a man tonight. His landlord. It was going to be with this knife. But there are other knives in the house. His landlord's a fisherman, and they always have a lot of knives about the place. Now I'm wondering how we became friends. I can't remember how it was an hour ago, before he told me about what he was going to do, whether I thought better of him, or if I always knew he was going to show me one day he didn't care about other human beings. I can't remember.

It's Liz, said the girl.

Wait.

You haven't told me yours.

Wait. Suppose your friend is about to kill someone. What do you do? This is what I'm most afraid of: that I go to see him later and there's no fisherman. No blood, no weapon, no clothes, no possessions. And I say to Helmet: What happened to the fisherman? And he says, What fisherman? You're remembering something that you dreamed as if it really happened. And I say: But Helmet, I remember. And he says: A memory of a man doesn't make the man exist. D'you see what I'm saying?

He sounds like a right wee bastard, this Helmet.

He's not wee.

I know the dog. I've seen it coming out of the newsagent with two copies of the *Courier*.

Two, I said.

I thought it was weird there were two. I followed it once and I saw it going into the house with both papers.

Christ, I always thought the fisherman hated the dog, I said. The trouble with Helmet is he's a psychopath, but he's too thick to be good at it.

I got up. Liz raised her head and her hair fell back, and she looked at me and blinked. Sometimes it's only when the looker blinks you realize how hard they're looking at you and how deep back the heart of the look lies. And that's in Visocchi's, over a half-eaten mini-pizza, a stainless steel teapot and a ten-inch kitchen knife. The seals were thickening. I took out five pounds and left it on the table.

I have to go, I said. That's for the steak. You have it.

Are you going to count seals? said Liz.

Later, I said. I go across to Tentsmuir. But there's others out on the sandbanks, closer to Monifieth. I was going to walk out there this evening. You could come.

OK, she said.

I made for Helmet's place. I left the knife on the table where I'd put it. I was trying to think how much I cared about Helmet. Not much. Hardly more than the money he'd cost me that day. Maybe I'd cared more before lunch. Liz was millions of seals, billions, just the way her hair bobbed against her bare neck, and those tiny golden shaved hairs, on the curve at the back.

At the cottage there was no answer when I knocked. The door wasn't locked. I went in. The house stank of smoked bacon. The dog ran up and started doing figures of eight round my ankles. I went through to the back green and saw the fisherman sitting on a chair outside his smoking shed, reading the *Courier*. He had reading glasses like Helmet's. Smoke wisped out from the edges of the shed door, held shut with a wooden twist latch. I stood in front of the fisherman for a while. He took no notice. A gull screamed on the glide over the shore, as if in ecstasy, or on ecstasy, after all, they must get dropped in the gutter sometimes. The smell was rich.

Where's Helmet? I said.

The fisherman said nothing. He didn't look up. Only his eyes moved, scanning text.

Where's Helmet? Where's Ian?

Eh? said the fisherman.

I was expected to remember the tosser's surname as well. Ian Colwell. Your tenant. I'm looking for him.

No tenant here, said the fisherman. I live on my own. Me and the dog.

You had a tenant. I was here this morning. I borrowed a knife from you.

I don't remember. Have you got it with you?

No. Where's Helmet?

Are you wanting to do business, son, 'cause I'm busy.

I heard you were branching out from smoked fish into smoked pig. I was thinking of making an order. D'you mind if I look in the shed?

I'm not taking orders, said the fisherman, lifting his eyes from the paper for the first time. It's all still at the experimental stage. I'm getting a grant from Brussels. I need to expand. There's not enough room here. He took off his glasses and tapped the inside pages of the paper. It's a communist paper, the *Courier*, he said. They're against private enterprise. They've been running a campaign against me. They're hand in glove with the council, you see, against the business. If they can't get you on planning permission, they get you on the fucking Clean Air Act.

I'm not saying I want to look in the shed, I said.

I'm not saying I'm going to let you, son.

Maybe someone walked in there by mistake and got locked in.

The fisherman folded the paper and put it down on the flagstones beside his chair. He took a tin out of his shirt pocket and started rolling a cigarette. He really did like smoke.

You can see the latch is on the outside, he said. If anyone's in there, it means I locked them in, right? D'you think like there might be a market for smoked folk? He laughed and lit the cigarette. With yellow skin like haddock! He laughed. See that commie rag? They ran a death notice of me this morning. It's part of the campaign against me. I wasn't too chuffed when I saw the death but then I thought hang about, if they all think I'm dead and I'm alive, there's bound to be some poor bugger who's died and nobody knows.

Why?

You think they can put a death notice in the paper and there's no death? I signed up once on a deep-sea trawler, spit new, superb, radar, sonar, stabilisers, it was like a space shuttle. A million and a half it cost. There were a dozen partners and it was named after the skipper's daughter. The *Tamsin L.* We were set for the first trip and the girl goes and gets herself kidnapped in Kashmir. Kashmir, aye. She was hiking there and they took her, the rebels. And nothing was heard for six or eight months. And we went to sea all the same. And the skipper too. We had two good trips. Listening to the radio, keeping in touch, but thousands of miles from shore nonetheless. I was on a fixed rate, the partners were on a percentage. I was doing all right and they were making an absolute mint. So we were back on shore and the news came in that the girl had been killed. They'd found her body with some others in the mountains with a message saying why they'd done it.

Why?

I can't remember, said the fisherman, shaking his head and waving his hand. They wanted to be free.

Free from what?

Free from having to kill people. They wanted the place to themselves. Anyway so the skipper had to fly out there, poor bastard, and identify the body. He was all set to go and he went to his partners and said, Look you're due to sail the morn, go anyway, go by yourselves, this is hard enough on me, why should you lose out. And they didn't say anything, they looked away, looked at the ground, they couldn't look him in the eye. They refused to sail. Eventually he realised it was the name: they'd never set foot in the boat as long as it was called the *Tamsin L*. So he said, OK, we'll recommission her, she'll be another boat. But not till I get back. Till then you can just sit on shore and drink your savings. And he flew off to Kashmir.

Only when he got there, who should he see waiting at the airport to meet him but the fucking lassie, his daughter! The local polis had screwed up and it wasn't her who'd been killed, they hadn't killed anyone, I can't mind now if she was ever even kidnapped or if she maybe just hiked around the Himalayas with them for a few months. So it was a big happy ending and they rode off on the 747 back to bonnie Scotland, five pages in the *Daily Record*, TV interviews and everything. And when the partying and the drinking's all done the skipper rounds up the crew and says, Right lads, we've got some ground to make up here. And it's the same routine again with the eyes, you know, they can't look him in the face. They still won't go. And he tries to tell them she wasn't killed, no-one died, it was a mistake, no need to change the name, everything was back to the way it was before, like they'd dreamed it all. It was no good. None of them could explain it, or maybe they could've, but nobody tried, they knew they couldn't go on the boat any more. He couldn't persuade them. There'd never even been a funeral, but as far as they were concerned they'd lived through the death of *Tamsin L*, and that was it.

Is it true? I said.

The fisherman shrugged and went back to his paper. I walked to the shed and unlatched the door. The hot salty smoke smothered me and I took a few paces back, intoxicated and coughing, eyes stinging. When it cleared I saw the dark space empty except for half a dozen rashers of supermarket streaky bacon pegged to the racks.

I turned and walked back into the house. Brynie didn't try to stop me. I opened the door to Helmet's room. Helmet wasn't there. The bed was made and the records were gone and without them there was no sign Helmet had ever been there. I looked out the window at the fisherman. He was sitting where I'd left him, reading, though he'd closed the door of the smoking shed. I left the house and went home.

I rang Helmet's number a couple of times in the afternoon and hung up without saying anything when the fisherman answered. I couldn't sit down or eat. I made a pot of tea and watched it get cold. I stood at windows with my palms on the glass, breathing on it, drawing crosses, hearts and smiley faces with the tip of my finger. I watched Gray Street through the binoculars, not knowing if I was looking for Helmet or Liz. I couldn't remember when I'd last seen Helmet in the open air. The pedestrians looked anxious and placid until two of them would start laughing for no clear reason. The sun was on its way down. I should have done something about Helmet. It was making me feel bad that I hadn't. It was only so bad as to be strong spice for the feeling good about meeting Liz later. And the planet'd spin like a tennis ball and get kicked off the

wall of sleep four or five times and lose its energy and which of
them'd be first to fade? I didn't know. But the thought of not
breakfasting with the fur hat worried me less than the thought
of not having a reason to go to the baker's in the morning.

I went down the road at six with the binoculars round my
neck and a seal sheet in my pocket and saw Liz in a print dress
sitting on the bench near the lifeboat shed, looking out across
the river. The sky was still light from the afterglow of the sun
but pricked with a blinding white Venus it looked a darker
blue than it really was. Liz looked up and smiled and turned
back to the river. I sat down next to her. Her hands were on
her lap and she was playing with her fingers.

It's too dark to count seals, she said.

I know, I said. D'you not want to go for a walk?

No, it's OK, she said. I thought maybe you had special
equipment for seeing in the dark.

I don't. Just these, I said, holding out the binoculars.

She took them and focused on Tayport. She watched the
cars scudding along the coast road for a bit. Then she stood
up and tried to look at the dark light-speckled humps of
Dundee upriver.

The lights keep skidding, she said. It's hard to keep still.

Here, put them on my shoulder, I said.

She came round behind where I was sitting on the bench and
put the binoculars on my shoulder, leaning her body against
my back.

There's a plane landing at the airstrip, she said.

I could feel her breasts press into my back and her heart
beating as she tracked the plane in. She moved away and
handed the binoculars back.

We began walking along the top of the sea wall. It was
easier than I expected to ignore what was coming in on the

tide as long as she hadn't noticed it. She said there'd been something on TV about the seals: too many old ones, not enough pups being born, they couldn't understand it. I told her how I made up the results.

Is that not really bad? she said.

If they knew the truth, it'd be worse. The real seals are having millions of kids, and most of them don't survive to be old, and the old tough ones get to be that way because they survived and know how to beat the young ones back until their teeth fall out and they're too weak to fight and feed themselves any more and they go away and die. I've been counting people instead of seals and it's the other way round. Too many old ones and not enough pups. And the pups start to think they're the tough ones. Time runs backwards and the young ones try to teach the old ones, try to share their wisdom, and if they don't listen, or they get too cocky, or they get in their way, they go out and fight. The scientists are looking at my figures and they can't believe the young seals are so special and the old ones are so common. They should start counting their own.

What are those? said Liz, stopping and putting her hand on my shoulder. She'd noticed. She pointed at the flat waves lapping the stones, pushing a zig-zag graph of sodden album covers up the beach.

I put my hand on top of her hand. It was cool and soft. I love you, I said.

She turned round to look at me.

What? she said.

I leaned forward and kissed her and found her mouth slightly open. Hers was the tongue to enter, buzz on mine and slip out. We separated. I heard the sound of marine engines on the river, cars and the hiss of the city as if my ears had just been unblocked. She looked at me like a nurse who'd had to jab a bucketful of adrenalin into a cardiac arrest case and was interested to see what was going to happen next.

You're going too fast for me, she said.

Yeah?

That only happened because of me getting interested in those LPs being washed up on the beach, didn't it?

No, I said. It was because of that, but it was also bringing forward something I was going to do anyway.

Fuck you, said Liz. I'll go away and come back later, would that be more convenient?

No, but don't let's talk about those albums. I did want to change the subject but would I have thought of saying I love you if I didn't? It would have taken longer otherwise. Did I not sound as if I meant it?

Liz began moving on and I walked beside her. She didn't look at me to begin with.

She said, Maybe you sounded like a man who finds it easier to change the names of things than do something about them. Like you're afraid your friend's too close to murder, and because there happens to be a girl next to you, the easiest thing is to cross out I'm afraid and write in I love you. But it's fear all the same, not love.

It's not like that, I said, and went quiet, because I couldn't think of anything else to say, because she was almost right. But we were walking on, leaving the records behind. We passed the harbour and approached the floodlit castle. It was a clear night. It would have been good to have lain with Liz on the beach, watching the stars and all the cosmic furniture. The floodlights and the streetlights were too bright. Through the fog of lights only the very brightest planets stood out. Years back the energy makers had gone on strike and there'd been power cuts across the district. We'd been grateful those nights,

when we'd hung our heads back with our mouths open and
tried to cover the whole speckled glory with our narrow eyes,
and the powdered field behind the constellations had seemed to
drift and not drift, move and not move. Then the lights of the
ground came on again. The energy makers had dared to strike
then. They didn't know Thatcher was coming. I was as angry
with them for a moment as with Helmet for not accepting that
she'd ever been. It was easy enough to confuse the past with
the future. I did it all the time. Liz was right. My mind was as
weak as Helmet's, it was filled with storms that had no names
or directions, colours that could never be remembered, events
with faces and dialogue that shifted with mood and age.

Is that a seal down there? said Liz.

We were on the beach, walking on the dry sand firthward
of the dunes, the tide half out. She pointed to a blubbery tube
rolling from side to side in the surf. We stopped.

I don't know, I said.

I'm going to look, she said.

Don't.

You said you came out to count seals.

I told you about that.

You could get one real one at least.

What if it isn't a seal?

Liz frowned and looked down at the sand. We go to the
police, she said.

I squatted down like a bird and watched Liz step away
alone through the ragged graph of jetsam onto the smooth,
wet, yielding sand of the recoiling waters. The first horn
of a crescent moon had risen over Tentsmuir, sheening the
lower beach, and Liz's feet sank neat black inches into the
sand, haloed with squeezed dry grains like charlatan snaps of
ectoplasm. She reached the body, bent down, skipped away

to avoid an incoming wave, pushed her hair back, turned to me, pointed at the carcass and called: One!

I got up and walked towards the creature. It was an immature seal, not long dead, its eyes missing, otherwise whole. I'd never learned how to sex them.

Thanks, I said. I'm a coward.

Yeah, you are, said Liz. I've never seen one this close before.

Neither have I.

What a shame.

They do die.

I know, said Liz, but it's still a shame. I suppose when my granny was laid out in the lounge you would have been the one to put your head round the door and tell us: Well, they do die.

I wish I could've. Only as you said, I'm a coward.

We walked on and I started telling Liz the dream. I was a detective angel, I said. An investigator. I could go anywhere, even through time, but I couldn't go into alternatives: only God could do that. The thing was I suspected he'd made the world – you know, earth – and then changed his mind, it'd just been one of the avenues he was exploring. But I couldn't prove it.

My dad's always doing that, said Liz. He makes things, then changes his mind and hides them. You should have looked in God's attic.

But I was sure I remembered the world. Even though I'd never seen it, the idea of it had got into me somehow, and it was killing me to think of how it'd been and then wasn't and I never would see it. Then I woke up, and instead of being relieved I was in the world I'd thought I'd lost, I felt terrible about losing the false memory of a real world.

How about not losing me? said Liz. Is there some point to this? What was God like?

Like someone who pretends to be very hospitable, but makes it obvious they can't wait for the guests to leave.

I like the real real world, said Liz.

You only get to touch it in one place at a time, though, and the rest crumbles away behind you.

You expect too much.

It was the best thing I'd heard about myself for a long time, and the place I touched, the beach, seemed very wide and deep.

Look, said Liz. There's another dead seal.

Another dark body lolled on the waterline a hundred yards further on.

Let's take a look, then, I said.

Are you not scared? she said.

We have to look, I said, taking her hand and leading her on.

Chefs' Night Out

ANTHONY BOURDAIN

TO BE HONEST, it didn't start with what Jimmy said. Or with the review. It didn't start last night, during that long, ugly bar crawl. And as much as I'd like to lay it off on the drinking, or the coke, or the pressure of the busy season – it just didn't start there either.

It was the lobsters.

And that steak. I think that steak might have had something to do with it.

That's where it started. Where things started to slide.

Understand; I've been killing lobsters for like, twenty-two years now. I've boiled them alive. Steamed them to death. I've torn them in half, chopped them into wriggling chunks for fricassee, for Lobster Americaine. Early in my career, when I worked at one of those seaside tourist traps – this one appropriately named 'The Lobster Shack', you could pick your victim out of a 55-gallon tank on your way into the dining room, and I'd kill him to order, have him delivered to your table steamed, broiled, stuffed, or baked – your choice.

I killed them in dozens, stacked their struggling bodies in heaps, five-deep in the heavy stainless steel and wrought-iron steamer, slammed the double doors shut, turned the wheel, and gave them the steam. I racked up, in one year, a body count that would have been the envy of a company-sized unit of angry Serbs. I was the Pol Pot of Lobsterdom, and you could smell the brackish cloud from the stacks of the dead blocks away from my kitchen. The drains clogged with the milky white albumen that bubbled out from inside their shells – it clung to my shoes, stained my clothes, collected under my fingernails.

And I didn't mind at all. Not one little bit.

One of my early chefs, an affable Frenchman from Alsace with a drinking problem, explained why, for Lobster Americaine, one must section the hapless creatures while still alive.

'The meat,' he said, 'she become tough.'

I said, 'Oui chef!', like a good German, and soldiered on, no thought at all to my victims' pain, or to some potential Lobster Nuremberg in the future.

Friends of mine complained of bad dreams.

'I dream I'm in a sauna,' said one, 'and I look out the door through the little window? And there's a big motherfuckin' lobster, wearing a bib, with a pitcher of a chef on it, and he's like, turning up the heat, man. His antennae are twitching, and he's making all sorts a godawful screechin' sounds. There's a whole buncha his friends, eggin' him on and cheerin'. They clappin' their claws together as he gives *me* the steam. Then . . . then, when I'm all pink and red and shit, they take me out and gang up on me. They split me up the middle and are like, cramming hunks a crabmeat and bay scallops in my chest, and I'm flopping around and screaming on the cutting board. Payback . . .' shuddered my friend, '. . . payback is a motherfucker.'

Never bothered me, though. I didn't dream about lobsters. For over two decades, it's been crunch crunch crunch, my 14-inch German steel chef knife coming down on generation after generation of bucking lobsters, cutting them into neat, one-inch sections. I prided myself on my precision, never overcooking. When I shucked, the claws came out intact, every time.

Though I am not a cruel man, I felt perfectly detached from their misery.

If you kill it, eat it. That's the moral threshold for me. Or it was, until recently.

Shoving food down a recalcitrant goose's throat until his liver balloons into foie gras? *Pas de problème.* I can live with that. Ditto veal. Somebody's gotta lock up a calf in a dark shed, induce anaemia to get those buttery soft, pale pink scallopines? Tough titty. Whatever torments my meal had to endure on the way to my plate is just too bad – if it tastes good enough. I can tell you that it's a good thing New Yorkers haven't acquired a taste for live monkey brain, or I'd really have a lot to answer for. Sorry.

So, fuck the lobsters, is what I always said.

'They too dumb to know they dead,' like my sous chef, Ricky says.

Lately, however, they've been on my mind. In disturbing new ways. And I don't like it.

Maybe it's the new presentation. I've been making Bouillabaisse, you see. It's something of a signature dish of mine. At the restaurant, we get thirty-two bucks a pop for it – it's a moneymaker. I don't just make money on the Bouillabaisse, either. One guy comes in for the Bouillabaisse, where the house makes, say, sixty-six per cent profit? You know he's going to bring in three or four friends, and they're gonna order chicken or salmon, or better yet, pasta – where I'm making seventy-five, even eighty per cent. It's powerful math, but a losing equation for lobsters.

Bouillabaisse, at my place, is a bowl of Prince Edward Island mussels, some New Zealand cockles, a couple of head-on Gulf shrimps, a sea scallop or two, and some assorted 'garbage fish' — meaning less expensive, less popular fishes which nobody would order if they weren't accompanied by lobster. I lightly braise all this in the classic seafood broth with saffron, garlic, leeks, tomatoes, shot of Pernod, and by the time the customer has washed it down with some wine, had a cup of coffee and maybe a dessert, he's dropped a day's pay. At thirty-two bucks, though, he wants — he *expects* a show; some artful presentation. The restaurant business, after all, is *show* business, and the easiest way to impress, is to go, as we say, 'vertical'.

So. I give them the head.

Not just the head. (Actually, all they get is half an undersized tail, and one measly claw.) What they get, the thing that razzle dazzles them and makes them oooh and ahhhh as my Bouillabaisse goes sailing by in the dining room, is the way we arrange the antennae on the head, perched magnificently in the middle of the bowl. They spiral regally upwards, in a bright, red, double-helix, six inches long from the head, like an appetizing-looking strand of DNA. Let me tell you: it looks damn impressive.

Sadly for the lobster, this effect is not easily attained.

It requires me, each morning, after a cup of coffee, a couple of aspirin, and a cigarette or two, to assemble the lobsters on my cutting board, and first, cut them in half. While alive.

You have to keep the antennae supple, you see. So you can work them, weave them into that stylish, concentric spiral. The lobster *has* to be alive.

Some chefs will tell you that you can, by stroking the lobster's back, put him to sleep before doing the deed. I don't do that. First of all — it humanizes them too much I think. And anyway, it's too damn time-consuming, singing lullabies to an oversized insect.

I simply whack them in half, as quickly and as mercifully as possible.

And it's not the wriggling and flip-flopping which gets to me – the way the severed halves move independently of each other, claws still opening and closing, tail skipping around blindly, seeking a brain to tell it what to do. I'm used to that. And when I stick my fingers up into the head cavity, scoop out anything resembling an organ or a gut, that's fine too.

It's the next thing that spooks me.

When I've got the hollowed-out heads lined up before me, like crippled soldiers, in an orderly row, their still brown and limp antennae awaiting my attentions – here's where the trouble starts. You see ... in order to get those antennae up, to hold them in place, to retain that graceful sweep skyward when I throw the whole head into the boiling fat – frying them so they turn red and firm – in order to do that, I have to first, drive a bamboo skewer right between the lobster's eyes, into its empty, but still twitching skull.

It's that one, horrible second, when the skewer is hammered home, the bamboo point burying itself deep in the lobster's empty brain pan, when *the lobster's eyes cross* for just a second: *that's* what's got me all fucked up lately. *That's* what's been bothering me. It's the expression on the lobster's face as he goes cross-eyed, like he's getting the message now for sure. And I expect, always, for the lobster to say something. An exclamation out of an animated cartoon, perhaps. Something like 'YIKES!' or 'DUHHHHYEAHHH!'

I find myself empathizing with the head. I imagine how *I'd* feel – some long, thin, surgical probe comes pounding down into MY cranium with swift, unflinching accuracy, straight into my frontal lobe.

What would I feel? A flash of steel-blue? The taste of metal in my mouth? Then oblivion? I don't know. But I think about it a lot. I even, in some sick, cynical, bone-tired part of myself, find myself *yearning* for that feeling – whatever it is – for deliverance, an end to consciousness, a blissfully vegetative state. Even the thought of my own stupid head, propped up in a bowl of fish broth and inexpensive seafood, a *rouilly*-smeared croustade extended from between my clenched teeth, my hair teased and fried into a vertical, if grisly, final affront to the dining public who I have come, in my heart of hearts, to loathe and despise with a burning, purple passion, even that whimsical image gives me a shudder of pleasure.

So, it was this lobster thing. I blame that for my unraveling. For my seemingly spontaneous, uncharacteristically violent reaction.

The steak had something to do with it. No question. But I'll get to that.

I haven't been any crankier at work. I was, and still am, I think, a terror on the floor staff, an enigma to my boss, and 'Dad' to my crew. Maybe I've been drinking a little bit more, but not during the shift, when I still confine myself to one shaker glass of margaritas, and two, maybe three pints of beer. I work in a fairly busy establishment, after all, even if it's a failing one, and one needs, in such circumstances, something to modulate one's natural, homicidal urges. It would not do, as one of my fellow chefs recently did, to leap over the line in a rage, bury my teeth in a particularly slow-witted waiter's nose and shake him like a dog. I never did anything like that, until last night. It's undignified.

No, I was managing to fall apart in private ways. Crying on the subway, for instance. Way to work – the morning commute, I catch a glimpse of another commuter's newspaper, a headline that says, say, 'HERO CAT SAVES TWINS' or 'TOTS KILLED IN FIRE', and I start weeping. At home, sometimes, on my day off, I'm laying around, smoking a nice fat spliff of hydro, watching the tube, and I start bawling over a car commercial, or a TV ad for long-distance telephone service. Those always get me. It's pathetic. A warning sign.

I haven't been answering the phone. I listen, on the answering machine, to the plaintive wails of my dwindling number of friends calling, and I lay there, immobile and terrified, like a trapped hamster, as their pleas to 'pick up, pick up, pick up . . . I know you're there . . .' turn to frustrated, defeated, droning. 'Pick up, pick up, pick up . . .'

I never pick up.

I just can't. I'm too . . . fragile lately, in my off hours. At work, that's different. I can still bully a waiter or a line cook into tears. But at home, outside my kitchen, I'm five foot ten inches of exposed nerves, hurt feelings, suppressed rage, envy and fear. If they knew, these people calling, how I felt, believe me, they wouldn't be calling. At this point in my life, anything anybody has to say to me on the phone is *not* going to make me feel better.

Something good happened to you you want to tell me about? Don't. Please. I hate you, am made miserable and unsettled by your relative good fortune. Your pride and happiness will only cause me to wish harm on you. Something gone wrong in your life? Don't tell me. My response will be inappropriate, inadequate, and will make me, on later reflection, feel guilty, will give me something *else* to regret. Best for everybody that I don't pick up at all.

You want to talk to me? See me at work. I know how to behave there.

Fucking lobsters. Cross-eyed, cannibalistic, dirty, carrion-feeding ... You don't bind their claws with thick rubber bands, they'll tear each other apart. And they got me all fucked up.

It's gotten worse and worse, right up until last night. The chefs' night out, when what the police report refers to as 'the incident' occurred ... when a group of Manhattan's finest culinarians got together (as we often do), and bounced from one chef-friendly establishment to another, eating for free at one late-night bistro (oysters and nori rolls at 13 Barrow), then drinks at Bar Six, then more drinks and darts and some pool at the Stoned Crow, then more drinks and some cocaine – after-hours at The Nursery, finally ending up at the shuttered, but still open for business Siberia, on the 50th Street subway platform: a grimy little corner of Hell's rumpus room-six stools, a juke-box, some tattered posters of Lenin and Kruschchev, picture of Kim Philby in the bathroom over the urinal, bleary-eyed Irish bartender, a come-stained couch. That's where the final conflict occurred between good and evil – where I resolved, in one brief, shining and senselessly brutal moment, the eternal struggle, and cold-cocked that yellow, rat-cocksucker with an ashtray, made myself the subject of restaurant legend for years to come.

There was me, Bobby, and my sous-chef Ricky ... there was Ronnie, known industry-wide as the 'Grill-Bitch', and Jimmy Sears with his cute new *patissière* (we were all sure he's fucking her), and Laurent, a taciturn chef from the Gascogne, and Maurizio, the Tuscan fundamentalist, and

Alex, the master of Flintstones food. I remember hearing Maurizio mutter, '*Minchia!*' when Jimmy hit the floor.

We had been discussing other chefs. Chefs not present to defend themselves. You hang with chefs, you better know that about us – that when you leave the table to take a piss, we're gonna be talking about *you*. Like a cabal of small-minded, provincial grandmothers, or Alzheimer-ridden retirees at some Florida compound, we'd rather gossip, duke it out over the last fruit-cup, than chat about lofty culinary concepts over a snifter of Calvados.

By the time we hit Siberia, half-mad from tequila shots and endless pints, and the occasional sniff of Ricky's blow, the mood was even more mean-spirited than usual. Jimmy, I recall, was going on about Brendan Ford – nominally his best friend, mind you, a revered elder statesman of the NYC chef scene. Jimmy didn't think much of Brendan's new menu.

'It's *gay!*' he explained. 'It's food for pussies! There's . . . there's nothing . . . nothing to eat!'

'He's so pretty,' said Ricky, sarcastically.

Brendan, who on another night, would have been with us at Siberia, was famed for his delicate herb-infused, elaborately garnished and presented plates. He was into weeds lately: grew them in his own garden, and his food tended towards items like Nearly Raw Fish in Sorrel Broth, Garnish of Lawn Clippings.

'Brendan. He is very talented,' said Maurizio, always the diplomat.

'Cocksucker can't *cook!*' said Ricky. 'Hasn't *cooked* in ten years! What's he *good* for? Walkin' around the dinin' room with a motherfuckin' clipboard? Air kissin' a bunch a dried up old rich cunts? Fuck that bitch!'

'He can cook,' said Laurent, weakly. 'He just doesn't lately. He's at . . . he's at . . . another level now.'

Ricky, a lifetime line-cook, and heavy lifter, didn't want to hear that.

'Yeah? Well I tell you, man . . . I ever go to prison? I hope Brendan's my cell mate. I be in smokes for the whole fucking jolt, sellin' that boy's ass. Last time that goof worked the line, fucking Jimmy Carter was president!'

I didn't like this. The part about Brendan not working the line. I think a number of us at the bar were made uncomfortable. It's a measure of your continued studliness – the hours spent behind the line, and I hadn't been back there – meaning actually cooked à la carte at a station during service-shaking pans, broiling, plating to order, for quite a while. I felt guilty about it. Ricky's contempt for chefs who never work the line – a feeling shared by most line cooks – hit disconcertingly close to home. I was glad that I'd spelled the saucier twice the past week. I need Ricky's good will. We all, I think, looked around, tallying up which of us still spent time behind the line, Ricky looking smug, his arms crossed, the comment about what he'd do to Brendan in jail made especially pungent by the shared knowledge that he'd done five years' state time for burglary.

Fortunately, the subject of conversation changed. To pussy.

Jimmy, a self-described expert on this subject, regaled us with a recent adventure. Rather tastelessly, I thought, as his newest conquest, the cute *patissière*, was sitting right next to him, hanging on every word. She nursed her beer while Jimmy described for us how he came all over a hostess's face. 'She looked like a glazed donut!' he guffawed, going on to detail how he'd 'walked her around the room like a wheelbarrow,' even doing a frighteningly realistic imitation of the noises she made when he pounded away at her with his (reportedly) donkey-sized dick. A few civilians melted away from the bar while Jimmy pontificated on the comparative merits of rear entry versus standup and carry, but all the chefs stayed.

You work fourteen hours a day, six days a week, come home smelling like you've been rolling around in sheep entrails and fish jiz — sex is not generally the first thing on your 'things to do' list. Most of us at the bar, tragically, had something less than active sex lives, and even more pathetically, we lived that part of our lives vicariously, through Jimmy, a notable exception to the rule. Jimmy, as the saying went, would fuck a barbershop floor if there was enough hair on it. Thin girls, fat girls, smart, stupid, fabulous-looking or ugly as hell, Jimmy screwed everything in sight. Married, living with a woman, still sleeping with his ex-wife, and juggling two or three regulars; how he managed it all was a miracle of logistics. Even more unbelievable was that anyone would sleep with him in the first place. Everybody knew how Jimmy talked. To fuck Jimmy was to share the excruciating sexual details of the experience with half the cooks in New York. His relentless coupling was like a soap opera we all watched.

Music was blaring from the Siberia jukebox — Steppenwolf, 'Magic Carpet Ride', I think, and my mind began to drift away from Jimmy's grunting and whinnying, in soft-focus now as he demonstrated some new sexual outrage in pantomime. I was thinking prep list for tomorrow, already loading in my mind, the cart I'd take up to the kitchen.

French cut Chix breasts.

Dry-aged shell steaks.

Veal bones for stock.

Sea Bass.

Salmon.

Arborio rice for risotto.

Crayfish for risotto.

Chanterelle and Porcini mushrooms . . .

A few more restaurant types arrived: a saucier from the Hilton, looking to move up in the world, came over, started ranting about his broiler-guy messing with his *mis-en-place*. He was fresh out of work, you could still smell Hilton-food on him, and he was all jacked up, still, with adrenalin – eyes bulging, sweat running down his forehead. 'Man stole my motherfuckin' kosher salt!' he shrieked. 'Can you believe it!? Right off my station!'

Two Ecuadoran pasta cooks from Le Madri came by, whacked out on aguardiente, one of them tugged my sleeve, roused me from my alcoholic torpor. 'Chef chef . . . You need me, my frien', next week?' Next week there were banquets almost every day, and I needed the extra help. I tossed them each two shifts and watched them both stagger toward the pinball machine. A small group of waitresses and bartenders pushed through the door, fresh from Blue Ribbon, another late-night cookie and restaurant hang-out. Somebody said they were hungry, and I saw Ricky pick up the phone. Ten minutes later, a porter from one of the hotel kitchens showed up with some stolen shrimps and a tin of caviar for us. We smeared fish eggs on potato chips, washed it down with Georgian vodka. People disappeared in twos to the bathroom, to pack their noses, handed off little packages, not so surreptitiously under the bar. The music changed, the Cramps, and things started to shift.

I'm usually a happy drunk. A sentimental drunk. When I've had too much, I get quiet, then reflective, then sad. But this time, I could feel the evil genie slip out of the bottle. I knew, even before it happened, that something ugly was coming.

Sure enough, that was when somebody, maybe it was one

of the recent arrivals, mentioned the review.

I flinched like a gut-shot dog. A palpable wince. Didn't say anything – just moved back and away, my balls scrambling up into my torso for protection, anticipating a boot to the crotch. I took another sip of vodka and saw that conversation had stopped, everybody looking now. Ricky, a perceptive young man, tried to change the subject back to pussy, but it was no go.

I heard, through the blood rushing in my ears, the words, '*New York Times*', a few choice excerpts – words burned into my brain weeks ago. I heard the word 'steak'. Then there was a pause. A long one. Even the waitress-bartender contingent saw that something was up, moved in closer, everybody sneaking looks to see how I was going to react. It was *me* they were talking about, after all. That fucking review, that motherfucking steak! *My* restaurant. *My* kitchen.

My comments were wordlessly solicited.

When I still said nothing, just knocked back my vodka and stared dreamily into space, focusing my gaze on a patch of mildewing acoustic tile on the low ceiling, that, that was when Jimmy, ill-advisedly, filled the silence with his own pithy, if rhetorical question.

Addressed directly to me. So there was no avoiding it.

So, of course, I *had* to respond.

Which I did.

Truth:

I hate the general dining public.

I think people should be licensed to eat in a good restaurant. Yeah. That's right . . . A long, and unnecessarily irritating process of testing and certification should be required of every would-be diner. To thin out the herd.

All the well-done eating, low-sodium, egg-white omelette nibbling, crystal worshipping, holistic vegan cocksuckers, the sauce-on-siders, the low-cholesterol, no butter, no cream, can you take that off the bone split for two geeks, the slack-jawed, bedwetting, mouth-breathing, fanny-pack wearing scumpigs and rubes, with their Hard Rock T-shirts and their wall-eyed, no-necked, overfed monster offspring in tow . . . they can get the fuck out of my dining room. *Now.*

The nauseating refrain, 'The Customer is Always Right' is exactly wrong. The customer is rarely, if *ever*, right.

This is, it is said, a 'service' industry. Jimmy says this all the time. Has no problem with it. Maybe that's why Jimmy is a success, and I, unfortunately, am not.

Serene, in his spotless, double-breasted chef coat, his name stitched in Tuscan blue over the right breast, Jimmy's got no problems administering roughage to the annoying foodies, trend-seeking Wall Street suits, blue-haired theater-goers, and all the rest of the waterheads and whiners who make up the great unwashed horde of dining public.

I explained my plan once to him.

Vouchers, I said. You waddle into my restaurant, I said, and you present your papers to a trusted lieutenant. Should your papers not be in order – say you failed the how to eat with a fork part of your certification exam – or a low score on the seafood section, that's okay, I explain. We'll take care of you. You won't go hungry. You will be generously offered a voucher. For another kind of meal, to replace the one which you have been politely (if forcefully), refused. A nutritious, but protein-packed sludge is yours, for reduced price, to be administered, say, in the rear loading area of the restaurant, out of view of the certified diners. Administered by trained nurses. Rectally.

I thought it was a modest proposal. Jimmy just snorted, scoffed. But then, he can afford to.

Jimmy, you see, is a brilliant cook. A theoretician, an innovator, a visionary, on the cutting edge of what the foodies call 'Asian Fusion', and what Ricky, my sous, calls 'Pacific Rim-Job'. Give Jimmy a couple a coconuts, some frozen shrimp, a few sprigs of lemongrass, maybe a jar of red curry paste – he'll have half of Manhattan lined up to suck his dick.

I work for a living. I've got to work harder to get by. So much of what we do is a hustle, a con, that when honest, beautiful food, conscientiously prepared, is ignored, or worse, destroyed by some ignorant shit-stain of a customer, the pain is near unbearable. Bouncing from restaurant to restaurant, year after year, my motley crew of talented young thugs and hooligans in tow, I've come to feel like the *Flying Dutchman* of the professional cooking racket. Always arriving on the scene too late. Checks are already bouncing by the time I first put on my apron, button up my cheap cotton/poly-blend chef coat. No name stitched on my jacket.

When my crew and I arrive, it's like arriving at the scene of a car crash, the bodies already taken away, but the cars, damaged and nearly useless, are what we have to drive . . . My latest owner, always looking doom-struck and trapped, standing there, caught in the headlights, his entrepreneurial dream of empire circling the drain for the last few times. We're the pros from Dover, me and my boys, here to get you out of this mess, fix things up, get you back on track. But we know, Ricky and me. You're never getting back on track. There's no hope. Like the lobsters, chances are, you're dead – you just don't know it yet.

One silly bone-headed fantasist after another. One more

egotistical schmendrik with too much money and not enough brains – believed what his friends told him when they used to say, 'You should open a restaurant!' Of course they don't tell him that anymore. They're not around. Now that the dining room is half empty and the deliveries are Cash On Delivery, and the owner stopped picking up their dinner checks, they don't come around much anymore.

After years of this ... I *know*, from the moment we first shake hands, before the interview even *starts*, the place has no chance. Failure has a very distinctive odor, and I've become very adept at recognizing it.

I smell it on myself.

But, I take these jobs anyway. Shit, I need the money. Got to take care of my crew. That the latest ill-fated adventure will surely end in bankruptcy for my new master is completely beside the point. We're used to that, my crew and me. We can, at least, be counted on to perform honorably, to go down with the ship. We give it our all, we really do. Willingly suspend disbelief, work each day like this, this is the big one. We fight the good fight, every day, every night, in the face of certain defeat. Dien Bien Phu, seven days a week. It's what we do. It's what I do. Feed on the remains of dying restaurants, the last scraps of expiring dreams.

My latest boss – let's call him Squirrel Balls (it's what the floor staff calls him), just last week, he's telling me his master plan to 'turn things around'. We're sitting over coffee in the empty cocktail lounge of his flagship restaurant-nightclub – the one that only a year ago was going to be the jewel in the crown of a chain of Squirrel Ball conceived restaurant-nightclubs which would span the globe from Syossett to Samoa ... anyway, he's sitting there bemoaning the weekend receipts, and I'm making the appropriate sympathetic noises, when he tells me about 'Cabaret Night'.

'There's a million unemployed singers, dancers, performers out there,' he said, hopefully, 'who'd just *love* a venue. Sort of a . . . a workshop, where they can work out new material, maybe get noticed . . . and we wouldn't have to *pay* them! I was thinking . . . I was thinking we could make Mondays Cabaret Night . . .'

I hear this, and I want to leap across the table, grab him by the hair, and twist a fork into his carotid artery. I've been through this part of terminal stage before, at other places. My last restaurant tried this knuckleheaded gimmick – invited a bunch of never-will-be performers to 'entertain' our already diminished clientele. These hideously inept yodelers would open their stupid mouths, let loose with some nasally inflected medley from Andrew Lloyd Webber, and the dining room would empty like someone had just cracked open a vial of anthrax spores or let loose a cageful of ebola-infected spider monkeys. 'Check please,' the customers would whimper, eyes looking longingly at the exits. 'I forgot . . . I left the gas on,' or 'I forgot my medication . . .'

I hear this, and I *know* it's not going to work. Okay. Maybe I say, 'Hmmmmnnn' and try to look thoughtful as I fight the urge to projectile vomit. It's no use you see, trying to reason with Squirrel Balls. I *have* to let him live in hope, don't *want* him to give in to despair. I mean, let's face it – if he knew the truth – if he had any *idea* of the truth, had any sense at all – he would have shut the place down six months ago, cut his losses, stiffed his creditors, and run off to an Indonesian archipelago island with the few bucks left to him. Sad fact is: I *need* him to stay stupid. So I shut my mouth, swallow my rage and frustration. Later I'll have a margarita.

Now, Jimmy. My friend, my mentor, former patron, former chef – gave me my first sous chef position, taught me everything I know about huac nam, jasmine rice, vertical food, infusions of herb ... *that* Jimmy ... He owns. He gets equity in his place. His place will go bust too. His partners? They're gonna take it the neck for some big bucks just like Squirrel Balls' partners. Difference is: Jimmy'll be fine. By the time the place goes down, he'll have raked off so much in skimmed cash, inflated salary, pilfered equipment, kickbacks, and 'consultant' fees, he can take a year off. His partners won't mind a bit. They'll have gotten laid off their proximity to Jimmy's shining star. They'll have had a few good years playing Good-Time Charlies, buying drinks and meals for their pals, getting furtive blow jobs from the never-ending supply of waitrons. They'll have done a lot of coke, gotten a lot of flattering attention in the papers, had a good time. When Jimmy comes back from riding the waves in Hawaii or wherever, announces he's gonna open a *new* venture, right across the street; his old partners might even put up some *more* money. It's fun to be associated with a winner. And Jimmy, though he's never once shown a dime in profit, is a winner.

I told him so. Just before I hit him.

I said, 'You're a winner, Jimmy. Everybody says so.'

Then I cold-cocked him. Clubbed him upside the head with an ashtray, right there at the Siberia Bar.

He went down like a stunned rhino on one of those nature programs. You know the ones: 'Zee rhino feels nussing as ze tranquilizer dart ...', usually delivered in heavily accented voice-over by some bucket-head in a safari jacket.

Afterwards, I 'went through the system', as the arresting officers called it.

When Squirrel Balls bailed me out, he wondered, on the way back to the restaurant, if 'this could be a *good* thing . . . You know . . . for *us*. The publicity and all.'

I had to say I didn't know.

'You could say it was a fight over principle,' he suggested, always the optimist. 'He stole a recipe or something. You could say that.'

No way, I had to say. Unethical. Even for me. It was me, after all, who'd been stealing Jimmy's recipes for years. Over time, I'd seduced away his sous chef with an offer of more money, stolen his best line cooks whenever I could. I'd even suborned one of his prep cooks, so he'd feed me information, regularly, on what was going on in Jimmy's kitchen. I wasn't going to step up and say Jimmy stole *my* recipes. That would be wrong. There *is* a limit. Plus, nobody would believe it.

The truth is, Jimmy said something to me that pissed me off. And I hit him. Hard.

Maybe too hard. I don't know. The way his head bounced off the bar on the way down, eyes blank . . . I don't know.

Information out of the hospital is pretty sketchy. They have him listed as 'stable', whatever that means. My prep cook source paid a visit, says that Jimmy, at least, is talking again, that he recognizes friends, is aware of the date, knows who the president is. That's good. As much as I enjoyed giving Jimmy a good whack – as richly as he might have deserved it, I wish him well in his recovery.

I am not a bad person. I'm glad I didn't kill him.

I'm glad I won't be grabbing my ankles for a crowded tier of Aryan Brothers at some upstate penal institution.

Even in a business where talking shit is an approved form of self-expression, Jimmy stepped over the line. And the threshold is pretty damn high. Verbal abuse, in our life, is an artform, practiced at a very high level of expertise, a culmination of a centuries-old tradition of heaping scorn and invective that dates back before Orwell and Escoffier and Careme and Vatel, to probably the first cave-dudes, smashing shellfish into the first bisque. It's a secret language, where 'hey, maricon', means 'hello, comrade', and 'suck my dick', means 'no thank you, valued co-worker' and 'gimme that fucking sautoir, you steaming puddle of reptile vomit', means 'hand me the pan, please. Thank you.'

In my kitchen for instance, God help you, you show up at work with a newly erupted pimple – if you're beginning to lose your hair, getting fat. You better get used to being called 'syphilitic labrat', 'fat-fuck', 'Pop'n'Fresh', 'Gut-Boy', people sayin' shit like, 'Michael Bolton called, he wants his hair back', or 'When's the last time you saw your dick without a mirror?' And that's okay. You can turn to a co-worker in my kitchen, suggest that he'd be better suited to mopping the accumulated semen out of the stalls at Peep World on 42nd Street, than murdering any more food on the sauté station. The threat of non-consensual anal violation is a constant rejoinder. No biggie. Call somebody a 'scum-sucking, treacherous, lying, spastic shoemaker', and you'll get a good laugh. But some things are off-limits.

The wife/mother/girlfriend rule, for instance.

You don't insult anybody's mother for Chrissakes. Pointing out that your entremétier's girlfriend was seen jacking off motorists on West Street, is a no-no, even if true. The word 'wife' is never to be mentioned at all. You can use the word 'mother', but only in Spanish, or as part of a larger word ('motherfucker' is used as punctuation, not as a noun). You don't want to break these hard and fast rules. Not in an environment where it's a hundred and ten degrees and crowded, and where everybody carries knives.

Jimmy didn't say shit about my Mom. He said something else entirely.

But I don't think my reaction was disproportionate to the offense. Not at all.

In my view, it was a perfectly foreseeable outcome to an ill-considered remark.

Even if I *am* flaking out a litle bit lately. Even if I cry on subways, at car commercials. Listen to 'Whiter Shade of Pale' six times a day, think Rush is beginning (God help me!) to sound *good*.

Jimmy was still in the wrong.

Since the incident, Ricky, my sous chef and director of covert operations, has been burning up the phone lines. A sous with a criminal mind is one of life's great joys, and Ricky understands the importance of a well-timed campaign of disinformation – the necessity of getting *our* version of events out there – before Jimmy gets out of the hospital and starts putting his own spin on things. A hint here, a hint there, the occasional outright fabrication – Ricky's a natural at this shit:

'Didjoo know Jimmy was a karate expert?' I hear him telling somebody. 'Yeah, bro'! No lie . . . And that kong foo, too. No shit. Man's got muscles on his muscles. Bobby stepped up in weight class when he hit that bitch, man. Motherfucker *deserved* it.'

By the time Ricky gets off the phone, the whole episode will have been written down in restaurant folklore as a win for the home team: Hero Chef Bobby Meyers, five-foot ten, spindly Jewboy, Strikes a Blow Against Elitist Media-Whore, the dangerous and unstable Jimmy Sears. Defends Honor of

Working Cooks Everywhere, by beating him with ashtray. Story to follow.

'I think I heard him say some shit about his mom,' Ricky's telling someone else. 'And Bobby's mom's got cancer, too. Can you believe it? Yeah. Stomach, I think. Damn *right!* I'd be pissed too. Should a seen Jimmy. He was cryin' like a little girl. Sayin', "Not the face, not the face . . ."'

I have to make a face at Ricky when I hear this. My mother's fine. She lives in Florida now – and Jimmy didn't have time to say anything once I picked up the ashtray. Still, you've got to admire Ricky's creativity.

If I'd had time to consider things, when Jimmy said what he said. If I'd thought about it, had the strength, the resolve, to just let the remark pass, pretend I hadn't heard it, then carefully, over time, planned a prolonged and painful revenge; Ricky would have been the perfect instrument. He can be positively fiendish. One chef who pissed Ricky off? Ricky started giving generous donations to an outfit called the North American Man-Boy Love Association in the poor guy's name, writing letters offering the services of the guy's restaurant to throw fundraisers for a group that advocates legalizing sex between men and male minors. Gave the guy's boss's office as a return address . . . I'm telling you, if Ricky had been working for Nixon, this would have been a very different country.

Waiting till the next day, tasking Ricky with the operation – that would have been the smart move. I'm sure it would have hurt Jimmy a whole hell of a lot worse in the long run than what I did to him.

But for instant gratification? Nothing beats a blunt obect, delivered quickly and unexpectedly to the side of the skull. Take it from me.

I did not set out to be this way: a bitter, envious, aging crank – a journeyman chef with a record for assault. Since the lobsters started looking at me funny, I've gotten a little over-sensitive, perhaps – a little thin-skinned. Abject humiliation tends to change a person. It changed me.

My early decision to become a serious, school-trained, European-style chef came after one particularly painful humiliation:

1973, Cape Cod, Massachusetts. I'd been working a summer job, as a dishwasher, my first restaurant. Elbow deep in a sinkful of dirty pots and pans, I'd look back over the line at the cooks, and envy them, swaggering, piratical young princes with a what-the-fuck attitude. They ate whatever they wanted, whenever they wanted it . . . They drank everything in sight, free of charge, fucked all the good-looking waitresses, stayed up all night shooting craps, playing poker, snorting coke and getting involved in varied and occasionally freakish sexual adventures. They smoked expensive, seedless weed, filled their refrigerators at will with stolen sirloins, lobsters, boxes of shrimp and champagne. The carried big, baddass, razor-sharp knives (which I thought was *very* cool) in leather roll-up cases which they slung over their shoulders like disgraced samurai, and they dressed in the height of outlaw style: artfully ripped jeans, faded Viet-vet type headbands, vaguely martial-looking double-breasted chef-coats, casually spattered with gore. They were cool.

Compared to the squalid conditions of the professional dishwasher, they were gods.

So, the first time one of them went off on a bender and didn't return, I stepped in, volunteered to work what was called 'the berry station' or garde manger. I happily cracked oysters on the half, made salads, plated desserts, filled champagne glasses with raspberries and strawberries. I bearded mussels, picked spinach, peeled potatoes and garlic and onions and did the scut-work for the big boys, the guys who cooked the hot food.

When the summer came to an end, when the regular crew began to fade away, off to work ski resorts in Colorado, charter boats in the Caribbean, restaurants in the Florida Keys, I got my chance, and moved up for the last few weeks before closing for the season. I worked fry-station, dunking clams, shrimp, flounder, scallops and french fries into hot grease for a while, until the broiler man got pinched for a parole violation and my moment arrived.

I was given charge of the broiler. The sheer pleasure – the *power* of commanding that monstrous, heavy iron and steel furnace, bumping the rolling grill under the flames with my hip, the way I'd seen others do – it was delicious. I couldn't have been any happier in the cockpit of an F-16. I felt like I could rule the world.

The next summer, my restaurant was bought by the owner of the better, larger, and busier restaurant across the street. Ciro, the new owner, was kind enough to allow those of us who'd worked the old place under its previous admin- istration to audition for our old jobs. I was thrilled, and headed up to the Cape from New York filled with hope and self-confidence, looking for that big-time broiler job, the big money, the position that would make me the studliest, ass-kicking, name-taking, take-no-prisoners motherfucker on Cape Cod.

I pulled into town I remember, wearing a spanking new Pierre Cardin seersucker suit – color: light blue. I cringe now, remembering it. The shoes, too, were blue. Here I was, hitch-hiking into a town that for all intents and purposes, was a little artists' colony, a Portuguese fishing village, where people dressed unpretentiously in work clothes, cut-off denims, army surplus. And here I was: in some deranged early Seventies bout of disco-inspired hubris, decked out in my batwing-shouldered Robert Palmer wear, come up from the city to show the local yokels how we did it in the big city.

I was so full of myself I could puke.

My audition took place across the street, at the usually jam-packed Ciro's. They were pounding veal in the kitchen when I arrived; the whole crew, on every horizontal surface, was beating on veal cutlets with heavy steel mallets for scallopines. The testosterone level was very, very high, like the locker room of a championship football team before the Super Bowl. My last crew had been adorable amateurs. These guys were pros, and they knew it. Everybody knew it. The floor staff, the management, even Ciro, the owner, visibly cowered when in their presence. Only I was too stupid to see how over my head I was.

I'd served a few hundred meals at a relaxed pace, in a not very busy joint in the off-season. These guys . . . these guys drilled out four, five, six hundred fast-paced high-end meals A NIGHT! Here it was: Friday, an hour before service, and I was informed I'd be working with Tyrone, the broilerman.

Looking back, I can't help remembering Tyrone as being anything less than eight feet tall, four hundred pounds of carved obsidian, with a shaved head and a prominent silver-capped front tooth and a gold hoop earring the size of a door knocker. While his true dimensions were proably more modest — you get the picture: he was big, black, fearsomely muscled, his size 48 chef coat stretched tight across his wide shoulders. A titan.

Unintimidated as only the ignorant could be, I started shooting my mouth off right away. Yapping about my old restaurant, what king-hell bad-boys WE all were, 'back in the old days', regaling my new comrades with humorous anecdotes of New York City designed to shock and titillate, generally portraying myself as a street-smart, experienced, thoroughly professional gun-for-hire.

They were, to be charitable to myself, not impressed. Not that this deterred me. I ignored all the signs – the rolling eyes, the tight smiles – and plunged on, oblivious to the huge amounts of food the other cooks were loading into their stations. I missed the determined sharpening of knives, the careful arranging of sidetowels, favorite pans, ice, extra pots of boiling water, back-up supplies of everything. They were like marines, loading up with ammo and sandbags, digging in for the siege at Khe San, and I registered nothing, blinded by stupidity and self-love.

I should have seen the practiced choreography of their movements for what it was; understood the level of professionalism and experience that allowed these hulking giants to dance wordlessly around each other in the cramped, heavily-manned kitchen, never wasting movement, turning from stove top to refrigerator to cutting board with breathtaking economy of effort. I should have understood the terror in the eyes of the floor staff as we got closer and closer to service period, seen the way these cooks spoke to each other in high-pitched, femme-convict patois, calling each other women's names for what it was – the end result of *years* working together in a confined space. They hefted three-hundred-pound stockpots onto the ranges, tossed legs of veal around like pullets, all the while indulgently enduring my endless, self-aggrandizing line of chatter without comment.

An hour later, the board was filled with more dinner orders than I'd seen in a lifetime. Ticket after ticket coming in, one on top of the other. Tables of ten, tables of six, deuces, three-tops, twelves, more and more and more of them, all containing dishes I'd never heard of with Italian, difficult to pronounce names. Waiters screamed ORDERING, food going out, more orders coming in, the squawk of an intercom, calling for food for an upstairs bar. Flames leapt out of pans three feet high, the broiler was crammed with rows and rows of steaks and veal chops, fish filets and lobsters. Pasta was blanched and shocked and transferred in huge batches into colanders, falling everywhere, the floor ankle deep in linguine, garganelli, taglierini, spaghetti a la chitarra, penne, and the heat was horrific. Everybody had sweated through their whites ten minutes in – the scratchy synthetic blend whites inflaming wrists and necks so that everyone's skin was pink and inflamed. Sweat flowed into my eyes, blinding me.

I struggled and sweated, and spun around like a headless chicken, hurried to keep up the best I could, Tyrone slinging sizzle platters under the broiler, and me, ostensibly helping out, getting deeper and deeper into the weeds. On the rare occasions when I had a second to look up at the long row of fluttering orders, the dupes looked like cuneiform or Sanskrit – indecipherable. I was lost, thoroughly, totally lost. Tyrone, finally, had to help the helper.

Then, grabbing a sauté pan, I burned myself.

I yelped out loud, dropped the pan, an order of Osso Bucco Milanese hitting the floor, and as a small red blister raised on my palm, I foolishly, *oh*-so foolishly, asked the beleaguered Tyrone if he had some burn cream and maybe a band-aid.

This was quite enough for Tyrone. It went suddenly quiet in the kitchen – all eyes on Tyrone and his hopelessly inept assistant. Orders it seemed, as if by magic, ceased to come in or go out for a long, horrible moment. Tyrone turned to me, looked down, smiling now, and said, 'Whatchoo want, white boy? Burn cream? A *band*-aid?'

Then . . . then he raised his own enormous palms to me, brought them up close so I could see them properly, so I could see the hideous constellation of water-filled blisters, angry red welts from grill marks, the old scars, the raw flesh where steam and hot fat had made the skin simply roll off – they looked like the claws of some monstrous Sci-Fi crustacean, knobby and callused under wounds old and new. I watched, transfixed, as Tyrone, his shark's eyes never leaving mine, reached slowly under the roaring flames of the broiler, and with one naked hand, picked up a glowing hot sizzle platter, moved it over to the cutting board, and set it down in front of me.

He never flinched.

The other cooks cheered, laughed their asses off. Orders began to come in again, and everybody went back to work.

I had been shown up for the loudmouthed, useless litle punk I was. Identified as a pretender, and an obnoxious one at that. Humiliated.

Ciro ended up kicking me down to prep crew at my old restaurant – one step above dishwasher on the food chain, and I slunk home that night in my Pierre Cardin hoping I'd die in my sleep. After a day or two of sulking and self-pity, I resolved, out of sheer spite, to become a chef.

I would go to school. I would apprentice in France. I would let a procession of evil drunks, crackpot owners, sadistic sous chefs work me like a Sherpa, until I became a chef. I would do whatever was necessary to become as good as, and better than, Ciro's crew.

I would have hands like Tyrone's.

Someday, somewhere, I would get to humiliate some other loud-mouthed little punk.

I would show them all.

So I became a chef because I'd been humiliated. I became a chef out of spite.

And I stayed a chef, for nearly two decades, until Jimmy Sears, for one brief second, made me a punk again.

Whatever Squirrel Balls says, a reputation for violence is not a résumé-builder. Not without three stars, anyway. Then it's okay. Three stars? Three stars, you can drink the blood of your enemies middle of the shift, stuff burning gerbils up a waiter's ass, parade naked and covered with brains and blood through the dining room, nobody gonna say boo. Not with three stars.

Me? With *one* pathetic star? Just getting through the fallout from this Jimmy situation is going to be plenty tough. The bastard could sue me. That would not be the 'good thing' Squirrel Balls is looking for. In this tiny, incestuous, dysfunctional family we call the restaurant biz, you can't go around braining your peers. Not with one star.

One motherfucking star.

The steak.

The *New York Times* . . .

Let me explain. One star is a death sentence. Not an immediate death, mind you, it's a long lingering passing, a coughing, wheezing, blood in your stool, gradual slide into obscurity and disrepute.

Finita la musica, papi.

See ya . . . Wouldn't wanna *be* ya . . .

Here's how it works:

Every Wednesday morning, every chef, every sous chef, restaurateur, cook, and serious foodie in New York City picks up the *New York Times*. They don't start by reading the front page. Oh no. Armies of disgruntled former Soviet republics could be swarming across the borders of Europe, raping the livestock and enslaving the populace, Hezbollah suicide bombers could be lighting themselves up in Disneyland, Elvis Presley could have risen from the grave to feast on the brains of young children; it wouldn't deter anybody for a second. They – we, all of us, are going to do the same exact thing every Wednesday: turn directly to the Weekend Section, second to last page – where the restaurant review appears.

We want to see if somebody we know got reviewed. We want that guilty frisson of pleasure that comes when an enemy, a rival, or better yet, a friend, gets trashed in the *Times*.

We know what to say if a friend gets a bad review. The usual platitudes: 'Don't sweat it, man, nobody reads that shit . . .' or 'it's not *that* important', or 'What do *they* know, anyway? Column's gone downhill since the last reviewer left', or 'She's prejudiced against ——————— food (fill in blank here), bro' . . . Everyone knows that!' We've mouthed those words of hollow comfort many times – while snickering privately up our sleeves.

Fact is, of course, that everybody *does* read it. That it *is* that important. That she *does* know what she's talking about. If you get three stars in the *Times*, your business triples overnight. You get two stars – you dodge the bullet; you can go on as before, hold your head high, no fault, no foul.

But *one* star? One star: you may as well carve a swastika in your forehead and rub a nice steaming loaf of shit in your hair – 'cause everybody you know, everybody you love, hate, like, respect, fear . . . is gonna read it, and laugh laugh laugh.

If they're anything like me, they're gonna photocopy the damn thing, hang it in the kitchen, so their cooks can get a good laugh too.

One star is a disgrace, a bad odor that will exude from your kitchen for years. Your cooks will look at you with shifty, worried, injured expressions, like sailors who, for the first time, have considered mutiny. Résumés will be secretly faxed. Other chefs will circle your staff like hungry buzzards, waiting to separate out the unhappy and disillusioned, pick off your sauté man, your butcher, your prep crew, your sous, even, one by one. Information will leak, hemorhage out. Your currency on the job market, and with your present masters, will drop considerably. You may as well put on a paper Burger King cap and start stocking the fixin's bar for all the respect you're going to be getting. Truth.

So, imagine. Late one Thursday night, not too long ago, I open up the *Times*, and with shaking hands, turn the pages, see *my* restaurant's name on the second to last page, see *my* name, with *one* cancerous star above it. Just imagine how I felt, reading, 'A hanger steak, ordered medium rare, arrived rare . . . Returned to the kitchen for more cooking – when it came back, it was still under-done . . .'

Now, I remembered that order. I still do. I sure as hell didn't know it was the motherfucking *Times* critic: but, it wouldn't have mattered . . . I swear to *God*, on my eyes, on my first-born male child . . . That motherfucking steak was *medium rare*. It was medium rare the first time. It was drop-dead perfect medium rare the second time. And nobody, *nobody* is gonna tell me different. Escoffier himself could climb up my leg with a thermometer in his teeth, and I'm not worried. That steak was medium fucking rare.

How could it have happened? Why? Why? Why?

It was bullshit. She was wrong. Maybe it was the light out there in the dining room. I don't know. Whatever I got to say about it – it's too damn late anyway. Nobody is going to believe it. Nobody is going to care. I got *one* star. That's all anyone will remember.

You know how I felt? Reading that review? You don't *have* to imagine.

I'll tell you exactly how I felt.

I felt like I had suddenly, and inexplicably, put on a fluffy crepe and organza cocktail dress, a rubber clown nose, roller skates, wheeled out into the center of Times Square, and allowed myself to get butt-fucked by a procession of crack-heads and circus freaks. On national television.

That's how I felt.

When the review came out, Jimmy said nothing. No conciliatory bullshit phone-call, no knowing references in passing conversation. During the whole evening, last night, of drinking and gossiping, he had made no reference at all to my fall from grace, my expulsion from the firmament of culinary stars. Maybe he didn't mean for it to slip out exactly the way it did.

But, then, maybe he did. Maybe he thought long and hard, waited until he had an audience, until everybody was watching – Maurizio, Laurent, Ricky, the grill bitch, all the various and sundry kitchen hooligans . . . all there, all watching when he finally let it go, stopped biting his tongue and said what was on his mind.

When he stood there at the Siberia bar, looked me in the eyes and said:

'So, Bobby . . . How does it *feel* to be a one star chef?'

That was when I said, 'You're a winner, Jimmy. Everybody

says so,' and hit him as hard as I could with a heavy glass ashtray.

I was trying to kill him. Certainly, if the ashtray had pushed right through his skull, popped out the other side, exploded Jimmy's head like some mush-filled piñata, I would not, at that precise moment, have been disappointed. I put everything I had into it – swung for the bleachers, the cheap seats. No Texas-Leaguer over the infield for me boy – I was looking for the home run – to knock Jimmy's smug face right out of the park.

Afterwards, though, when old Jimmy still hadn't come around; when he hadn't responded to the water thrown helpfully into his face by Maurizio, Laurent gone, others melting away from the bar, the grill-bitch arguing with somebody over whether to 'call an ambulance' or 'clear air passageways' or 'commence CPR', . . . that's when I started to worry about maybe I hit him too hard . . . started to take stock of my situation and wonder how bad it was going to be.

Jimmy was bleeding from a tear over his left ear. Connor, the Siberia bartender, suggested strongly that I disappear. There was a lot to recommend this strategy – Jimmy's patissière, I noticed, was conspicuously gone – to call the cops, I imagined. I had only a few minutes if I was going to hot-foot it out of there . . . But I looked around, and knew, in an instant, that *somebody* here would blab. A whole roomful of people saw what had happened and one of them would give me up. Running would make things worse. I pictured myself getting hauled out of work during the pre-theater rush, shackled and in handcuffs through the crowded dining room and thought that wouldn't look too good.

So I had a couple shots of vodka, stood there waiting for them to come. Connor, quite nicely refused money for the drinks. I seem to remember Ricky, slapping me on the back, covertly whispering, 'Good one, Dad,' in my ear.

Two paramedics arrived first, with two paunchy uniform cops right behind them. Jimmy was loaded onto a gurney, hauled up the steps, bundled into an ambulance with flashing red and blue lights. I saw the little blonde patissière follow them – probably intending to ride with her still unconscious chef to the hospital.

When the two cops began to take statements, I could see the unease on my friends' and drinking companions' faces when they asked the big question: 'Okay. Who hit him?' Faces turned away, eyes drifted down to the floor.

Nobody wanted to be the first to snitch.

I made it easy for everybody, raising my hand weakly, a sheepish smile on my face.

The fatter of the two cops snapped on the cuffs, hands behind my back.

I remember how incongruously tender they were, the way they shielded my head with their hands as they shoved me into the back of the patrol car.

It was the lobsters' fault. That look in their eyes – when I drove the skewers in . . . the way their eyes crossed. 'Duhhhh . . .'

I think, in my mug shot, I had much the same expression on *my* face.

And that fucking steak. How I wish . . . what I would give for *that* not to have happened.

That didn't help at all.

When I got out of the lock-up, I went straight to work. Got a standing ovation from my crew. Ricky said all the right things, then got to work making some calls, doing what he could to fix things. He looked happy.

Ricky will dine out on this story for a long time. He'll get laid off of this story. He deserves to. His version, with any luck, will become the authoritative, the official version. By the time Jimmy gets out, whatever he has to say will seem like whining. I hope he's okay. I'd like to think he's making a full and complete recovery. And that he won't sue me.

I'm not a bad person. Really.

Things just got out of hand. I was vulnerable cause of what's been happening lately. Jimmy hurt me. I hurt him back. That's what happened.

God, please don't let Jimmy turn into a vegetable.

Don't let him sue me.

Let me bring honor to my clan.

Let my customers eat specials – the whole roasted sea bass or the Osso Bucco in particular. Let them order fish – properly cooked, not incinerated into dry, leathery slabs.

Please, God, strike down my enemies – but make sure I've got an alibi when you do it.

Save me from vegetarians and the lactose-intolerant.

Deliver me from the tyranny of the food critics, for they know not what the fuck they do.

Allow me, at all times, to see into the hearts and souls of my crew, so that I can better guide them to my way of thinking.

Keep me from treachery and conspiracy and mass defections.

Protect my sous chef from harm or temptation.

Save my pitiful, failing restaurant.

Let the lobsters feel no pain, nor malice 'cause of what I do to their heads.

I swear, before God: that steak was medium rare.

Teeth Shall Be Provided

EMER MARTIN

THE ASMAT MAN was sleeping on the skull of his father when his wives woke him up. His village had been at war with a neighboring village but something was different. Four frightened wives told him the whites had destroyed the enemy village and now were here. He hung a light bulb around his neck and went to face the Dutch invaders. The Dutch had machine-guns and the Asmat had knives and wooden spears. In all the blood, misery and ripped bodies, his light bulb remained unbroken. Wounded, he clung to the ground as the women's screams punctured the bloated evening. All their hate, fury and fear hissed out into the immense alluvial swamp. The white tribe picked about the bodies nervously. Men's groans hummed close to the wet earth as their world deflated. The ghosts of the jungle took note.

'I'm so hungry I could eat a nun's arse through a cane chair,' Aisling proclaimed as she sprawled naked on Fatima's bed.

Her body was big and freckled, her flesh was soft and caved into her rolls and curves. She traced a bitten nail down jagged stretch-marks that streaked like silver lightning through her thighs. Fatima, in contrast, was clothed in a kimono that was a mile too small for her. Bony legs and arms slid out from the material. White clay was caked into the lines of her long black fingers giving her hands a zebra-like quality. Both women were six foot tall, towering over the petite population of Tokyo like beings from another planet. Fatima sat up in her basement apartment and ceramics studio.

'You're always hungry after sex,' Fatima said.

'At least I've quit smoking.'

'Did you smoke after sex?'

'I never looked.'

Aisling grabbed her girlfriend's long dreads and tugged her head back gently.

James F. Burns had an appropriate name considering what he was about to convince the President of the U.S. to do to 300,000 people he had never met. The Secretary of State was always the hard-liner when others were trying to convince the President to make peace. The Japanese might be ready to surrender if they could keep their emperor. Their new foreign minister was appointed to do just that. But Burns wouldn't let it go. Truman was throwing a few last-minute personal things in a bag. He was really thinking about Stalin and the upcoming Potsdam conference. The Soviets were ready to march on China. Japan would be next. The Soviet Union and the United States were allies but the plotting against each other had already begun.

'If the bomb explodes I'll certainly have a hammer on those boys,' he mused as he ran his fingers over the bristles of his toothbrush sending a delicate shower of stale water in Burns's eagerly nodding direction. 'We've spent enough on the damn thing.'

On the thirty-second floor of the Hotel Ana, Aisling tied a leash around Hiro's neck and pulled it hard.

'We're going for a walk today.'

He whimpered in fear and she stroked his head.

'It'll be good to get out. Look down there. Tokyo is just about to fizz up all its lovely neon veins.'

They looked down; their eyes scanned past the long buildings, down to the intersecting highways at the crossroads of Akusaka, Roppongi, Toranomon and Kasumigaseki, the car lights just coming on, forming a faintly glowing, soundless pit of snakes whose ends and beginnings slithered beyond sight. A moon suddenly appeared from the smog like an eyeball popping out of a socket. Aisling tenderly but firmly took off Hiro's tie and jacket.

'We're going to have to hippen you up a tad,' Aisling scolded him. 'Let's get you some club-kid clothes. How about that? Mr Business mogul in some shiny platforms. Oh the things I could do to you.'

'I can't go through the lobby like this. They'll see me,' he protested.

'Ah whist will ye. Look we'll tuck the leash in your shirt till we get outside. Where I'm taking you none of your colleagues will ever venture. That I promise. Now let's get cracking, I've to meet up with Toru in just over an hour.'

'Where?' Hiro's soft eyes expanded to an unappealing mixture of terror and pleading.

'Shibuya.'

'By the dog statue!' Hiro was aghast.

'Appropriate huh? That's why you like me and not some cheap unimaginative whore.'

'But everyone meets there. My kids could be there.'

'All the more fun for me and anxiety for you, Sweet thing. Now I'll be out in a minute. Don't go anywhere.'

Aisling went into the bathroom and straightened her tie. She tied her long red bush of hair into a pony-tail. Her breasts were bound. Opening a carved wooden box she removed a beard and moustache and attached them with spirit-glue to her face. With her imposing height, broad flat face, and the way the Japanese would expect anything of a foreigner, she passed. Back in the bedroom she extracted a small folded packet from her breast pocket. Pouring a white powder mound onto the bedside table, she divided the stash into two lines as thick as Fatima's fingers.

'What's the word for this in English?'

Hiro accepted a cut straw.

'Devil's Dandruff,' she told her eager pupil.

He snorted the coke and was just sitting back when, without warning, she kicked him across the room with her long leg.

Hiro got up off the floor looking hurt. 'I don't know if I like you as a man.'

'No one likes me as a man.' Aisling did not adjust her voice. 'I've never given anyone reason to.'

Shooting down in the elevator, Hiro tried to assert himself with a dog leash tucked into his shirt, the leather collar visible.

'Don't take me by surprise like that. There are rules.'

Aisling grabbed him by the testicles and the arm. 'In the research for my trip I've come across the Asmat tribe who greet each other like this. Something for the missionaries to get used to. The tribe's ancestors claim to have been carved from trees by Fumeripits the God. Then he drummed them to life.'

'Primitive people,' Hiro winced, but made no attempt to fight her. 'Surely you are not impressed with jungle stories of stone-age people.'

'Wood-age, Hiro. Stones are kind of hard to come by in

a swamp.' Aisling let go of his testicles. 'And our own tribe does claim to be descended from fish.'

'Evolution is a scientific fact. Great minds worked it out in Europe, not savages living in mud huts.'

'Look Buddy, we didn't crawl out of the water to become us.' She adjusted her tie as the doors opened and some giggling women watched them exit. 'We crawled out when trapped in dried-up pools.'

'So what?' Hiro scurried as fast as he could to the taxi rank.

'No you don't. The Subway tonight.' She steered him away. 'So what? We were seeking the same. We failed to do so in time. What we became was incidental but how we treat each other is unforgivable.'

'Fish was a long time ago.'

'We mammals did so well out of that great explosion 65 million years ago. Do you think that's what we've been longing for all along? Another chance? Another huge bomb?'

'Aisling. You are obsessed. Your friend, Toru, tell me what to expect?'

'He's from Hiroshima.' Aisling shot him a cold look.

Toru waited for them under the bronze statue of Hachiko the dog. Sticking his fingers into the depths of his perm, he pulled on a spring-like curl. A true sentimentalist, he always managed to squeeze out a tear or two when he thought of this dog. A monument to waiting. He came early on purpose to elongate the anticipation, his nerves exposed to the passing minutes and the constant expectation. Toru grew up hearing the story of the dog who for years waited outside the *eki* every evening for his master to return from work. When the master died, the dog still came and waited. One day the dog died on the way to the station and everyone missed him. Hence the statue. This was a true story, Toru thought with satisfaction. He smoothed the crease in his trousers and got on with waiting. A surprise tear fell onto his slender yellow hand. Toru bent over and licked the tear. Aisling had taught him to drink his own tears. Got to keep yourself to yourself. Never know when you might need that tear. Mustn't go shedding these tokens about the city streets. Tonight Aisling had promised to bring him her one and only client. She was a monogamous whore. Toru knew that Hiro had been in her English night-class and later would go to the bar where she hostessed at night and pay to talk to her. He was improving his already excellent English after having been raised in America by his scientist father. Aisling said she was bringing Hiro clothes to go clubbing and Hiro would furnish Toru with a new outfit while he was at it. Aisling said Hiro always did what he was told. Toru waited, then curled up dejectedly under the bronze animal when they didn't come.

On the swamp shore Pierre-Dominique Gaisseau was filming the Asmat carving their giant *bis* poles from felled mangrove trees. The Asmat carved side by side, noisily chatting and laughing. Others sat and drummed the souls of the dead into the wooden personalities that were taking shape in the tree trunks. Grinning, toothy, big-dicked, the elaborately-carved trees cackled with unavenged ghosts. The man with the light bulb around his neck bit down on a sago grub and grinned somewhat toothlessly at the white man who seemed to be the boss. Sago grub tasted, looked and felt like human brains. As if a door had just opened in his brain, the Dutch police officer intercepted the dark smile and instinctively ordered the French film crew to pack up and leave at once. Gaisseau nodded to his people and they made off into the river back to where they came from. Not before they managed to negotiate a deal and take the giant twenty-foot *bis* poles with them. The ghosts reluctantly vacated the poles as soon as the Asmat handed them over. They hovered in the air that was like mud to them.

Late at night Aisling bent over the curled Toru and shook him awake. He stared up at her with a wounded expression.

'Poor Toru. I knew you'd wait for me.'

Toru sat up suddenly and inspected her face. Her eye was swollen and blotted with a bluish-yellowish bruise, her forehead was scabbed over and caked with grit, her chin was cut wide open. He almost smiled.

'I knew you would come.'

Aisling patted the statue. 'It's funny even the dog looks Japanese.'

Toru slid his thin arms through hers and purred as she stroked his head and whispered, 'I have to go home Toru. Fatima will help me.'

'We're not going out?'

'Ah, Toru get a grip, would ye look at me?'

Aisling bought Toru a small gift on the way home to Fatima. Fatima sighed as she opened the door and saw the two of them. A big battered Irish woman and a tiny slender Japanese man with glitter blusher on his cheeks.

'What happened to you this time?' She led her girlfriend in and sat her down. Standing back to assess the damage.

'She bought me this in the subway,' Toru beamed, trying to show Fatima a tiny packet of glitter make-up. Fatima ignored him.

Aisling shrugged. 'I was with Hiro. I had him on a dog lead. It was ok. We'd done it before but I went to get a coffee in Kentucky Fried Chicken and there were these American Servicemen . . .'

Fatima nodded, that was all the information she needed. She started boiling water and taking down the first-aid kit. 'Thanks for bringing her home, Toru, now you can go.'

'Leave him be,' Aisling winced as Fatima dabbed alcohol on her chin. She still had the mustache on but they had cut off the beard. 'He was waiting in Shibuya all this time. Hiro escaped, he must have gone back to the hotel. They weren't interested in him so much. They heard my voice ordering coffee . . .'

Fatima silenced her by placing a finger on Aisling's swollen mouth. It was apparent that she did not want the details. A fourth person sat in the room as Fatima ministered to Aisling. His name was Sadao and he only spoke Japanese but was accustomed to letting them idle on in English. He had long hair to his waist and was bare-chested. Spending much time in the gym, each of his muscles was defined and Fatima used him as an artist's model. Toru had brought him to her one day. It was the only thing Fatima was grateful to Toru for. Usually, she dismissed Toru as a street creature. After all, when Aisling found him, he was bouncing with fleas, but mostly she resented his devotion to her lover.

'They didn't take everything, the fuckers.' Aisling produced a packet of cocaine and poured some out on the kitchen counter. The four gathered around and hoovered up its contents with alacrity.

'Why do you have to dress like a man, it makes me sick and it gets you in trouble.' Fatima rubbed her nose and sniffed heartily.

'Jesus, Fatima, half our fucking friends are drag queens.'

'They're giving up power, you're trying to take it.'

'So?'

'You're buying into the system with this uniform, these designer suits Hiro buys you, and all your S&M bag of tricks. It's imitative.'

Aisling shook her head and waved the straw about. 'As my father would say, "You've your tae in a bucket." It's not merely imitative, I'm subverting the power dynamic.'

'How?'

'I'm taking on a role and I don't need a dick, just a costume. Why else would they want to kill me as soon as they suss me? I'm showing them it's a game they're playing too. There's nothing real about men and women.'

'You know there's a huge missing female population with infanticide and bad health care for girls and now you're erasing yourself too.'

'Strange that I should have made it so far when they stamped me out at birth.'

'You piss everyone off eventually. How many beatings can you take? I mean I'd never say you deserved them but I'm an African Lesbian in Asia and I've never got beaten since I left home.'

'Everyone loves Aisling just as she is,' Toru protested.

'The drag queens don't like her because she's too macho. The butches don't like her because she goes in and out of butch. She has no regard for anyone's traditions. She's the worst kind of tourist. Here she is in Japan and she blows her nose in public, she always forgets to take off her shoes, she eats walking down the street . . .'

Aisling looked bored with Fatima's ranting. Toru went to the bathroom and changed into a silver mini-dress. He tottered forward in giant platforms. Aisling grinned as she watched him waver towards her.

'Those are what I call from-the-car-to-the-bar shoes. Let

me call you a taxi child of grace. You'd be lucky to make it up the stairs.'

'Let's go, Ash,' he said. 'It's midnight. The city will be nicely tuned now. Get in the mood. Sing me a song.'

'What do you want?'

'"The Last Rose of Summer" or "Danny Boy".'

'Oh, Toru, all that mush will get you in trouble.'

'I hate those songs,' Fatima said. 'And you're not going out in that state.'

'I can't put a beard on, Toru. It'll have to be a girls' night tonight.' Aisling walked to the bedroom and loosened her breasts, marked and red. Toru helped her into a silk blouse and billowing purple silk pants. 'I think I may have lost Hiro as my one and only client. Oh well. File it under "A" for "Another-brilliant-career-down-the-drain".'

'I have a man I don't want if you want him,' Toru whispered, making sure Fatima was out of earshot. 'He is a Buddhist monk with tits. I swear, he has tits like a woman. Lucky man. Very clean. He has a dog and the dog has its own toilet. He has trained the dog to press a pedal and flush. I have so many now, you take him over. He's easy. No sex. Two hours' nipple stimulation and that's all. Good pay.'

'Two hours? Jaysus, I don't know about you Toru, but my mind would wander. Forget it, I'll go on my trip to Indonesia early that's all. I wanted to go to Bali and then on to a few islands and then to Irian Jaya.'

'Irian Jaya,' Toru said the words in fear.

'Pure land it means, that's all.' She stroked his cheek. 'I want to pay a visit to the Asmat before the Indonesian government puts them to work or the missionaries convert them. Already the Jesuits have them smoking tobacco and wearing knickers.'

Fatima brooded in the doorway. 'One night in wouldn't kill you.'

'I've yet to test that theory,' Aisling said, combing her long, red, frizzy hair.

'I thought when I met you, you had some kind of philosophy but now I'm beginning to worry that it's all just random to you. Each day you're hammering against a window-pane not knowing what blocks you. Like an insect. Do you have any ideals left or is it all just kicks, pricks, and clits?'

'Fatima. Let me tell you a story. When the Reverend Ian Paisley was giving a fire-and-brimstone sermon, he was thumping the pulpit shouting, "In hell there will be wailing and gnashing of teeth." And a trembling old lady piped up, "But Reverend, I have no teeth." And the Reverend stood to his full height, surveyed his expectant congregation and roared, "TEETH SHALL BE PROVIDED,"' Aisling threw her head back and roared, splitting the scab on her chin until it bubbled with blood. 'That's my philosophy baby, in a nutshell. TEETH SHALL BE PROVIDED.'

'Is that story true?' Toru asked.

'All stories are true.' Aisling turned to Sadao and spoke in Japanese, asking him did he want to share a taxi but he glanced nervously at Fatima and muttered that he was staying the night. Aisling walked out, slamming the door, not to offend but because she always slammed the door.

Fatima called to her in surrender. 'We need toilet paper.'

In the taxi, Aisling pulled up Toru's dress. His cock and balls were strapped firmly out of sight and he was wearing black lace panties. 'Well, well what have we here? From-the-bar-to-the-bed panties.'

Toru giggled, and opened his hand like a magician; two ecstasy tablets on display among the glitter in his palm.

Hours later, as they tip-toed through the fetal goo of dawn, Aisling stopped at a convenience shop in the station. She caught sight of herself in a mirror and realized that she had gone out with her mustache on and no one had the guts to tell her. Or maybe they just didn't give a shit. She counted her money but couldn't afford the six-pack of toilet paper, so she ripped the plastic and took a single one out. The shop assistant was so taken aback that he didn't object. 'I'm trying to cut down,' she told him in Japanese, nodding towards the single roll.

At Potsdam the allied leaders posed for photos after issuing the Potsdam Declaration. They wanted unconditional surrender from the Japanese. They refused to guarantee that the Emperor remained. The Emperor was God to the Japanese but a war criminal to the West. One westerner pointed out that to the Japanese people, killing the Emperor would be synonymous with crucifying Christ. But in the dog-fight for world supremacy, Truman needed a fist to slam down on the world to show who was boss once and for all and he had to do it before the war ended and he couldn't do it to Europeans. An inferior race had the nerve to bomb America. It was beginning to look logical to the American war leaders. Truman paced the room without much thought in his head but with growing excitement. He smiled as he reached up and pulled the string on the ceiling fan.

Back at Los Alamos, the scientists had carved their giant totems in the desert, and they gave them to a soldier. The soldier named the H-bomb plane after his mother, Enola Gay, and the bomb was christened Little Boy. It was as if he wanted to be born again.

Fatima touched Aisling. Their legs were long and entwined,

their arms were interlocked, their faces were nose to nose, their lips open, their tongues spiraling into each other's heads.

'Let's go dancing,' Aisling said.

'Can't we just stay here for a night?'

'I'm going away. I want to say good-bye to all the freaks.'

'Say good-bye to me.'

'I told Toru I would go out.'

'For Christ sake,' Fatima said as she sat up. Her small breasts jiggled and Aisling instinctively reached for a nipple. Fatima pressed Aisling's hand close to her heart. 'I love you.'

'I love you too, Fatima. Tell me, what's with this Sadao character? I'm not jealous or anything but I was taken aback. You've never had anybody else except me in all these years. And a man at that?'

'There are more than two sexes, Aisling.'

'I think I know that,' Aisling said. 'Are you trying to get back at me for adopting Toru?'

'Toru is a lot cleaner these days. I've noticed you've scrubbed him and have him speaking English like an Irishman.'

'It's a useful skill. I taught you too.'

'Nobody but you could have taught him that fast and that perfectly.'

'Toru is brilliant. A genius glistening in the garbage.'

'I can't see it. I can only see how you teach.' Fatima bent her head and then lay back down by Aisling. 'Aisling, I wish you could tell me how long you'll be away. I can't bear missing you. Why do you have to go? You were only back six months this time.'

'I'll stay with you tonight,' Aisling whispered. 'You have your art to do. You're a Buddhist. I've no Gods. I'm trying to do the whole thing by myself. Travel is the only recourse

I have to make my life longer. You should read the book I read. You'd want to come too.'

'Stay just a few months longer. Make it a year this time.'

Aisling rose white, naked and big, out of the bed. Her hair was bristling and alive under the whirring ceiling fan. '*To the road. To the road. What is left of life is but little and the journey before you is long.*'

Michael Rockefeller was one of the heirs to the greatest fortunes in the United States. His family had made their money in steel. He was studying ethnology in Yale and preparing to go on a trip to Dutch New Guinea. His friend helped him pack his bags. She had prepared a first-aid kit for him. They moved about the large room as the sun spilt over the furnishings and dust particles shook and hovered in the bright air.

'I'm going to bring more ceremonial poles home for the museum.' Michael pushed his steel-rimmed glasses up the bridge of his nose.

'What do they use the poles for?' His friend sat on his bulging suitcase as he tried to fasten it shut. A shirt was sticking out the side so he made her get up and they folded it neatly and put it back in.

'The Asmat believe death is unnatural. As far as I can understand, every time there is a death it has to be avenged. So you can imagine that they are constantly fighting. They have to place the enemies' heads in these huge carved poles. It's the only way for the spirits of the dead to be at peace.'

'Fascinating! And I suppose they eat each other?'

'Yes.' Michael smiled. 'Yes, in fact they do. At least they did until the Dutch tried to put a stop to inter-tribal warfare and cannibalism. I'm not sure if they are still head-hunters. It's very remote but I have contacts in Agats, the missionary post, quite near. It was great the last time, perfectly wonderful. I feel different out there. I can't describe it. And safe, so don't worry. They only avenge those who have killed members of their tribe and as far as I know no white man has touched them.'

'We'd better go down for dinner. And try not to tell your father all this, Mike. I'm not sure he'd want his son going among savages.'

'As Governor of New York he's among savages every day.' Michael shut off the ceiling fan and closed his bedroom door.

The Asmat men canoed up to the shore and leapt out to pull their chosen mangrove trees onto land. The women howled and snarled. They had weapons in their hands. Their eyes were painted with black stripes and their chests were pocked with beauty scars. Straw hung from their ears as their screams shook the swamp from its sleepy water patterns and rattled it into battle. Splashing into the river, they shot arrows and threw spears. One man was hit in the shoulder but he was not the target of the women's venom. The jungle spirits were. The women fought the spirits and rid them from the felled trees. When the trees were finally dragged by the men onto the shore, the women felt satisfied that all the spirits were gone. Now the trees would be ready for the dead souls. The mood was festive. Dead souls crawled into the massive trunks and settled. Waiting once more to be carved into form.

On the fridge in the basement Aisling had stuck an advertisement for Miss Vera's finishing school in New York. The picture was of a person in a long black dress with a bulging crotch clutching their head in consternation. The caption read: 'Even the Simplest Evening Gown can be Ruined by a Penis.' Toru read it and giggled, then he showed her his belly button and nipples, red and newly pierced. To match the piercing in his eyebrows and ears. He was wearing silver track-suit bottoms and a black jogging bra over his flat chest. He handed the little packages to Aisling.

'What are these?'

'Nicotine patches.'

'I've given up smoking.'

'No,' Toru said. 'They're not for you, they're for the men in the swamp. You told me the missionaries had them smoking and now they have to work for the tobacco.'

Aisling threw the packages into her case. 'Toru you want me to go liberate the Asmat?'

'I think you should.' Toru nodded seriously and sadly.

'Before they become asthmatics.' She watched his face to see if he caught the pun. The ultimate test of her teaching.

'Sing me a song. "The Last Rose of Summer".'

'We'll go to a club and I'll sing for you on the street. I want to leave before Fatima comes back. She thinks I'm going in two days but I'll just bring my bag out on the town and head straight to the airport from there. The good-byes panic us.'

Soon Tokyo coughed them out of the subway. The street narrowed as they walked and the buildings grew. It was two days after the beating and Aisling still felt shaky. Also, she was drug-lagged. She and Fatima had stayed in bed all night and drank wine and did coke. Her brain felt like it was growing inside her head, softly expanding against her skull. In a Yakatori-Ya, she put Toru on her knee at the bar and sang.

'Tis the last rose of Summer left blooming all alone,
All her lovely companions are faded and gone.
No flower of her kindred, no rosebud is nigh,
To reflect back her blushes and give sigh for sigh.

'I need money Ash,' Toru said. 'I can't stay with you all night.
I have to go. Sadao is moving into Fatima. I was staying at his
flat and now I have nowhere to go. I need money or I have to
sleep in the streets.'

'Moving into Fatima.' Aisling's eyes burned. 'Here am I
singing to you. You little flea sanctuary.'

'Oh, I'm clean now, Ash. I was on the streets that's why.
No more fleas. You boiled my clothes and washed me in all
those smells.'

'I guess I'm going and he'll be company for her.'

'I only got him as a model for her. He spends all day in
the gym and she told me she wanted muscles.'

Aisling took out a wad of yen and halved it. 'Go to Michiko.
Give her this for rent for a few months. She's in need of cash
and can share her place if you behave.'

'But your trip.'

'I have too much money. Take it. When I come back
I will teach you to write English and read it. Then you
can teach.'

'Not much money. Fucking is better.'

'But you get thrashed all the time, Toru. One day they will
kill you. You have the worst taste in johns. The more violent
they are, the further you go.'

'The more they fight, the more they pay.'

'You know I read yesterday that once you could smell
burning flesh in the Tokyo sky. During the American fire-
bombing the pilots said they could smell it from their planes.

Now the buildings reach that height to reclaim the spirits of the smells. Burnt smoked souls.'

'But how do they reclaim it?' Toru asked, popping a chicken ball into his mouth.

'At night they now have the windows to condense on. It relaxes them.'

'I miss my aunt in Hiroshima,' Toru said suddenly. 'But I like it here. My grandmother was under the atomic bomb. She gave her sheets to the museum. They were all black rain. But my aunt she was in the womb that day.'

'The Americans had to avenge their dead. Their savagery is wildly inventive, they made your aunt into a pinhead. Not to worry, you are Japan now Toru.' She fiddled with a curl that hung from his forehead. 'A neon slut phoenix. Smashed by men and cruelly risen with commerce in your heart.'

Toru liked that and tugged at her little finger. 'Sing me the end of the song.'

'No. People are staring at us now.' Aisling instinctively touched her moustache. A man in the corner read a newspaper with the headline roughly translated as 'Yet More Mentally Deranged Foreigners on the Streets'. 'There might be trouble, let's go to the bar.'

'Which one?'

'Well, since I'm a man tonight we'll go cruising like you wanted to do on Tuesday.'

In the bar they met a man. Aisling bought him a drink. When she was a man she walked without her hands ever touching her sides, and took up space when she sat. She drank by throwing the liquid to the back of her throat instead of in sips. Most of all, she never smiled. That was what convinced. That was what had been hardest at first. You forget and smile. Women smile all the time because they have to. Japanese men smile more but Gaijin men don't smile if they are not happy or amused.

There was a back-room in the bar and Toru led the man behind the curtain. The dark had bodies moaning and grunting; the dark was thick with smells. Solemn as a priest, Aisling went behind the man and sodomized him with her dildo as Toru stood in front with his cock in the man's mouth. The man leaned over a chair and wrenched a happy sigh from deep within. Aisling and Toru smiled at each other as they skewered this stranger. Deeper and deeper they pressed as if to touch one another through the host and consecrate the act.

Aisling looked out of the window onto the dark runway as the plane landed. There were packs of wild animals yelping beyond the wings. The dogs of Indonesia. Aisling preferred it when there was no jetway and she had to cross the runway to the buildings. She thrilled to be walking among these giant machines with their lights and stairs and huge wings like holy animals. The wide space that stretched to fences and fields was not a human space. But she had never seen dogs on a runway before. They stood just at the periphery of the lights with their heads bent, long necks sloping, eyes concentrating on the people traversing their territory. The dogs were linked to the planes in a bond of empty hunger, flight and distance. Like white birds on elephants, here the skinny dogs and immense planes were in symbiosis.

Weeks later, she left Bali and took boats to islands that got smaller and smaller and more lost in the sea as she stepped ashore.

On one such island she walked the white coral road and saw a shadow above her shadow. Glancing into the blue empty sky she could not find the object that could possibly throw this second shadow. The shadow was small and shook above her own elongated shadow. She saw a village on stilts in the distance and hesitated, thinking of the commotion she would cause arriving in their midst with a blot of a shadow above her own body shadow. But as she came onto the dusty strip of bamboo houses, the second shadow disappeared and she attributed its sighting to heat or casual madness. The people came out to gawk at her. There was a hypertension in the air as if they were all peeled raw. In every village these days there was a bearded European anthropologist. This one gave her some stewed tea and kept patting his bald head as if he couldn't quite believe his hair had gone forever. He informed her that the people were engaged in ceremonies of a highly unusual order, whatever that meant. He was there to record them. He had a video camera and it had taken a while to get permission to film. She casually told him the story of the shadow and he was amused and translated for the people.

The people panicked, some falling into trances, and one man sewed his lips together with a big splinter. A woman bit into rocks, cracking her teeth. The anthropologist told her she was upsetting the ancient rituals. That night Aisling woke on the floor of a hut to find a carved wooden effigy with stained red coconut hair, long like hers. With fright she stared at this voodoo creature and it stared back with shell eyes. She knew when she wasn't wanted and left the island in the morning on a passing fishing boat. The anthropologist was furious at the interruption of the ceremonies by the crude arrival of an Irish tourist. He fumed when the people began to draw her image and take her as an omen. He frantically hopped about trying to destroy the images and get them back on a pure route but they seemed utterly

absorbed by the double-shadow phenomenon. This big, poll-
uting, red-headed woman with pale skin was being carved into
their totems.

Michael Rockefeller sat and had a good dinner with the
missionaries in Agats in New Guinea. The priests told jokes
and stories about their unlikely flock. Tobacco was the only
way to control them and make them listen to the word of
their God. With tobacco they could stop wars by threatening
to withdraw supplies. It was a dubious peace but it sometimes
worked. One priest told Michael that the Asmat up at Otjenep
had been carving poles and might be amenable to trading.
The poles were meant for the spirits of the dead to dwell
in until these spirits were avenged by a severed head from
the offending tribe. But it was quite easy to buy the poles
since the spirits could leave the carvings and take over new
poles if necessary.

'Very considerate of them,' one priest said and they all
laughed.

'Oh yes,' another told Michael. 'The spirits are remarkably
flexible when it comes to trading.'

Early in the morning Rockefeller loaded a little boat with
fishing hooks and tobacco for trading and set off. The outboard
motor droned through the great swamp for miles and miles.
He thought he caught glimpses of brown faces in the jungle
sombrely watching but maybe it was just the hypnotic glare of
the water and the sodden trees and the constant noise of the
engine that brought about the occasional flash of hallucination.
Michael came to the village and saw the great poles. They
were about twenty feet high with intricately carved figures,
phalluses and praying mantis. Delighted, he put down half
the fee and promised the rest on delivery. The man with the

light bulb fingered the fishing hooks, grinned and nodded and they all ate together in the male-only longhouse. Rockefeller returned that evening before sundown to the government post in Agats. He nearly broke his leg on the wooden boardwalk with its loosely set rolling logs. His glasses slipped off and he quickly caught them before they could slip forever between the wood and into the murky river. As he placed his glasses firmly back on, he stared straight ahead; the brown leaf huts on their slender multitude of stilts were mirrored in the water.

First the Americans sent out a plane to drop radios and recording equipment onto the streets of Hiroshima. The Japanese who were up that early fiddled with the equipment in wonder, not understanding. Tension was high among the crew aboard the *Enola Gay* as it flew through the sky towards the city. They had maps with the Initial Point marked. They were looking for a bridge in the middle of the city beside a dome.

Toru had spiked Sadao's drink because Sadao hated doing drugs and Toru could not tolerate such weakness of character. Fatima had remained inside her basement, glazing her sculpture. She had been stoic on discovering Aisling gone, but Sadao was afraid of her. He sensed a fierce sorrow beneath this calm exterior and did not want to be the one she lashed out at. As usual Fatima worked while they all played. Her exhibition was coming up and Aisling had promised to be there for it. The life-size sculpture was of a boy walking while balancing a severed head on top of his own head. Sadao had been the model. Both heads looked alike. In contrast, Toru had been inconsolable when Aisling left, worse than ever before. He had grown so dependent. Fatima had found herself unwillingly comforting him.

The club was on the twenty-fifth floor. Tokyo reeled about them. The cars pumped with music and everyone was eating and dancing and drinking or hurrying to eat and dance and up here they were drinking and drinking and now Sadao was cursing Toru because his brain was crawling like some hairless gray rodent through the teeming streets between the spike heels of women's knee-high boots and the drunken stumbling of men – while his body was up on the twenty-fifth floor, an empty host with no power but his senses. He got sick on his own feet and Toru tut-tutted and kissed him on his ear. Much to his horror, he felt Toru's tongue snake into the cavity and leave it wet and tingling.

'What do you most want to do that you can't do?' Toru asked.

'Take me away. I want to go home. Fatima will kill me if she sees me like this.'

Toru sighed deeply, said good-bye to his myriad of club kid friends and with surprising strength dragged Sadao to the elevator.

'My brain has gone, I have to get it back.' Sadao closed his eyes but opened them as the darkness he found inside his hollow head was of a disgusting nature. They shot down the insides of the building.

'Your brain will be back soon. It just needed a walk and a little independence,' Toru assured him genially as the doors opened onto a marble lobby.

Two hours later Toru was massaging Sadao and he was enjoying it despite himself. They sat in a dark corner of a transvestite bar in the Golden Boy district.

'Aisling and I used to come here at first when she began to teach me English. I spoke a little when I met her but now

I speak like an Irish queer. You see I used to wander around Peace Park looking for tourists to practice my English. I'd bring my aunt with her head shaved, just a tuft at the top to make it look pointy. Radiation bait. The tourists always wanted to know. Sometimes they had white faces and no English. I hated those ones. I met her by the atomic dome. She was inside even though it is forbidden. I saw her looking from out the broken window. It was my aunt she saw and came immediately. My aunt loves her. You should get her to teach you when she comes back. She is the best teacher in the world. That's her gift. I come here because it reminds me. In the beginning they didn't trust her because she wasn't in drag. They thought she was just a man. And Gaijin too. Aisling could go anywhere in Japan as a man but the other Gaijin they always looked at her as if they couldn't figure her out and it made them so mad. But for us she was Gaijin first and so naturally strange and funny. I swear they might have even let her into the *ofuro*.'

'That's the one thing I would like to do, go to the *sento* and take a bath.'

Toru stopped his hands and beamed. 'Let's go.'

Sadao reddened. 'Toru, I can't, you know that.'

The two men walked into the bathroom with white towels around their waists. The *ofuro* was a large stone pool and the mosaic tiles were slippery and beautiful. Already, there were two men cooking in the steaming bath. Toru skipped over to the taps on the wall, took a bucket out of the stack and handed it to Sadao who stood mute with fright. There were little wooden stools with holes in the middle and he was staring at them in horror. Toru sat on the stool and put his cock and balls into the little hole and began soaping and washing with the water from the bucket. He kept the towel on his lap and Sadao sat down gingerly and followed suit. They filled the bucket many times and rinsed away all the soap. Sadao had tears in his eyes.

'I always wanted to come here,' he whispered. He wanted to thank Toru but Toru understood. Smiling radiantly at him, he indicated to the big *ofuro*.

'Ready?'

Sadao would never be ready but he followed Toru and shadowed him as he crawled into the bath. The other men weren't even looking. One of the men had tattoos and a finger missing. Sadao remained very still in the scalding water, his legs were drawn to his chest and he had never felt happier in his life. His brain re-entered his head in this soup of men. Four men in the hot water in silence; and this was paradise to the young man of twenty-two. Not long ago Toru had introduced him to the African woman Fatima who appeared to love him. Maybe not with the same intensity that she loved the strange white woman but it was a more soothing love and he had never been able to let anyone touch him before. He had been stone for so long. Fatima was well known as an artist and when he was with her people deferred to him and gave him respect. A chance meeting with this little drag queen had kick-started his life just when the dark things inside of him had been untangling, gaining strength and reaching out to kill him. He had been propelled along darker and darker corridors, the stench growing thicker and thicker, doors shutting and locking behind him. Sadao had been contemplating suicide every waking hour rather than be overtaken and immobilized. Until Fatima had cracked in some light.

While the men were at the baths Hiro had paid Fatima a visit and she did not try to hide her distaste as he sat before her in his beautiful suit.

'I have to have her back. I must know when she returns. I thought she would return to the hotel that night.'

'When she's beaten she always comes to me,' Fatima said coldly.

'Tell me when she is coming back.' Hiro was a man accustomed to getting his way.

'I never know that. She just comes and goes without regard for any of us casualties she's left behind.' Fatima was a woman who made sure she never gave way to men like Hiro. Hiro stared at the sculpture of the boy.

'Can I buy the statue?' he said on impulse, feeling giddy to be on Aisling's home ground.

'Come to the exhibition and make a bid to the gallery.'

'I had so much until I took those evening English classes. She was recommended to me by all the executives as the most effective English teacher in Tokyo. I grew up for a few years in America in the Fifties so I just needed to improve and learn to write better . . .'

'Aisling told me she met you in the bar where she hostessed.'

'That too. I started going there for drinks after the class. I saw her walk down the street once. She was reading a book like other people listened to a Walkman. She was reading and walking, not looking up at all. Big strides and everyone was jumping out of her way. She made reading look so dangerous.'

Fatima stood. 'Well, Hiro-san, when Aisling comes back I'll tell her you called by and she can phone you.'

Hiro clenched his eyes. 'She stripped me raw. She opened the night and showed me worms of light.' He wiggled his fingers at her.

Fatima frowned, he was a creepy guy and she wanted him out.

'Maybe Toru knows more than me. If you give me your number . . .'

Hiro's face contorted with hatred. 'That gutter child. I heard about him. He is *Buraku-min*. You wouldn't know what that is but we in Japan know. They are not human, they are dirty and, like animals, they have four legs. They have been outcasts for centuries. I warned Aisling but she did not take heed. What a joke, someone of her caliber running with him . . .'

'Get out of my fucking house.' Fatima approached him, she was several inches taller and he immediately stood and walked towards the door.

'If it is the only way and he does know something, give the untouchable my phone number.' He handed her a card and glanced at the statue once more. 'Why does it have two heads?'

The vanity of the artist made her more amenable as he was genuinely taken with her piece. 'My little cousin in Mozambique was captured by South African funded bandits and made to cut off his friend's head and carry it on his own head all the way back to the camp. He was ten years old and they trained him as a soldier. The war is over now and I might go back and help out. Many children are killers. They have to be de-programmed. I was contacted by my embassy and asked to return.'

'Yes Aisling has shown me your picture in magazines. But I thought you were Nigerian.'

'That's where we met but I'm originally from Mozambique.'

'But your English is perfect. What is your mother tongue?'

'Portuguese.'

'I see.' Hiro walked to the door. He was an elegant man with a young face for a man in his fifties. Fatima almost let him stay just to talk about Aisling. Hiro bowed to her on the way out, 'So she colonized us all.'

Aisling was told by everyone that the missionaries would not take her into the jungle as a woman. But she had a trick or two up her skirt. She swam around the lagoon with some Australian surfers. The beach was a half-moon of light sand and palm trees penciled the dunes. Schools of strange fish parted and regrouped as she nosed into their flowing formations. She sat on a rock and the surfer handed her a towel, tiny crabs scuttered up the fissures.

'I wonder what all the poor people are doing now?' She smiled at him and he laughed.

When she was alone, she bound her breasts and put on her beard. Swaggering towards the mission camp she talked to a thick-set blond man in his sixties. He lived in a small prefab house with his son, a red-headed dark-eyed sly man. There were no women around. There were no books anywhere except religious books. She spotted blond hair dye in the bathroom. The father's. It seemed a strange vanity for a missionary in this part of the world. They took her money and agreed to introduce her to some Dyak natives who would take her into the jungle for a spell.

'I just want to see the jungle. I'm acclimating myself before going on to Irian Jaya.' She did not want to speak too much as her voice was never deep enough.

'Borneo's not a hiking place, the jungle can kill you. We can only land a plane if they beat a clearing in the trees, otherwise you're on your own.'

'Kalimantan. I haven't heard the name Borneo in years.'

'Ha! Names change, sure they do, but the wild man is still here.'

The father flew her to a camp and the Dyaks, accompanied by a few young children, brought her into the trees away from the paths. For days they walked and at nights they camped. She was empty-handed and yet they raced ahead sure-footed and laden with supplies. Once inside the jungle, the tribe began to strip down naked and Aisling was constrained in her loose T-shirt and baggy shorts. Insects got caught in the folds of the material. She trusted the Dyaks that it was better to wear nothing but she shook her head and they laughed at her misplaced modesty in their forest.

On the third day she felt a stinging on her back and the world blotted out like sudden icy ink running down the inside of her eyelids. 'I'm blind,' she said in English, pointing to her eyes and shaking her head. They began to undress her and found a bee in her clothes but then found her breasts and the babble of their tongues bubbled to a frenzy as one man pulled down her shorts. They tied her to the tree and placed water in her hand. All of them seemed to leave.

It was hot and she felt she was in the insides of the world and she'd never get out. She was being digested by this darkness, the long intestinal whorl of the jungle. Dream, she thought, dream of something worse than being swamped by a private night in deepest darkest Borneo.

She dreamt of the American soldiers that spotted the bridge, the initial point they had been looking for. Colonel Tibbits gave the order that introduced a global atomic age.

She dreamt of four men in a boat. Two missionaries, one anthropologist, and Michael Rockefeller, the heir to the world's most famous industrial fortune. It was a clear Saturday morning and they buzzed out from Agats towards Basiem. They talked little and at the mouth of the river their engine got swamped. It was only a small outboard motor but it was all they had. The two young missionaries jumped off the boat and said they would go get help. Michael and the anthropologist watched their arms strike through the water as they themselves were tugged out to the open sea. Night came suddenly and they glanced at each other in the fragile boat. Both held onto the sides to steady the tiny craft. They were far off land now and did not know if their companions had made it back to get help. Unable to sleep, the hours of darkness weighed like giant stones on their web of hope. Michael, at one point, put his hand in the water. Fearful of sharks, he withdrew his pale limb and placed it on his leg looking at it for a moment in a sudden flash of objectivity. As if it was a limb alone. Belonging to something else.

Aisling dreamt of Toru's grandmother. Wet black rain streaked from a leaking sky, marking every white thing she had hanging outside. How she scrubbed those sheets, scrubbed and scrubbed, then later gave them to the museum. That morning, hanging her sheets, she was hanging them before the world. Her neighbor was humming in the yard – minutes later her guts lay outside her belly and she shoveled them in as she died. Her brother in the house, his arms outstretched, his bones exposed, ran to the river with the others to drown.

She knows now, pain contaminates.

You weren't in their dreams until you cracked their heads like eggs off the side of bowls. Burned their children until their fingernails peeled away from their hands. They were women, children and prisoners of war; forced laborers. They were not at the conference table. They were not at the war. They were another species – combustible.

Black ash burnt them as they spun in circles in that flattened town. Soft ash swayed onto their limbs as if there were no violence in it. Like later you said you did it to save lives. They were small after all, down there. Soft ash, black rain, and she was pregnant when it fell. Her child was born with a pointed head and a tiny brain. In the months to come she was nursing her, thinking (even those who were untouched were dying from it) and she was thinking. What you could have done on the journey home, when you left them behind? Spinning, disintegrating, burning; in the black rain falling.

The Americans felt very sleepy after the release of the bomb. Adrenalin ebbed away. They smoked cigars, ate sandwiches, and drank pineapple juice. 'Then we took a nap,' one of them said, 'as the plane just kept boring holes in the sky.'

When President Truman was told of the successful mission he exclaimed, 'This is the greatest thing in history.'

The sun came up and the anthropologist and the rich man hooked their worried eyes on the coastline. It was a relief to see it but they were floating away. The anthropologist begged Michael not to try and swim for it. There were sharks and it was at least six miles by the looks of it. Michael stripped to his underwear. With his glasses tied around his neck the world was blurred and the coastline was a suspended green streak. He took two petrol drums to float on and slid into the water. The men looked at each other as he clung to the side.

'Come with me?'

The anthropologist shook his head, and Michael said, 'I think I can make it.'

One man watched from the boat as the other's pale limbs split the water and grew fainter and fainter. The man sank his head in his hands, his fingers clawing at his ragged hair, and the sea slurped oblivious at the bottom of the boat.

Aisling's dream was snapped in half as she was yanked up off the jungle floor by the two missionaries.

'I heard your plane in my dream. I thought it was the *Enola Gay*,' she told them excitedly. Her body was alive, a mass of ants and leeches and she was still blind. They roughly kicked her and dragged her by the hair to the machine. When she was sitting inside the plane they thrust a bible into her hand. On the flight back to the base her sight came back, first as a blur and then it cleared up as if she had just put on a pair of glasses. The blond father was shouting at her, and the son who had put a blanket over her nakedness was sniggering and licking his lips and tapping fingers off the palm of his hands as if making signals to the deaf and dumb.

'*Come down and sit in the dust, O virgin daughter of Babylon, sit on the ground: there is no throne, O daughter of the Chal-de'ans: for thou shalt no more be called tender and delicate . . .*'

'I beg your pardon,' Aisling was surprised. Her body was covered in bites and lumps. 'Where are the Dyaks? Did they go get you? I want to thank them.'

'*Uncover thy locks, make bare the leg, uncover the thigh, pass over the rivers . . .*'

'You guys are quite the conversationalists, aren't you? Real Oscar Wildes of the jungle.'

The son's eyes bulged. He kept glancing back at Aisling, afraid to catch her eye.

'*Thy nakedness shall be uncovered, yea, thy shame shall be seen: I will take vengeance, and I will not meet thee as a man.*'

'Oh that's why you picked that passage, I see,' Aisling rolled her eyes. 'Very clever.'

'*Sit thou silent,*' he roared over the engine's noise and she tried to concentrate on the view. '*And get thee into darkness, O daughter of the Chalde'ans: for thou shalt no more be called, the lady of the kingdoms.*'

'I never was buddy, I never was,' Aisling muttered and pulled the blanket around her. She still had a beard and that made her laugh out loud. The son looked at his father in fright and the father pounded the plane through the sky roaring ferociously.

'*Thou that art given to pleasures, that dwellest carelessly, that sayest in thine heart, I am, and none else beside me; I shall not sit as a widow, neither shall I know the loss of children.*'

'I have a friend like a child and I have a wife in Tokyo. A beautiful wife . . .'

Aisling had not known how long she had been blind in the jungle after being bitten by the bee. She was hungry and when she saw the son peel a banana, she leant forward and snatched it out of his ruddy hands.

'*But these two things shall come to thee in a moment in one day, the loss of children and widowhood: they shall come upon thee in their perfection for the multitude of thy sorceries, and for the great abundance of thine enchantments.*'

'I'm impressed you know this all by heart,' she told him as she munched on the delicious banana. 'The nuns back home never taught us the bible. The bible was for the Proddies. We learnt lots of Yeats though. Let me see if I can drum some up for you. *For the good are always the merry, save by an evil chance, and the merry love the fiddle and the merry love to dance.*'

The father's voice rose to a high pitch: '*Thy wisdom and thy knowledge, it hath perverted thee . . .*'

'Oh, the big "P" word. That's not the first time I've heard this.' Aisling gave up, falling asleep in exhaustion.

He banged the plane on the ground and she jolted awake. The father got out from the cockpit in fury. She did not know if she could walk. Her legs were wisps of cloth and her brain was a spinning top inside her skull. A husky man's voice croaked out of her dusty dry throat. 'Water, I need water.' The son glanced around as if checking for his father. Then he straddled her legs and ripped her beard off her face. Aisling cried out in fury and passed out, her chin red and stinging, the blanket falling away.

An hour later Aisling was whacking the blond father on the arm and screaming, 'Your fucking idiot son. Tell him I charge for shit like that. You better get me out of here or I'll lodge a complaint. I'm going to the police.'

'Look lady or whatever you are,' the man's pudgy face was beet red but Aisling was two inches taller than him and bore down on him with eyes like a dragon's. He faltered but went on, 'I've alerted the authorities and you best get out of Indonesia because . . . you've no choice, they're revoking your visa. Go back to your scum where ever you came from. I fought in World War II. I was only fourteen but I lied to fight. We didn't make the world safe for your kind to go fouling it up. I fought the nips and I saw what they done. I was only a child in Iwo Jima.'

Aisling scowled. 'I don't give a shit for your stinking war. I don't like your kind either, you're scum to me what you do out here. I need clothes. I left mine behind. Get me trousers, anything. We're about the same height.'

There was a trash bag of women's clothes in the wardrobe. He found a pink floral dress with a food stain around one of the buttons.

'My wife left me. She's back in North Carolina,' he said, as if to make sure she knew they were not his. He fingered the dress and turned away in disgust as he handed it to her.

The father beat his son with a belt when the son slunk in. The son squealed like a piglet and ran to the other room to watch the big, demented, red-headed woman, with the loose dangling breasts walking away between two policemen. She was wearing his mother's dress. She turned around and shouted back at their prefab house: 'TEETH SHALL BE PROVIDED!'

He heard his father chanting in the kitchen, '*Therefore shall evil come upon thee: thou shalt not know from whence it riseth: and mischief shall fall upon thee; thou shalt not be able to put it off: and desolation shall come upon thee suddenly, which thou shalt not know.*'

Three days after dropping the first bomb, the American soldiers were writing messages to the Japanese people on the shell of the second. —To Hirohito with love and Kisses— then the crew signed their names. That day was so cloudy they could not see the city beneath. Finally, with relief they spotted a hole in the cloud and they dropped the bomb into it. Looking back, they reported a horizontal cloud over the city then a vertical cloud growing out of it. They said the atomic cloud was unbelievably beautiful and colorful. In Nagasaki there were human beings who did not see the beauty and they were burning with it. One of the crew said, 'It would've been immoral to have that bomb and not use it.'

The dry scuttle of leaves on the cement outside sounded to Fatima like a fire crackling, but bringing cold, not flames.

She and Sadao had sat up all night in fear. Fatima looked at her watch and declared it time for the work day to start. Fatima was running through town. She had always been so self-contained and confined to the space in the basement. For years she had made her art while keeping her life motionless as a panther in the crouched attentive moment before the strike. Now she ran to her former enemy, Hiro.

Hiro was uncomfortable and angry that she had come directly to his company office. The staff were deferential but he knew they would be curious as to why this tall, black woman with long dreads was so breathless to see him. However, he was sure she brought news of Aisling so he ushered her politely into his large office.

'The four-legged one, Toru. You were right about him. He has killed us all for sure.'

Hiro raised his eyebrows but did not speak. He was on his own territory and, with the door closed, felt in control.

'He drugged my Sadao and took him to the baths. Now Sadao is being pursued. Do you understand? Someone followed him home. A man covered in tattoos with a four-fingered hand.'

'Yakuza?'

'It seems like it. We are being watched. They might give us a beating for kicks. I mean they do that sort of thing. To prove things to each other. What will they do?'

'Aisling. Is she back? I've waited for a call.'

'I can't be beaten. I won't live like this. Sadao . . . one more beating will kill him. He has told me he will not live through the bruises again. We are not Aisling.'

'And what is Aisling?'

'A punching bag for the tribe,' Fatima faltered. 'She was

so brave. I never told her that. I was always kind of disgusted when she came home.'

'What do you want me to do?'

'I have a brother in New York. We will go there. Aisling will come to you. Here is some money for her. Tell her to join us. Tell her to keep away from the basement or they will attack her too. Those men who hunt us now will not follow us out of Japan.' Fatima, normally so composed, fumbled in her bag for a thick envelope and gave it to Hiro across his huge neat desk. Hiro took the money and put it in the drawer. He felt an uncontrollable excitement and could hardly contain himself as Fatima walked to the door, worry etched in the lines on her severe face. When she was gone, he opened the drawer and stared at the envelope. Flipping his shoes off his feet, he wiggled his toes.

It only took a day before the anthropologist was saved in his little drifting boat. The governor of New York flew to the swamp to search for his son. Armies from all around the world dispatched boats, helicopters and aircraft carriers to the scene. With tobacco they were able to get the Asmat to search in a thousand canoes for the young man.

Far up river the man with the light bulb sat on the shore and told his colleagues to float logs down the river to block the invaders. As they chopped trees his light bulb splintered and cut the brown flesh on his chest. He sunk to his knees and bitterly tore it from around his neck. His wives, who were dragging a big tree to the water's edge, glanced at each other and the oldest one ran to him while the others worked on.

The anthropologist packed his little bag back at the missionary base and stood on the rough boardwalk looking out into the low green mess of the swamp.

Michael was never found.

The sky was not radiant as Aisling walked from the underground station to Fatima's basement in Tokyo. Winter was already splintering the pale blue sky and gray was seeping through. There had been no dogs on the runway the night before to see her off. She had been thrown out of Indonesia and she had watched in vain for their yellow eyes beneath the wings.

The basement was empty, rectangles of dustless floor where the furniture had been removed. The studio had one sculpture left with plastic covering and marked 're-delivered' from the gallery. She had missed the exhibition. Aisling took the covering off the statue and saw the figure of Sadao with a severed upside-down Sadao head on top of his own. Loneliness screwed into her, boring her insides out in a coil. She lay down on the floor at the foot of the statue, underneath the ceiling fan. For hours she stared at the edges of the blades piled with dust. She almost died, though she was too afraid of death to go near it. She could not wear her life anymore. It chafed and itched and burnt and was too tight. But then, naked and cold, she could not face her death.

'More than ten years Fatima,' she said. 'And every day I thought of you every hour.'

'Come Hibushka,' Toru whispered. 'I will take you home.'

Aisling turned on the floor and faced him. She had not heard him come in. He was weeping.

'You are too easily moved,' she said through her own tears. 'Those tears, you drop those tears as if you can come back to them.'

'I'm taking you home,' Toru said. 'I can speak but you can't go until I can read and write. Remember?'

He wiped her blackened dusty face and placed his bag underneath her head as a pillow. Then he covered the statue with the plastic and knelt down beside her.

'We must go, Ash. It is not good to be here.'

'Where is she?' Aisling sat up.

'There were men looking for Sadao and they left for America, to Fatima's brother.'

'America? America?' Aisling leapt to her feet and grabbed her bag as if to run to America.

'Come home with me to Hiroshima.'

Aisling was silent for a minute before answering.

'Your mother will throw me out as usual and I'm broke. I can't face the streets just now, child of grace. I need some creature comforts.'

'I will get you good cardboard and you can sleep in the alley like last time.'

'You weren't the creature I was thinking of.'

'My aunt misses you.' Toru's aunt had microphelia, a condition caused by being radiated in his grandmother's womb at 8:15, August 6, 1945. Aisling shook her head and went to the door. Toru followed like a dog at her heels as she stumbled through Tokyo, spasms of neon seizing up the stalks of buildings. A whole city shivering with lighted words. With the last of her money she bought him a meal in a bar. Gulping down whiskey after whiskey she began to talk a little, 'I'll go to Hiro. I need some money fast. Do you have any?'

'I spent all you gave me. I have some drugs left for you though. I knew you'd need some.' He was eating rice and left his chopsticks sticking up in the bowl. She stared at them in fright and felt like slapping him. He saw this and carefully removed them. 'I have two train tickets on the Shinkensen for us.'

'Toru, Toru. X-ray club kid. Prosthetic prophet bringing me the bomb for convalescence.'

'My mother was five when the bomb fell and she doesn't remember it. But there was a typhoon that winter when many got killed in the little houses they built on remains of the town. She remembers the wind. My uncle was ten and he was in the center doing war work on buildings. He was vaporized I think. My grandmother kept his burnt fingernails to give to my grandfather when he came back from China. She found them by his lunch box. We gave his lunch box to the museum with the burnt food inside. My grandfather wanted to keep the fingernails but my grandmother gave them with the sheets.'

'I'll go to Hiro. He'll give me the money. I know Abraham, her brother. I used to teach him English in Nigeria. He'll be in the phone book. How could Fatima be with a man? I thought she was of the school of thought that your brain shatters as soon as the dick enters, unless you're charging.'

'Yes but Sadao did not have a dick.' Toru held the bowl to his chin and gobbled some rice.

'I beg your pardon?'

Toru looked at her, not comprehending.

'What the fuck?' Aisling translated.

'He was born with a sex they couldn't be sure of. So they cut off his dick which was very tiny and unsure. He said the surgeons make all the unsure ones into girls because it is easier. But he was XY just like I'm Z. Ha! I made a joke Ash, did you like it? He was very sorry about what the doctors did.'

Aisling signaled frantically for more whiskey. 'Where are those drugs? Break them out.' She shook her head. 'But I know all about that stuff. Intersexed babies are one in two thousand. I was always looking out for them. Medical science has only started interfering this century to normalize them.'

'They make them into girls.'

'Yep. The surgeons say, easier to poke a hole than build a pole. I suppose as well they think it's better to be an imperfect woman than an imperfect man regardless of your chromosomes. Hey, women are imperfect anyway. Poor Sadao.'

'But it didn't work out for him.'

'It rarely does. Jaysus! How did you know and I didn't?'

'I don't think you need a dick to be a man or a cunt to be a woman.'

'But why did you never mention it?'

'I never thought it was important and he was very private. I gave him to Fatima because he had muscles and that's what she asked for. He was very happy. Almost happy. I never saw him so happy. He said the doctors gave him hormone injections when he was a child but they made him sick and when he was fourteen he grew a mustache and no tits and that's how he found out. His parents wouldn't let him stay when he decided to be a man. So he was on the streets with me. When I knew him first he was very scared. He had no money but when he got some it all went to the gym. I brought him to the baths when you were gone. Some man saw us and wanted to hurt us.' Toru shrugged and looked at Aisling. 'Sing me a song.'

'Toru, right at this moment I'm contemplating whether to kill you or not.'

'My mother thinks I am like I am because of the bomb.'

'Well the fall-out must have been quite something worldwide.'

Hiro played his broad feet off each other under the teak office desk and frowned. Aisling had come to him and he had offered her an apartment in the Ginza district with all the expenses paid. They had not mentioned Fatima. He could not let her go for she would go forever and life was a chain of needs. One link to him was Japan: his company, his wife, his two children. But she had linked the other side, bound it to the rest of the species and he could not snap that now. He fiddled with the pen, clicking the nib in and out. She had sexualized everything. His bare feet rubbed off the carpet. He could hardly keep his shoes on these days. There was a picture of his father on the wall. His father had been a medical scientist who during the war had worked in Operation 731. His father never talked about it, but now the newspapers were full of newly revealed details. Hiro had read of this research place where they vivisected Chinese prisoners of war. They operated on them all without anaesthetic. They pickled whole Chinamen in giant jars. One laboratory journal reported that, 'Usually a hand of a three-day-old infant is clenched into a fist but by sticking the needle in, the middle finger could be kept straight to make the experiment easier.' They floated air balloons with fleas carrying the bubonic plague in the direction of America. They would have loved to have such a tidy A-bomb to themselves. The Americans had promoted his father when they discovered the operation during the occupation. They had wanted the data for themselves. It was all kept a secret. After all, the Americans did their own experiments on the Hibushka who survived their two bombs.

Aisling had been agitated and refused his money. Thinking she might turn violent, he had a small knife in his pocket that he fingered. But she had not been violent or even so authoritative as usual. In fact she had begged him. That was his offer and she would come around. A big fancy apartment and expenses paid, but no money in bulk. His conscience was clear, using the money in the envelope he had purchased the statue of the boy carrying the head and had it re-delivered to Fatima's basement apartment and studio. He looked at his hand and clenched it into a fist, sticking out the middle finger. He looked at his father and then looked at his own feet. A blank row of toes, no surprises there, no evil in the feet. The feet were the very end of him and where the indifferent world began.

'Toru, one day the moon will die and the sea will fall into the sky and we will all be as dead as each other.' Underneath the flat train floor, the machines screeching, cranking, churning them onward. As always his mother would throw her out. It was alleys for her at the end of the ride. And then his crazy affectionate aunt, her triangular head like a torpedo pointing to the past. Flashed in the womb when she was just a pink fishy underwater creature, grasping. Just ripe to receive the imprint of the age. Aisling would sleep on Hiroshima's ground between cardboard walls, while he and his aunt stretch like mad cats in the sky on the twelfth floor.

There was a table between them and Aisling showed him photos from the book, *Ring of Fire*. 'I never did get to see the Asmat to wean them off tobacco and strip them of their underwear.' She had a loose black and white photo of Michael Rockefeller. He was inspecting his expensive Nikon camera surrounded by fierce Asmat with shells through their noses. Toru touched the bolt he had just got put in his own nose and smiled.

'So what happened?'

'They ate him.'

Toru was distraught and Aisling, pleased with this reaction, continued. '1963, they found him washed up on shore, face down in the mud and panting. They only needed one white man to avenge all the ghosts. One white man for the Dutch machine-gunning their village a few years before. The Americans needed 300,000 sacrificed for Pearl Harbor.'

'So sad.'

'Don't you see? They didn't pick a poor anthropologist or missionary. They only needed one person from the white race and they went for a Rockfeller?'

'But he was innocent, Aisling.'

'So was your grandmother, her children, and all those 10,000 Korean prisoners of war. Hey, not only did they kill him but they made him pay half for his poles.'

'Why did the Dutch kill the Asmat in the first place?'

'Typical European logic. They wanted to put an end to the cannibalism, the head-hunting, the incessant warfare. So they machine-gun the whole village.'

Toru touched Michael's face. 'His poor mother and father.'

'The father ended up Vice President of the United States. He died while having sex with his mistress. I'll tell you Toru, those Rockefellers knew how to die. What does it matter anyway? Listen to what I'm saying, one day the moon will die and the sea will fall into the sky. We were fish Toru, fish, all of us here were only fish, not thinking of trains. We didn't crawl out of the water to become us . . .'

'I don't know why you are so happy,' he interrupted her. 'I think this was a terrible thing. He looks so young. Only twenty-two. No one deserves this.'

'Ah Toru, that's why I'll always be a disgruntled peasant and you'll forever be a queen.'

Toru took the photo and clutched it to his heart. He would not give it back and so they remained silent and he eventually fell asleep. Carriage after carriage paraded to Hiroshima. Fatima must have hated her to leave without a note, without a word. Now that the numbness was wearing off and Toru's stash of drugs was running out, she would have to accumulate the fare to America. That would not be easy from an alley in Hiroshima. Ugly buildings flashed outside, containing lives of utmost complication. This country was too old for its new structures.

Wake up Toru, she thought, look at Mount Fuji. Through the smoke-stacks, through the telephone wires, through the thick glass, and I'll look through your eyes; spotless leopard, stripeless zebra, cuntless slut, footless centipede, wingless bat. Honest trickster. I can taste the tin in you.

Sometimes the lights went out and they rattled unseeing. Whooshing the black like splinters into the heel of darkness. Night bled the light back in breaths, they flickered towards one another. He was sitting with pursed lips, a sure sign that he was thinking. He never spoke his thoughts, he only answered hers, and yet she felt he would die for her, in this spitting light.

The train was reflected on both sides, printed onto the night. Three trains: one hard center and two reflected wings. But it was the wings that were flapping them home. We have no fires Toru, no haunts, no flooded waters inside of us, but here Toru, I see rock gardens in your eyes. An inscrutable laying out of stones. Tell me the truth. You are taking me to Hiroshima, at this the very worst time of my life, the time I have lost the most, if not the all. You are taking me to Hiroshima, to cheer me up?

Now he was looking with pity at the photo of the young man. This planet as suddenly disposable as his tears. Tears, Toru, tears. Keep them inside your head. Wash your skull with private waters. Your buried burning thoughts. I can see them fluoresce from here.

Fatima had a ceiling fan in Tokyo. And like the dust on the edges of the blade, they were chopped into existence off-guard, and became dirt. They were dirt when they were static, but when travelling in the air, they were an undetectable substance to be taken in in unsuspecting breaths.

This train, this trunked-out snake, moving to scatter them again. For the cloth can not eradicate the dust, but the cloth, and the swipe of the train, sets it spinning again and once again their lives were teeming in the room, glittering in the sunlight, floating in the rare water of the air. In their drowned sea-bottom lives, the train rushed them home to Hiroshima.

Toru sat up suddenly.

'Aisling, I love you, why can't we be lovers and you not go to Fatima?'

'Oh Toru, I've told you this before. You have a penis. I'm not into guys.'

'I'll have it chopped off.'

'You don't want to do that. Believe me.'

'I'll wait for you.'

'Like the dog at Shibuya?'

'Like "The Last Rose of Summer".'

'Jesus Toru, get a grip!'

'Ash, if you leave me who will look out for me?'

'The patron saint of gender outlaws.'

Toru smiled as she wiped his nose with her sleeve and carefully adjusted the new bolt. 'Is there really a patron saint for us?' he asked.

'Sure.' Aisling racked her brains as he sat hopefully in front of her. Then her face lit up in relief. 'St Francis the Sissy!'

On arrival, Aisling picked up a map in the tourist bureau. It read, 'Hiroshima – the town famous for Japanese pizza!' Toru was in the bathroom, shedding his fantastic skin, becoming a brown pea-hen when justice should have let him fan his tail. Lions have manes, and deer have antlers but the twentieth-century male has chosen to go unadorned. Aisling wondered, if she had been a drag king at the seventeenth-century French court, would she have worn silk stockings, face powder and giant curly wigs? Toru approached her in a track suit. His face was pale without make-up. Poor wee Toru. His grandmother had been a shoe-shine lady at the old station. His grandfather a butcher. Unclean professions. Show me the beauty of radiation, the hope side of the despair coin. She gave him a hug and kissed his curly head. He knew it was the last time he would take her home. He knew her journey was a good-bye. After Hiroshima he would never see her again. They clung to each other amid the station shops, the open face of the building letting in an approaching winter that cut them to the quick. Outside, pieces of their lives and bits of their dreams flashed in bulb after bulb of light with the Kodak/Coca-Cola world, forming whole patterns out of the fragments. Totems of the commercial world. Aisling held Toru at arm's length to inspect his face. Tears slid from the gutters of his eyes.

'We blossomed after the bomb didn't we?' he said. 'Didn't we just blossom?'

Last Rites

JOHN KING

THE ICE-CREAM SELLER leans through the cell bars leering, threatening sex, swearing I fuck you good, fuck you very good, fuck you so hard you never walk again, my friend, but I say nothing, just clench my fists, knuckles tight, ready to kill him when I see a chance, if he breaks into the cell and I'm forced to defend myself against the ice-cream rapist, and I'd enjoy killing him because he's a sick man with his cock hard at the suffering of others, a coward peering through bars that protect him, someone who deserves a dose of instant justice, the worst sort of criminal seeing his big chance, and I stare straight into two black-ringed eyes but find no pity, no light no soul, the five other prisoners around me tired and quiet, huddled against cold stone walls – buried alive in police custody.

I need stitches in my cut head but the guards all say tomorrow-tomorrow, moving their hands and mouthing sounds, inspecting the bloodstain patterns on my legs and chest, thick red blobs from the slice in my forehead, thin threads woven into material, thicker blood crusted and stretched across the bone, and I shiver as the sea wind blows through a glassless barred window, telling the ice-cream sadist to fuck off and leave me alone, but still there's no decency in his face, he shrugs and smirks, and now I'm really aching to wrap my hands around his neck and crush his throat, batter that cropped head against the floor, see the skull split in two and teach this man a lesson, but I know it's not going to happen and that murder won't set me free.

I turn my head away and focus on the sleeping figure opposite, a hollow-faced old-timer with holes in his shoes and rips in his clothes, smells like a tramp and must be at least sixty years old, someone who should be sitting in an armchair in front of a warm fireplace watching the flames dance, but instead he's a frozen hunchback trying to survive, bones jutting against a filthy grey cardigan, rooted to cold concrete, and I follow the trail of small brown freckles along the ridge of his nose imagining him as a young boy with everything to live for, a big smile and endless dreams, seeing myself in the past and future, at first young and full of life, next old and broken, and I'm sitting across from this old man, know nothing about him, and I'm no better off, worse maybe, but I don't go right down this road because I'm aware of the face at the door, can see the ice-cream skull from the corner of my eye, guess that if I pretend I don't care he'll go away, probably enjoys the reaction, have to show him he's nothing, concentrating on the sunken cheeks of the old man, the freckles of a boy who's grown up and accepted that life isn't as fantastic as he once believed.

When the ice-cream seller finally leaves I stand on tiptoe at the back of the cell gently shaking the concrete grille showing off a tempting view of a flickering city, street lights low and throbbing, citizens deep asleep writhing in dreamtime erotica down in the harbour where they caught me in the red light, leaving the scene of a crime, a knife and a glass, it means nothing now, my only wish is to break through the grille and run towards the docks through this barred hole to the world, get lost in the back streets and become invisible, back to the docks past the brothels and bars, the stink of ouzo and pretty women coloured with red lipstick, laughing and chatting and making the most of every minute, an unseen nobody minding his own business, smiling as he passes, climbing the gangplank, stowing away on a tanker sailing to Turkey, Egypt, Brazil, anywhere, I don't care where I go as long as it's a long way from this cell and the years of prison waiting for me on top of the mountain.

But there's no escape and the drop is too far, it's impossible even to see the ground from here, a long jump that would smash my spine and turn me into a cripple, backbone splintered and legs crushed, unable to escape and forced to wait for morning hoping someone will discover I'm missing, suppose I'd be glad to be found and taken back inside, or to hospital, but there's no real chance of breaking through the grille, a policeman walking past the door bringing me back into the cell, a vintage rifle slung over his shoulder, chubby face peering through the bars checking we're asleep inactive unconscious, broken drifting snores of six tired men, frightened and defeated and branded scum, the insults fired fast and angry, these ice-cream sellers and judges enjoying the same sort of sex, with their power politics and sadism, verbal violence means harsh words, the prison sentences much worse than the insults.

I feel claustrophobic in this cell, six of us packed tight, trying not to think what it will be like in the prison, but worse than the confinement is knowing I won't see the people I love for a long time, not properly, they might come and visit but it's not the same, because if someone is sick and dying I won't be there with them to say goodbye, if they're in trouble I'm powerless to help, and this is the second big fear I have, because every man is scared of being raped in prison, it's a terror inside me and I've heard the stories and the lawyers were whispering in court, kicking me when I was down, small minds twisted, handcuffed and unable to fight back, and now I have this new terror, that I won't be there when my mum is on her death bed and it makes me sick inside because at least I know that if they try to rape me I'll kill them, sooner or later, never surrender, pick my moment, but what will I do when the authorities inform me that my mum and dad are fading, gasping for breath asking to see their son, why doesn't he come in their final hours minutes seconds, the scene right there in my head, I can feel tears in my eyes but men don't cry, specially not now in front of people, and I'm strong and push the sadness right down.

The only thing that really counts is what's coming next and I move quickly from the window, dropping my trousers to squat down, pretending to use the hole in the ground, keeping my head low so I don't meet the guard's eyes, tracing patterns in concrete, the small plastic bin where prisoners put their toilet paper, black and brown stains on thin white squares, newspaper headlines and a sour sickly smell, I can feel the bile in my mouth, and when I hear the guard's footsteps and know he's carried on I move as far as possible from the toilet, the stink of ancient shit and freezing air coming through the bars, sit knees below chin in the corner without a blanket hoping the night will pass quickly, that I can get through this period of my life, I have to be right here in the moment, sharp alert ready for anything, the resigned expression on the policeman's face lingering, knowing I'm on my way to something the lawyers and judges call hell on earth.

I sit for a long time with a head full of sound, thoughts making my brain speed, the cut in my forehead aching, a steady thud, treble and bass mixed feedback, have to concentrate, be aware of my surroundings, looking at the five men around me one by one, slowly, taking my time, the old-timer snoring gently all bones and hollows, a young junkie with skinny limbs and huge brown eyes staring at the wall, two middle-aged men asleep on their sides, thick heads delicately resting on small pieces of beige cardboard, their guts spilling out over thick black belts, a nervous character twitching with rapid eye movement, pale dome skull shaved clean with a deep scar gashed right to left ear, the light above us dim and never turned off, a bare featureless grey cell with nothing to make it stand out from every other grey featureless cell, not even some angry graffiti or funny cartoons, just the smell of shit and piss and decay, the wind coming through the empty window keeping the three ingredients circulating.

The old man must be in here for vagrancy, because I can't see him as a bank robber or murderer, and who would send an old man to prison for petty theft, while the skinny kid has to be drugs-related and the nervous bonehead some sort of conman, while the two fat men are probably here for minor violence, but I don't know, it's just me thinking and wondering and I have no way of knowing whether the man next to me is a gangster or a child molester, a shoplifter or a serial killer, looking at the bonehead again I see him differently, working with stereotypes, fascist or communist, lover or fighter, there must be segregation, catching the junkie's eyes drifting from the point on the wall, as though he's been trying to drill through the stone using supernatural will-power, wondering if he's doing the right thing, thinnest arms and legs I've ever seen, hidden by clothes but still obvious, his massive eyes the eyes of a good-natured cow.

My thoughts drift and I try to sleep but it's hard, not even a half-sleep of jolts and electric shocks, I'm too tired, because I now know there's no such thing as mercy, picturing those furious faces of authority screaming and drowning in racial hysteria, pointing accusing convicting punishing for a crime I've hardly committed, the prisoner surrounded by violent faces, the ice-cream prowler outside the court selling cones in the corridors of power, smiling and whistling at the bad boys in handcuffs, all these faces twisted and drawn tight over too-big skulls, heads full of festering hatred for a novelty foreigner outsider troublemaker, lies fired in a language of specifics I don't understand, but it's easy enough to pick up the anger and danger, stamping feet and banging fists, the judge's eyes rigid in their sockets, a righteous man indignant and vicious, demanding retribution, insisting on a strict punishment, something to fit the crime.

I go back to last night, standing in a busy harbour bar, minding my own business, a glass of cold beer in my hand, travelling the world, a man comes in, big man drunk and spoiling, invincible, drinking heavily because he's happy to be free at last and he starts talking to me, he speaks English, he likes England, tells me how he's going to find a prostitute and take her deep inside one of the red light's dirty back alleys, same wind howling in from the sea washing away her disease, he's just been released from prison and will let the air blow away the stink of the institution, yes, he's going to take a whore with sagging breasts and chewed nipples into a quiet corner and lick away her mascara, stretch his patience to the limit knowing the longer he holds back the better it will be when he cuts her face, tempted to blind her but knows this will take away the sight of her mutilation, understanding that paying men will fuck the blind but rarely waste their money on girls who can't keep their faces pretty, business turned off by the sight of knife grooves in powdered skin, a nasty affair, far better to move on to the next girl.

Strong and proud walking into the bar, ordering ouzo and beer, standing at the counter drinking the ouzo in one swig, looking into the mirror and seeing his face, the knife in his pocket, a foreigner who he tells his story to, how he's come from the prison on the hill, three years for raping a fucking prostitute, can I believe that, and he makes me feel sick with my head hazy and his ideas festering, and when I tell him what I think he nicks my head with his knife and I use my glass, defending myself, the two of us spilling along the bar kicking over tables, customers moving away as we stumble outside where I stand in the middle of the pavement, and he backs off, leans against a wall, bleeding, and I know I'm the outsider, that it's me who's going to have to explain myself, feel the blood seeping between fingers running into my left eye, looking side-ways and seeing the owner inside talking to his telephone, calling the police, and I turn around and very quickly walk away.

I turn left and right, make more turns so nobody sees where I'm going, and five minutes later I'm lost and walking through a small door and up a narrow flight of stairs, a red carpet and purple couch at the top, a pink light and corridor of green doors, small white dog yapping and pretending to nip at my heels, black-haired gypsy madam asking me what I want, strong perfume and a big smile, I can have anything I want, young and old she has them all, anything I desire, but I'm bleeding and awkward, she offers to clean my cut but I say I don't need a woman, hurry back down the stairs, dog's barking ringing in my ears, start looking for somewhere a bit more private where I can hide and recover, and looking back now, as I sit here convicted and sentenced, remembering the mess I made of the man's cheek, I know I should have picked a plain-looking girl and told her she was beautiful, bought a night's sex, chosen the one on the purple couch with the sagging breasts, crying in the corner, treated badly by a customer, small nicks on her face and arms, but I made a mistake and walked straight into a police patrol, and before I know what's happening they're out of the car and I'm pressed against the wall, flashing lights and a siren, taken to the station for questioning, next morning sent straight off to court while the man who cut me gives evidence and has the door held open for him as he leaves.

There's little justice in the legal systems of the world, without exception administered by the rulers for the rulers, a chance to vent frustrations on those who merit no respect in the pages of their precious rule book, and because I'm the foreigner I'm down at the bottom, and the legal profession is sleeping in comfort while we shiver in the cold, innocent and guilty thrown together, more names and bodies locked away, counting sheep in their sleep, judges and lawyers with gardens to roam through muttering hypocritical ideals of decency and order, tucked up in warm goose-feather beds, whitewashed suburbs where police patrols are regular and efficient, intestines blocked with dead lamb, skin oily from the finest olives grown in the finest manicured groves.

Time moves backwards in this cell, a tiny forgotten corner of the world, and though I want to think forward to the day when I'm released I go back instead, to when I was a boy and how things were so much easier, there were no real problems then, everything seemed simple, and I have to move my legs for the old man who has suddenly woken, as if he's remembered something important, and I can see his mouth moving, teeth decayed and gone, only sore gums left now, and he heaves himself up and walks past in a daze, drops his trousers, and because there's no door we're forced to shit in front of each other, no paper either, small but painful humiliations, the old-timer's gut exploding and splattering stone, the junkie leaning his head back, and I tuck my face into my knees feeling bone against bone, kneecap against skull, the smell of the old man strong and sick, filling the cell as he cleans himself noisily, using the water jug, tries to wash away the mess.

He stumbles back to his place by the wall and the stench slowly fades, it's a long time since I slept and I feel myself sinking at last, but there's a sharp scream that sends a razor into my heart, the sound of metal rattling, and I'm looking up at the skinny youth shouting through the bars, banging his fists against the door, hauling his body right off the ground kicking with the back of his feet, shouting something down the hall, the two fat men rubbing their eyes and looking annoyed, shouting at the boy who pulls out a small penknife which he opens and holds out for inspection, the old man not bothering to move but the bonehead running into the toilet, the junkie digging the three-inch blade into his arm halfway between elbow and wrist, running it down and opening his forearm, slumping back against the wall repeating a word over and over, don't know what it means but I can see he's suffering, needs help, his whole body trembling, the word a mantra, eyelids fluttering, blood oozing from his arm.

One of the two fat men goes over to the door, calls to the guards, and it must be the sound of his voice because within seconds three policemen are charging into the cell yelling at the kid, pulling him outside so roughly I wonder if his arms will snap, they take him away, last officer out locking the door and looking back inside, says something to us that the others understand, and I want to know what he said but I can't communicate, I've got nobody to talk with, try to find out, and the bonehead says hospital, then heroin, and putting a sheet of clean cardboard over the blood sits down and turns his back, the two fat men talking as they lay down exactly as before, old-timer blowing his nose into his fingers and wiping the snot on his trousers, so I do the same as the others, get on with life, sit back down and lean my head on my knees, try to sleep and forget.

Morning comes with the face of another guard at the bars, calling me over, opening the door to take my hands and put on handcuffs, almost gentle the way he does this, gesturing me along to a desk where a group of uniformed men discuss my fate with jabbing tongues, and once the papers have been signed I'm given to another more important uniform who, with a second man, leads me into the street, and once outside I notice how the citizens nearby stop and stare at my chains and cut face, a mixture of emotions, disgust to sadness, and I'm pushed into a car that fires fourth go and we start moving as a burst of rain hits, the driver darting through light traffic, water swamping the gutters, a flood to wash us all away, flashing windscreen wipers slashing the torrent, turning in and out of narrow streets, the city yawning and coming alive with a mix of *bouzouki* and Orthodox prayer, clear water cleansing everything.

As the rain stops its freshness is immediately replaced by the smell of burning flesh, smoke entering the car as we pass a bazaar, brilliant red-orange-yellow-green fruit merging with chunks of black meat, the solid colours of vegetables facing streaked limbs, a vivid display of gutted and skinned bodies, rows of goat and sheep heads, skin sliced and peeled leaving a mesh of white fat tissue and red veins, big trusting eyes frozen in the shock of death, and there's no hint of respect for differences of anatomy, castrated hacked with knives and machetes, treated as worthless, just taste sensations, animal necks thick with congealed blood, chopped cut ripped maimed abused mutilated slaughtered, the screams of innocents falling on deaf ears, laughing men elbow deep in guts, friendly creatures facing the butcher's blade – without rights.

There was a photo I saw once of a man who was about to be hanged, and he was being held from behind by several soldiers as he struggled to break free, don't suppose he wanted to run because there was nowhere to go, there were walls around him, just didn't want to die, and even though it was a still picture it was obvious he was pulling back, he was dressed in a white Jesus gown with his head at an awkward angle trying to escape the noose, face twisted with horror, knew he was never going to see the people he loved again, parents and wife, brothers and sisters, his own children, and the soldiers were swarming around him in newly pressed uniforms, braid on their shoulders and bushy moustaches neatly clipped, boots polished, eager to do the right thing, faces glowing with the knowledge that they were right and the condemned man was wrong, that the criminal was evil and they were decent, handling the prisoner as if he was a naughty child who didn't know what was best for him, dealing with the logistics of getting the rope around his neck, ready to snap vertebrae, a clean kill, humane execution, and I felt sick but there was nothing I could do because he was already dead and his killers kneeling down before their god.

When I was seven or eight I caught a butterfly and put it in a jar, I wanted a pet and it was beautiful, and we didn't have enough room for an animal where we lived, but because I was a child I didn't understand that the butterfly had to breathe, so it fluttered around in the jar and I watched its wings move and the whole time it was slowly choking, and I went to play soldiers but when I came back it was at the bottom of the jar, sitting there motionless, and when I opened the lid it didn't wake up and suddenly I knew it was dead, Mum telling me that because butterflies are so pretty they only live very short lives, which was sad but almost fair, then later I realized it was me who'd killed it and I felt guilty because it was a beautiful creature and it hadn't had its day of life, and I understand that life is too short to waste but it's too late for us now, the goats in the bazaar with their heads stripped and the butterfly slowly suffocating in a glass jar, a chained prisoner force-marched to the slaughter.

The driver parks and I'm taken into a clinic-hospital where the staff look at me as though I'm subhuman, it's been deemed fact, an animal without rights, less than human, taken along a bright hallway into a big airy room, ordered to lay down on a padded table so my head can be stitched by an old nurse, a grim-faced witch with yellow eyeballs talking with the police, and I watch the reactions around me, appreciate the relaxing of other accusing glares particularly a younger nurse beautiful with short black hair, because I'm off to a world of men, this woman seeing me as some sort of innocent, not guilty of rape murder other forms of perversion but chained for the duration, simply defending myself, but there's no less hate in the older nurse's face, her needle poised, bitterness bleeding hate covering my face with a white death's hood cotton shroud, ready for what the scientists call humane execution, frantic inside my thoughts confused as she cuts a circle where my spilt head aches, and I'm waiting for the smell of the bazaar thinking about the cut vocal chords of vivisection pigs, nobody hears them scream, they can't shout out, nobody listens once you're out of sight, but I'm still alive behind the shroud watching the witch through thin cloth fighting the paranoia but imagining her syringe full of poison and will-destroying chemicals, a woman who enjoys experimenting on the prison population, but I push this idea away, preferring a medical profession that serves and helps the most vulnerable members of society.

I close my eyes as the sewing needle digs in, half my head drugged and numb as the poison flushes into the blood stream, through the chambers and into my heart, can almost hear the valves creak, a vicious god-fearing monster weaving her pattern, a religious right-thinking devil woman, the drug killing nerve endings and washing through me, a chemical potion brewed in broken test tubes heated over a fire, skeleton hands pulling the wound together, no fine needlework for this man, the spite in her bones flowing along the needle as she pulls the thread tight, sharp point digging in hard skewering skin, this frustrated woman knowing what she can get away with, slipping, losing the thread for a few seconds, casting spells under her breath, picking up again as the voices rise and fall, my mind floating, voices chattering in the ceiling.

When I left home six months ago we had dinner together, my mum and dad and sisters, sitting around the table, laughing and telling jokes, the sun coming through the window, and I can remember the heat on my arms and the dog sitting under the table, we have more room now, waiting for the old man to drop something, always does, asking if he can have some bread for his gravy, telling us a joke so unfunny we all laugh, and laying on this table I feel the same way, that I'm part of a dream, that this is all too stupid to be true, I can't believe it's happening, I should be able to stand up and tell everyone that the joke's over, it doesn't make any sense, and I can feel my face cracking, I'm smiling now and glad the hood is over me but wondering what the nurses doctors police would think, whether they'd feel insulted, angry that I'm not treating the situation seriously, but I can't help smiling and laughing, sounds more like a cough.

The woman finishes and stands back in the shadows, a small smile on pursed lips, flush of satisfaction in her belly, and I'm helped upright by the police, walking on distant feet tripping into the car, engine connecting first time, the crank of gears in my head as we move through grey streets where people gather on shabby corners, rain replaced with a pulsing sunlight that lightens the concrete, my eyes adjusting and brain sharp, then fuzzy, the man in charge turning to me, now he can speak English, saying I feel sorry for you, I don't think you deserve this sentence but nothing can be done, it is too late now, the law is the law, but the time will pass and even though it will be hard you will come out with a knowledge few others have, and I try to laugh and say I'd rather stay stupid but the languages are different and he raises his shoulders and looks away for a while, thinking, turning back with more words, his tongue skipping.

He says the prison is a sewer for junkies perverts murderers every type of killer and petty criminal rotting and ripping at each other packed shoulder to shoulder, men society has banished to a crumbling castle high above the city, the guards there criminals themselves who have gone over the edge and broken the rules, enjoying the warning despite himself, the surge of power and fear he creates irresistible, and I don't like what he's saying but feel sorry for him somehow, because maybe he's a decent man inside, and I'm pleased when he slows down and controls himself, tells me I'm not to worry too much because things aren't as bad now, better than the old days when the convicts' heads were shaved and the men had to parade at six every morning, because now they're left to rot, there's nothing to do and the regime is more lax, I wonder how far I'd get if I headbutted him and kicked the car door open, ran off and tried to lose myself again, second time lucky, get down to the docks and a free ride home, go back to the brothel and buy the girl on the purple couch, follow her along the hall through a freshly-painted green door, a big double bed and stuffed opium pipe, cold beer and salty cheese, if I had the chance now I'd stay there for a week, maybe longer, only get up for a hot bath, scrubbing away the last twenty-four hours, but I'd be shot down before I left the main street, wounded and beaten to a pulp, crucified for embarrassing the authorities, making them look bad.

As they lead me into the station the policeman's last story is playing in my head, about the man who killed men and women, put them in his freezer, thawed their bodies out when he wanted sex, then returned them to the freezer afterwards, better sleep with my eyes open, very funny, they all have to turn the knife in your gut, he can't decide whether he wants to scare or reassure me, feels guilt, says I shouldn't worry, half the prison population is there for drugs offences and as long as I keep off the heroin I'll be okay, because he himself has heard stories about the drugs available, good money made by corrupt men, though it could be a rumour, and apart from the drug prisoners there's a lot of thieves and a few embezzlers in with the killers, but he hopes I'll stay clean while I'm there and not be tempted, accept my punishment.

Back in the police cell I sleep for a while as the chemicals gradually wear off, don't know how long it takes but there's still light coming through the bars when I'm shaken awake by another policeman, yet another new face, can't get my thinking straight, pulled to my feet and handcuffed, taken up stairs by three officers, one whose face I never see jabbing me in the kidneys, a single soft punch so I move faster, should understand his language, broken words, faint pain, I don't care about him, maybe it shows, going into a room where a huge man stands in shirt sleeves leering the same way as the ice-cream seller, the same person except he's grown, ghost face muttering I fuck you good, fuck you very good, fuck you so hard you live a crippled, spine-snapped, legs pasty and withered, junkie prisoner, sentence increased, old man with bones sticking through my clothes, might as well carve my arms up, ice-cream melting in the sun, back home in summer, dead butterflies, fuck you good my friend, have to clear my head, panic in my belly, crippled by narcotics, got to think straight as I'm ordered to drop my trousers and lay face down on a steel bench, can't manage it try to resist feeling hands around my waist, trousers and pants pulled down bent forward over the bench, drugged and defenceless, laid out like a slab of meat . . .

For a prescribed injection syringe overflowing spouting transparent oil, the needle sharp but the doctor careful, I know they can shoot whatever they want into me and there's no such thing as a clean needle, because I'm without rights stretched out on the bench one of those mutilated animals in the bazaar with little protection putting my trust in common decency, the goat's throat slit by laughing butchers, these policemen giving me my medicine, men doing their jobs, my head clearing with relief once the injection has been completed, medicine to stop infection, told to stand and pull up my trousers, and I'm led from the room part of the production line but I feel better, much better now, back down the stairs to my cell, home safe and sound, sit down and wait as more prisoners arrive, one youth crying almost hysterical, punched hard in the face by an older man, nose bruised as the ice-cream seller arrives, wants to fuck us all before the van is ready to take its cargo to the castle on the hill, and I really have to fight the temptation to grab him through the bars, looks over his shoulder and sees that the police are coming, hurries off.

Two hours later the drugs have faded and I see everything clearly as we're handcuffed two-by-two in the cell, then taken outside Bible-style heading for the ark, except there's no women allowed, surrounded by police, other guards waiting with their rifles pointing at us, willing to kill men in the street without knowing their crimes, whether it's murder and necrophilia or stealing a loaf of bread, it doesn't matter, they'd gun us down for trying to escape, for insulting their authority and not showing them the respect they feel they deserve, and if there's one thing not worth doing in this life it's embarrassing those in positions of power because they don't like it, don't like it at all, this is what they live for, their reason for existing, and I go with the others, hands together as if I'm praying.

We climb into the van and have to wait ten minutes with the door locked before the police are ready and we start moving, this prehistoric machine rocking its prisoners side to side, everyone silent except a small demented character talking to himself non-stop, excited one second then secretive, whispering to an invisible friend, nodding through the tiny windows as if he can see a way out, and there's no escape for the wicked as the van starts moving uphill, the skinny kid from last night sitting at the front with a bandage along his arm, next to the bonehead, the two fat men behind, van slowing down as it struggles with the slope, a heavy smell of exhaust fumes, the mad man suddenly singing a song and tapping his fingers on the seat in front, a hard face turning and saying something, I can feel the anger in his voice, the song replaced by more whispers, a hymn maybe, everyone else trying to get a last look at life in the outside word, the van moving slower and slower, our heads straining, knowing we're almost there, a heavy atmosphere filling up the van.

Seven solid towers root the prison in rock, this mountain fortress standing firm against the rain and wind battering its walls for hundreds of years, giving nothing away, and I look up at the walls as we leave the van wondering what's on the other side, we're about to enter another dimension, another universe, and even though I'm scared I'm ready for anything as the steel gates slowly swing open and a group of prison guards stand in front of us preparing to welcome the new arrivals, and we shuffle up the three steps, white plaster giving way to blocks of stone, a small barred window over the entrance, and I'm through the gate and inside Seven Towers, gates shutting behind us, our police escort fading into the background once they've taken back their cuffs, and the guards start shouting orders and we hurry further inside the prison, pace cranked up, hurried through a smaller gate until we're crowding into a small court-yard, the man in charge running down a list, naming names and pointing his finger, bouncing on his heels he's so excited.

There is confusion for a while before two guards take me to a cobwebbed room where I stand in front of a huge sweating man, his skin soaking wet in the middle of winter with perspiration seeping through a thick green uniform, his yellow teeth packed with gold nuggets, a dirty man who never washes his mouth and stinks of rotten meat, moving his head forward as he tells me to drop my trousers, but this time the drugs aren't confusing me and I know this is the real thing, something worse than chemical terror, worse than paranoia, because this is the worst thing that can happen, the reality, and the room has tiny chapel-like windows that send long shafts of purple light to the far wall illuminating a billion specks of dust and it's beautiful and I could be in a tiny village church somewhere full of kindly pacifists but beauty doesn't matter any more because I can either refuse or hope for the best, so I take the middle path and do what I'm told, ready for this fat bastard if he turns into a homosexual, I'm going to work my fingers into his eye sockets and blind him for life, even if they beat me to death afterwards I'll pluck out his eyes, dig my thumbs right in and make him suffer, because I'm at the end of the line with my cock and balls out on display knowing I'm forgotten and on my own, that these men can do anything they want.

His iron fist punches me in the stomach and the stinking mouth screams abuse, one two three four five times he hits me, I have to stop counting as I double forward, holding back because as soon as he turns into a pervert and tries to rape me I'll take his eyes out, and I'm strong inside knowing this because the punches don't matter, they'll never take me alive, I know this, it isn't a threat but a promise, he hasn't crossed the line yet, I expect a punch or two, that's what they mean by justice, the man kicking my right knee under the joint so I stumble, both thumbs ready, feel spit on the side of my face, and I stay standing among the sudden chatter of language, the guard who's hitting me laughing, wanting a reaction, maybe he wants me to cry or moan, beg even, but I suffer in silence and stand straight again and he stares between my legs, thumbs bent, ready to dig in deep and scoop out his eyeballs, I look at the ground staying humble and he's gesturing for me to pull up my trousers and go with two of the laughing guards.

I'm led along a narrow courtyard and put my right hand on my heart, find it's beating fast, and to my left there's the outer prison wall and to my right an inner boundary, and we pass prisoners guards lawyers standing around talking, the wonders of the world threaded around the outer limits, police and thieves drinking thick black coffee, trusted prisoners doing their work, a good percentage of men turning to look at me as I pass, the new arrival, foreigner, new boy, but I remember that this is a port town and there are other foreigners in here, and I don't feel any hatred just curiosity, guards taking me into a store-room where a tall thin man in a neat black jacket nods as the guards explain the situation, showing he understands, raising his eyebrows, learning about my offence, saying something which starts them laughing, going back and forward to a row of wooden shelves, a dank musty smell filling the room and the same dust as before, but there's a more healthy feel here, a place where things gets done, there's some sort of order and I can tell the store man takes his work seriously, a calendar nailed to the wall with mountain photos, white peaks and pure blue skies, crosses marking the days, black kisses counting down.

The store man gives me a white plastic bowl, white plastic spoon and a coarse dusty brown blanket, even have to sign my name, and the thin man walks along his shelves straightening blankets as we leave along a short dark corridor and come to a burst of light, a bright space in the middle of the various blocks, barbed wire topping smaller walls, standing still waiting for a trustee to find the right key and unlock a blue door, the paint blistered and flaking as he pulls it open, one of the guards urging me inside, but I know where I'm supposed to go, one step ahead, the industrial lock and iron bar slamming shut behind me.

I stand for a few minutes at the edge of a near-empty courtyard pocked with craters, three men on the other side clicking worry beads and glancing over, lowering heads, bored, the coughing of one man smothering the clicking beads, and I see that there are two levels to my block, two long rooms one on top of the other, black bars over broken windows, slates missing from the roof, jagged glass catching the sun, an argument in the building rising and falling again, followed by laughter, and I think back to better days because being a child was a good time, I saw things differently, and I'm hungry now, seeing my mum and dad sitting at the table with eggs in their shells and pieces of toast cut into strips, toast soldiers marching into war, dipping into the yoke, a yellow blob with the marg, sending me off to school, little soldier going into the playground to learn life can be hard and people spiteful, everything a battle that needs to be faced and won, or at least survived, all a question of will, and I'm going to come through this, the wind picking up and clouds smothering the sun, weather changing fast, clearing the yard, the men opposite hurrying inside, and I stay where I am thinking of that butterfly, how it suddenly came back to me last night in the cell, all these years later, and I think of how life changes so suddenly, that this is my first day inside.

Standing by the gate I feel stronger than I did sitting in court, while I was being held in the police station, in hospital with a death's hood over my head, at the station face down on the injection table, riding the convict bus up the hill, arriving in Seven Towers and being punched in the gut with my trousers around my ankles, and I've come through this and I'm learning fast, and maybe I'm lucky in a way, because you can feel sorry for yourself for a while, consider the mights and maybes, the past and the future, but then you have to move forward and deal with the moment, so I tuck my blanket tight under my arm and walk towards my new home and another sort of life, knowing this is where it all begins.

Hope

LAURA HIRD

1

AS THE AMBULANCE blares towards the Infirmary, I try to look as out-of-it as seems necessary. Can a hundred paracetamol kill you? That's what I told them so they wouldn't make me vomit. The driver tells me not to worry, he's only put the siren on to emotionally blackmail his way through the traffic. They can't pump your stomach with paracetamol, can they? When Julian swallowed them that time, all the blood vessels burst on his face and his tongue went black. Or maybe that was the Cabernet Sauvignon.

The wee lassie that attached me to the monitor looks about twelve. She looked pissed-off when my vital signs showed up normal. I know how to read them having watched dad slowly die on one. She and her even tinier mate have just carried me from the middle of Saughton Park to the main road. I called 999 from the phone box outside Davie's, then staggered over there.

When we get up to the hospital, I wait until they're busying themselves with the ramp and stretcher before pulling free of the monitor and leaping out into the glow of A & E. As I hit the ground running, I'm halfway across Lauriston Place before they register what's happened. The driver is a fast-moving blur behind me as I sprint into Forrest Road. By the time I get to Desiree's flat in George IV Bridge he's obviously re-read his job description and given up. I have no complaints about the NHS. I've always found it very hospitable.

Desiree's out for the count by the time I arrive, having just received a cassette stuffed with supergrass from Eartha in Botswana. A rather misguided children's charity gave Eartha a grant to go over there, bugger little African boys and post marijuana to his pals for six months. It makes you realize what Live Aid was really about. I'm going to send them a proposal. Get out of here. Go somewhere hot.

I knock back half a glass of red wine and skin-up before bothering to look up and see who's here. There's always a full complement of people in this room. Some come once, can't handle the slagging fags and never return. Others visit weekly or every few days. Some never seem to leave. Desiree and Eartha usually hold fort but in their absence it is rather like a chat show without a host. Splinter groups have been established. They are all probably bitching fiercely about one another. Noticing a woman in her sixties sitting with the pigeon sisters, I wonder if she's our Betty Boothroyd for the evening.

I slowly start to take in everybody else although I know it's fruitless. There's never any talent here. I've had my cock sucked by a couple of them but only ever through blind drunkenness or unbridled desperation.

Jason squeezes my shoulder and hands me a copy of some

literary mag from the north-east. He wants me to look at a poem he has in it and watches my reaction as I read. It is a self-obsessed navel contemplation and as predictably shit as the rest of his stuff. Jason's high opinion of himself really makes me cringe. If there's one thing I hate it's those poor-me-tormented-artist types. Handing the magazine back I feign interest none-the-less and ask if he has anything else in the pipeline.

'I wish. Nobody's interested these days if it doesn't have a body count. Nobody wants real literature any more.'

'Couldn't you stick a few gruesome murders in to keep the punters happy?'

He stomps away, feigning offence.

As I spark up the joint, I turn my attention back to the pigeon sisters. Coo is in the midst of an astronomical phase and has been boring the tits off us all for weeks with his black holes and supernovas. Doo has started going to saunas again to illustrate his disquiet. As Coo rambles on about Stephen Hawking's universe, Doo keeps trying to get the conversation down to his level.

'Honestly though, if they have the technology to leapfrog galaxies surely they could get a better voice for the poor guy.'

The old woman chortles.

'. . . don't you think though, a nice wee Sean Connery or something? Intershtellar coshmanaughtsh. Much more believable.'

Coo is blushing and flustered.

'Oh, you're such an ignorant prick. Your brain's the size of a sixteenth. There's no room for anything new in there,' he says, banging his temple for emphasis.

'Oh come on, sweetheart, that R2D2 voice. *Exterminate, exterminate!* I ask you. He's like a walkie-talkie doll.'

Coo clatters his chair dramatically, proffers his back to Doo and attention to the old woman.

'I've never met him before tonight, honestly. Intelligent conversation, please, before I lose all faith in humanity. What are your thoughts on cosmology and the search for dark matter, pray tell?'

The old woman winks at Doo and smiles.

'I'm awfully sorry dear. I watched a couple of that chap's programmes, the Sunday night things, and the only thing that struck me was that so many imminent scientists have subscriptions to *Penthouse.*'

The comment seems to focus everyone's attention on her.

Shirley drapes an arm around me. I hadn't even noticed he was here.

'Speaking of which, Dionne, I'd like you to meet Hope, my auntie. She's been festering away in her huge New Town penthouse since my uncle died. I thought we could do with having someone old and wise round for a change.'

'Hey, less of the wise,' she smirks, raising her glass to me. 'Dionne, is that your real name?'

I can't even remember why or how we ended up addressing each other in such ridiculous ways and suddenly realize how sad it is.

'Martin . . . Martin Bell strangely enough.'

'Now he IS an alien,' Doo butts in. Hope blanks him.

'Then I'll call you Martin if you don't mind. These Las Vegas names are all very well but I prefer Hope to Despair.'

'Absolutely.'

Numerous joints circle the table. When Hope is passed one she takes a long draw then blows a smoke ring. She's cool. Not as old as I thought at first, maybe just late-fifties, with a

Vanessa Redgrave sort of clumsy elegance. Intrigued, I pick up my drink and go over.

No sooner have I sat down than Shirley has his big arse squeezed on the back of my chair and whispers unsubtly in my ear, 'Auntie's climbing the walls in that huge flat. See if she fancies a lodger. You must get out of that smelly place you're in.'

I push him away, awkwardly, as Hope frowns and shakes her head.

'Honestly, Angus, I'm not senile, you know? I do still have control over my power of speech. I've no doubt Martin does too.'

The room erupts in laughter. Angus! He told us his real name was Andrew. No wonder he makes us call him Shirley. We try and out-do each other with crap Angus/sheep-shagger jokes until I notice Hope's eyes starting to glaze over and don't want to seem as arse-ish as the rest of them.

'Come on girls, it's like the *Sunday Post* office party in here. Anyone would think we were smoking real blow.'

The door goes. It's a couple of guys Shirley knows from the Traverse, very fuckable but straight, I've already asked. In line with flat decorum they immediately uncork a bottle of Jacob's Crack and start skinning-up. The effect the youngest guest has on the assembled queens is rather like that of a discarded fish supper on seagulls. I regale Hope with my observation.

'And he thinks I don't get out much!'

It's nice to have someone look me in the eye when they talk to me without reading something into it for a change.

'I didn't even know Shirl . . . Angus had an auntie, or a family for that matter. I just assumed someone had found him in a cabbage patch in London Road in the mid-Eighties and handed him in at the Laughing Duck.'

Hope pulls a face.

'We don't really have a family as such. First and second generation black sheep, far too garish for beige people like them.' She gestures to Shirley. 'His father's a church elder, you know, not that the implication of that is what it used to be.'

Replenishing my drink from one of the army of bottles, I offer her some. Fumbling in a carpet-bag by her side she produces a half-bottle of Ten Year Old MacAllan and pours herself a navvy's measure. Shirley materializes like the shop assistant from Mr Ben, topping up Hope's glass with hot water, blood orange juice, a spoonful of Tate and Lyle and a stir.

Hope gives him a smile of appreciation, takes a little sip and hugs herself.

'It was my only pre-condition of coming here tonight. I bring my own bottle though or he tries to palm me off with that revolting Grouse nonsense. Even with their Sunday clothes on I can still tell one from the other.'

'So is that your standard tipple?' I ask her, amused at her extravagance.

'Only when there's someone else to do it for me, or if I know I'm really going to be hitting the sauce. It dehydrates and rehydrates me simultaneously. I never get a bad head, just a good night's sleep.'

I'm completely sold on hot toddies and begin wolfing down the wine, briefly scanning the girls as I swallow. Coo seems to be having most success with the Traverse dreamboat. The rest sulk round them, having one of their little joint-rolling conferences. I don't think I've ever met any of them when they've been straight. Mind you, neither have I. I'm only ever straight at work, sometimes. Turning back to Hope I take a long sniff of her drink and go mmmmm.

'Finish that red muck and have one if you wish. Don't let

the rest of them near it though or I'll end up on the red muck too.'

I'm flattered that she seems to have singled me out like this and feel a need to disassociate myself from the rest of them. They suddenly seem so childish, superficial.

'So you're having some accommodation trouble I gather.'

Not wanting to sound like a dosser after Shirley's *smelly place* comment I play it down.

'I'd like a bigger place but they all want a deposit and a month's rent in advance and I resent handing £800 over to some horrid little Jew before I even spend a night there.' Oh shit, the anti-Semitic lapse was maybe a bit much. Hope is smiling and seems to have appreciated it though.

'Indeed.'

'Besides, I spend so much time at work I never have time to look at anywhere.'

'What's your line of work?'

God, how embarrassing. 'I manage a bookshop near Stock-bridge. Not really what I intended to do with my MA in Fine Arts but you just can't get funding to produce a portfolio these days.' Does it sound like I'm hustling her? Fuck, I'm just being honest.

'Couldn't the Arts Council help you out?'

'Erm . . . oh yes. I suppose I could try them.' Shit, shit, shit. She'll think I don't know what I'm talking about.

Supping her toddy, she glares at me as if she's trying to suss me out. Just as I convince myself she's realized what a twat I am however, she says very matter of factly, 'There's bags of room in my flat. I'm not out of my mind with loneliness as Angus seems to think but you're welcome to stay while you look for somewhere. It's Northumberland Street.'

Northumberland Street! Isn't it that gorgeous Georgian

street that all the queens stay in? I'm instantly fantasizing about leaving my shit-hole in Haymarket behind, along with two months' unpaid rent, a huge phonebill for chatlines and a kipper down the back of the cooker. I knew there must be a reason I pulled the ambulance stunt to get up here tonight. You never see cabs in Whitson. Nobody can afford them. God, I'm sitting gouching without having responded to Hope's offer.

'Seriously, you wouldn't mind?'

She laughs as if I'm joking. 'What's to mind? You're not a sociopath are you? Angus can vouch for you, can't you Angus?'

Shirley tries to focus his attention away from Traverse-boy. Jesus, don't they get bored being so lecherously queeny all the time? He points at the blood orange carton, not understanding.

'No dear, I'm just wondering if Martin here would be likely to run off with the family silver.'

'I'd let him. Silver's just so passé. Make not bad ashtrays I suppose.'

Jesus, do people really have family silver? I'll be lucky to get a sixteen-piece Argos special with two chipped saucers and a plate missing when mum pegs out.

Angus gives me the thumbs-up regardless and immediately turns his attention back to Traverse-boy who I've decided looks like a young Christopher Walken.

Hope grabs my hand and shakes it till I hear the bones crack.

'See how we get on anyway. Better than throwing money at a horrid little Jew. I've known a few myself.'

I shake back enthusiastically, consciously more firmly than my usual flaccid-penis-in-the-palm thing.

'That's great, honestly, great.'

People are so stupid. They trust implicitly anyone who shows the slightest interest in them. It's loneliness I suppose. Other people can't seem to be comfortable with their own company the way I can, pathetic really. I can make myself like Hope though. I can make myself like anyone.

2

The following day, I go for a few swifties in the New Town after work for my nerves then make my way down to Northumberland Street, to see the flat. As I try to work out the house numbers, I see Hope struggling towards me, two Vickie Wine bags clanking from each arm.

'I thought I should rejuvenate my drinks cabinet if I'm going to have company. Please don't say you're a whisky puritan like myself, I've rather splashed out on lesser things.'

As I wrestle a couple of bags off her, she begins making her way up the steps to one of the houses. It's like a fucking foreign embassy. Then we're on the way up this plush and seemingly endless stair. For a second I think she owns the whole thing. Fuck, these New Town places are only three floors but they seem infinitely higher than normal stairs. By the time we finally reach the top landing, I'm knackered. Hope smiles at my wheezing, looking decidedly un-exerted.

'I only keep this place on for the exercise. It's either that or starving myself. I can't abide overweight people.'

The front door opens onto a very long, polished-floored

hall. Old film posters are pasted to the walls like they used to be outside cinema two at the Filmhouse. I wonder who stole whose idea. Some of them would be worth a fortune. *The Wizard of Oz* looks like an original, *Lolita*, *The Servant*, *The Sweet Smell of Success* – they all look old. Pasted to the bloody walls though, worthless.

'This is absolutely fab. Did you do it yourself?' I ask her, gesturing to a poster for the original *Desperate Hours*. God, Bogie was such a man.

'Good God, no. I don't have the patience. They were my husband's babies. Completely film-mad he was. We saw a lot of them together. They remind me of it, in a good way.'

All over the ceiling as well. God, it's so cool. I'm trying to see how many I recognize as she leads me to this enormous kitchen. In the centre is a huge, cast-iron cooking range, over-hung by dozens of stainless steel utensils. Honestly, every cooking implement (and some more suited to the interrogation of political prisoners) you could ever dream of. At the top of the room, by the window, is a massive china sink, like the kind you get in art classes and a gorgeous chunky oak breakfast table. It's like a bloody hotel kitchen. I think of the windowless boxroom in my current flat with ochre grease a centimetre deep on the walls. The walls in here are a fresh-looking Habitat green with a gorgeous abstract-print linoleum floor. Opening the vast fridge door, Hope begins transferring bottles from her bags.

'What's your poison? Wine, beer, champagne? There's spirits in the other room if you'd prefer.'

'Anything, I don't mind.'

Hope extracts the Moet with a flourish.

'How about this to wet our whistles? Carry it round with us as I show you the place.'

Popping it open she hands me a glass with a bowl the size of a grapefruit and pours us both one.

'To you and your kindness.'

She pulls a face and switches off the kitchen light.

'Spare me the sentiment, dear, please, it lulls one into a terrible false sense of security.'

First on the right is this gorgeously enormous bedroom – big brass double bed, polished floors with a couple of extremely expensive-looking rugs, ornate lead fireplace, with a view right down towards Stockbridge and into the houses of all these rich, lucky bastards. A lovely mahogany wardrobe and chest of drawers, massive old pirate's chest. This must be Hope's room, asbsolutely exquisite.

'What do you think then? Will it do until you find somewhere else? Don't worry about money. Cook me the odd spaghetti carbonara if you must.'

I'm utterly aghast, already imagining the reactions of the people I'm going to invite here, the ones who try to make me feel inadequate because I don't have my own place. Fuck them and their mortgages.

Hope seems so keen for me to stay, and for free. There will most definitely be a catch but I'm damned if I'm going to worry about that before it makes itself apparent. Could I finally be getting a break?

There are another three bedrooms, all immaculate, like mine, and Hope's, which is packed to the gunnels with books, antiques and boxes looking for a home. You can barely make out her bed amidst the intense camouflage of clutter. Our rooms are at opposite ends of the hall, however it is hers, rather than my own which is conveniently next to the main door. We have a bathroom each, both with Liza Minnelli dressing-room bulbs round the mirrors, perfect for blackheads. It's like the bloody Caley Hotel.

Eventually we retire to the living room which is so wonderfully chill-out it's unreal. Again, big, chunky armchairs with ethnic-looking throws over them, massive fireplace, again, antiques absolutely everywhere, loads of plants.

Hope puts the Moet on the table in front of the fire and switches on an art deco lamp in the corner of the room. A stretching flapper is illuminated against the lamp-post of her stand.

We seem to become embroiled in this intense conversation as soon as we sit down. There's none of that ridiculous small-talk that Edinburgh people usually use to keep people at a distance till they've decided what to dislike about them. Hope seems to have angles on everything that I'd never even contemplated before and seems able to make any topic interesting. She sells all these wild concepts to me and is encouraging enough to make me think up a few of my own. It's so refreshing. The Scots used to be renowned for their love of a good argument. Now they just bottle it up and go daft. As we finish off the champagne, having smoked a few joints, I start going on about the Holocaust.

'It was more like a revolution if you ask me. Honestly, if there was a major revolution in Britain tomorrow the targets would be the same. All these wee enclosed, self-perpetuating groups of wealthy people – the Jews, Freemasons, homosexuals, the aristocracy. You know? They're all we're-all-right-Jack types?'

Whilst I realize I shouldn't really be advocating the gassing of gays I feel like I've suddenly understood what it was actually all about. Like I've just realized how we colonize things – bars, professions, streets, and can be protesting for the right to be accepted one minute and watching someone's grandad take a dump through a hole in a wall the next. I don't want to be gay, I never have. I hate gays and that contempt they have for everyone else. I see it in myself and I hate that too.

In the midst of regaling Hope with my new homophobic philosophy I start to panic that I'm going too far or that I'm getting a bit anything-you-can-think-I-can-think-sicker. I'm pleased with the bit about recognizing it in myself though. It makes me seem quite sorted I think. Hope re-fills our glasses with two huge measures of a seemingly precious bottle of Glencoe though, so she must have appreciated it.

'Oh, I'm a great one for extremes myself, my dear. The middle-ground has always bored me silly. Someone once said I should set up a fascio-communist alliance. My politics sort of dangle somewhere along the Bering Strait.'

Although her comment is intended to put me at ease, it unnerves me and I begin to worry about her being more intelligent than me, thinking I'm an arse. Why am I having this sudden downer when I had coke-like confidence a minute ago? To overcome my negative thoughts I study the stack of CDs by the fireplace, mainly classical, bloody boxed sets – Mozart complete piano sonatas, the whole *Ring*, loads of Bach and baroque stuff which I love, musicals, hundreds of film soundtracks.

Hope tells me to put something on and I start to panic again as I'm certain I'll pick the one she hates, the one she's ashamed of. I'm taking too long so I plump for Debussy and start going on about him dying of fright when he heard the noises of battle coming towards him. Then I realize I'm taking the word of a music teacher, fifteen years ago, who probably made it up in a fruitless attempt to make the pupils more interested. Change the subject, quick!

'I've not noticed a television in the flat. Are you a non-believer?'

'Can't stand it. The real opium of the masses. I can't tell you how many good friends I've seen wither to death in front of the box. It's worse than cancer.'

Oh well, there goes *Late Review* and *Eurotrash*.

'It can be terribly manipulative, I suppose.'

'I'll say. Wasn't it originally supposed to be educational and impartial? Bloody propaganda! If I want to learn about something I'll go to a library and make up my own mind, thank you.'

'Not get your opinions prescribed to you by multi-nationals,' I manage to slur out, replenishing my confidence somewhat.

'Precisely!' and she clinks her glass against mine.

My sense of well-being gathers momentum again as we begin joking about the things that make life worth living. It's amazing how many queer wee things we have in common – Bob Fosse musicals, DH Lawrence, really fishy seafood, Talk Radio and the demise of Caesar the Geezer (and she was snooty about TV?), the Questionnaire in the Saturday *Guardian* being the best bit, sitting amongst cows and the smells of London Underground, tar, carbolic soap, baked potato shops and these little white bits you cough up sometimes. Jesus, and I thought I was the only one.

Then we start on our dislikes. We resolutely agree on cars, media witch-hunts, people who tell you to cheer up just because you're not grinning inanely, the tragedy of bad smells during beautiful moments, snoring, mothers who don't need to work but do (hi mum!), the Irish (both sides) and people who break wind in public. Then Hope doesn't respond to my *women who have abortions because they want a life* (hi again, mum, I didn't want a brother anyway). If that doesn't make me paranoid enough, she then comes out with *thieves* and *people who rip off the Health Service* in quick succession.

I don't know how long I sit with a stupid look on my face before managing a measly, *people who go on about their sun tans* (Hope and myself are both peely-wally and interesting) and the fact that the *Daily Record* is the biggest-selling newspaper in Scotland. I realize how crap they are as soon as I've said them but it's too late now anyway. These little rushes of unpleasantness are starting to get the better of me and I want to go. She can't see me puking in the toilet before I even move in.

Wolfing down the remainder of my whisky, and stifling a subsequent boak, I say I'll have to go, work in the morning, all that shit. Hope welcomes me to stay the night but I want back to my moisturiser and my Ribena and just that pile of rubbish I call home. Once I've moved it here, this will be home. That is the nature of rubbish. As I won't be able to flit for a couple of days (the landlord's always snooping around for the rent on Wednesdays and Thursdays) I give her my work number in case she changes her mind. I'm only thinking about the good bits by the time I get in the taxi. Northumberland Street, you cunt.

3

I busy myself for the next couple of nights hassling the local grocers for cardboard boxes and savagely disposing of a lot of my belongings in the name of a lighter-travelling existence. Having to work until six both nights doesn't help. I have loads of annual leave to take but it's not cost-effective. Besides, I'm saving it up for a big blow-out, maybe a cruise. Generally, the majority of my working days are spent constructively anyway, i.e. not working. Hope and I have a few long phone calls at my boss's expense. It's good to have someone intelligent to talk to for a change.

I'm lucky if I get three hours' sleep on the Thursday, my last night in Shitsville as I'm thinking about that gorgeous flat and the people I'm going to show it to and potentially good times with Hope. Life does smile on me sometimes. I must take advantage of it this time.

Leaving for work the next morning for the last time is glorious. My excess baggage lies strewn for the binmen along Haymarket Terrace, like the staff of Number Ten bidding farewell to an outgoing Prime Minister. Though I leave ten minutes after I should have opened up, I take my time to gaze at the shit-stained road for hopefully the second last time. Who buys second-hand books at ten in the morning anyway? I've been running the shop on my own since my boss retired three months ago. He just pays the bills now.

Cutting down Palmerston Place I walk along the Water of Leith. The smell of rotting vegetation is as refreshing to me as sea air. As I pass under the Dean Bridge, I recall a fuck I had down here with an old wino a few years ago. He could only summon a semi, but it was huge. I had shaved pubes at the time, which really drove him wild, but he stank of rotting liver. An old bloke walks past with his dog, jolting me out of my thoughts with a ridiculous, *'Cheer up, it's not the end of the world.'* Christ, we were just talking about that the other night. People do actually still say it. I give the old tosser a smile anyway. He has a complexion like an uncooked beef sausage.

It's 10.25 by the time I get to the shop. In the unlikely event that Callum, the owner had phoned to check I'm in on time, I'll just say I forgot to switch the answering machine off. No messages though, no calls and no customers for most of the morning. Leisurely speeding myself up with black coffee, I listen to Classic FM and throw myself into the *Scotsman* crossword. Sometimes I really like routine.

A Goth-looking lassie comes in about 11.15 and tries to sell me a bag of John Mortimer. How is there so much fucking John Mortimer, John Galsworthy and Raymond Chandler in the world? I think they breed with each other on the shelves at Barnardo's. Having regaled the lassie with my observation, she looks suitably embarrassed, then slopes back to Transylvania.

Occasionally in this shop I'll get offered a little gem but generally it's scruffy twenty-somethings who sell me course books, get used to the extra money then bring in their film books, then the Penguin Classics till eventually it's the spanking new never-read book club editions and they come in with tears in their eyes. I take books off these student bastards I know I can sell for a couple of hundred pounds, get them to sign for enough money for a sixteenth, then stick a two or three in front of the £7.50 when they leave – everybody's happy! Stewart only pays me £120 a week, after tax. I'll be saving £45 a week on the flat now so that can go straight in my Premier Investment Account. The rest of my money usually gets tied up in debts I haven't been able to dump and my blow. For entertainment I usually aim to fiddle about £50 a day which is piss-easy via a subtle combination of over-charging, under-ringing, altering figures and private sales. The shop only takes about £150 a day but Callum hasn't checked the accounts in ages. The cancer will finish him off in a few months anyway. He's not going to waste his time book-keeping now.

By closing-up time I'm pretty excited about the move but starting to feel a bit edgy about cohabiting with a woman I've only known for three days, who's older than my mother. I don't want to end up like some Tennessee Williams toy-boy. Do women her age still want sex? Surely not. Is it obvious enough that I'm gay? She is all right though, I'm sure. I know I was pissed but we've been fine on the phone since and we have a laugh together. Besides, I read somewhere that mothers are supposed to be the new fashion accessory.

4

One taxi journey is enough to transfer the few worldly belongings I haven't binned, to Northumberland Street. I supplement my kipper down the back of the cooker with the old mustard-seeds-on-a-damp-carpet routine. The three boxes of junk and expandable case full of clothes only take two treks up and down the stairs. A previous entourage of books and records were sold long ago in less-flush days. My current occupation is a symptom of this.

Hope flutters around as I feather my new nest with my minimalist belongings, trilling along to a Kurt Weill CD. Adding a few postcards and random drapings of white muslin, I roll a joint. Unwinding with the first few puffs I take it through to Hope with a bottle of Bowmore I got her on the way back from work.

'For me, darling? How sweet.'

'Just to say thanks, you know, for letting me stay. I'll find my own place as soon as I can.'

'If you'd rather be on your own, that's fine. You're welcome here though, no rush. No more presents though, ok?'

She hands me back the spliff as I follow her through to the living room. I'm expecting a whisky but she puts the Bowmore in a cupboard and squeezes past me into the hall again.

'I'm going to be away for the night. You don't mind do you? You won't be scared?'

'Erm, no, that's fine,' I stammer, slightly taken aback. 'Going anywhere exotic?'

She slings a shawl dramatically around her shoulders and grimaces at me.

'Not exactly, well not unless your idea of exotica is line dancing in Loanhead.'

I laugh too forcefully.

'Oh I know dear. I went there with some friends about three months ago though and I'm completely hooked. Pathetic, isn't it? Anyway, it's one of the few places I can go and still feel faintly glamorous.'

Biting back a mumble of patronizing clichés about being good for her age, I settle for a simple, 'I know the feeling.'

Then the front door's open and she's rushing out excitedly.

'Try to enjoy yourself and if you do burn the house down, make sure it looks like an accident – insurance, you know? I should be back tomorrow evening sometime. Be a good boy,' and she pats my cheek and launches down the stairs. I feel quite stunned for some reason as I wave over the bannister at her. As she gets to the bottom she shouts up, 'I go to the occasional rave as well,' then I hear the stair door slam. It's more than I do. Going back into the flat I stand and stare along the huge empty hall. My huge empty hall. Fuck two years of celibacy. I'm bringing a man back here tonight.

5

Time seems to pass so quickly as you get older. It seems as if *TFI Friday* is on every night of the week. My system never gets time to recover between drinking bouts. What the hell, it's predominantly wine I drink, which is good for you anyway. Drinking is preferable to eating. The choice between two bottles of claret or a meal is a simple one. Eating's time-consuming and makes you look so bloody bad. I'm lucky if I have one proper meal a week but I still look fat. I can feel my ribs through my jumper but I'm terribly podgy about the abdomen.

Going to my enormous, gorgeous room, I stick Garbage on, uncork the bottle of red wine I bought myself and roll a massive spliff. Striding about, knocking back the drink, I look at the view down to Dublin Street and across towards Stockbridge, into the lives of all these rich fuckers and I think here I come, you bastards, here I fucking come.

I sit down on the bed and begin fantasizing about all the different people I'm going to bring back here. What their reactions will be. Then I have a prolonged dwam about slapping this little chicken I have my eye on about the place and almost get a hard-on. When I come to, it's 9.45, and the wine's nearly finished. Two and a half hours have vanished. This happens a lot these days. I go into myself and can't find the way out.

Forcing myself under the shower, it feels fantastic after the dirty, fibreglass tub I've been subjected to for the past three years. Feeling suitably invigorated I study my nakedness in the bathroom's full-length mirror. Jesus, my belly gets bigger every time I look at it. Maybe I should shave my pubes again. It might help me feel hornier.

Despite my liberating flit from Haymarket I feel strangely drawn to my old local. Faggots have been slowly streaming into it over the past few years and it's now more or less a gay bar but with the odd hairy-arsed workman. The other guys remain unconvinced and refuse to go there with me.

I want someone with me tonight though, an accomplice, someone to do all the talking while I stalk my prey. Jesus, listen to me. Who am I kidding? I'm beginning to think I'm completely unshaggable. Some speed might help, but it always makes me psychotic and I feel like topping myself for about a week afterwards. It's just the physical act of snorting it I like. It goes pear-shaped after that.

Once I'm outside and fully conscious of where I am, I see sense about my Haymarket idea, and allow my feet to drag me easterly, to the Phoenix. As I swing into a room full of vodka-breathed people it seems not a bad decision. I always see someone I know in here, I think, a second before seeing Simon, a guy I know from Thin's who's usually good for a bit toot. Standing at the bar with him I begin to think my life is either charmed or I am psychic.

Simon gets me a double Black Label Smirnoff and Diet Coke. It's so cheap in here it's untrue. We go up the steps, sit looking down on the bar and I painlessly score a gram off him. There is a guy at the juke box with his dog, acned ugly bastard but wearing football shorts which I love. There's something about that flimsy layer of fibre between me and a cock. My ultimate fantasy is to be at a football match, standing beside some wee kids and their dad, someone like Duncan Ferguson getting tripped-up in front of us and his three-piece falling out the bottom of his shorts. I saw a photo of that very phenomenon in a magazine a few months ago but I thought of it first. I made Duncan's balls fall out.

Simon starts telling me about his friend in the City with pneumonia, being on his last legs. The last time I saw the guy was about two months ago in the New Town. He had on a cropped t-shirt to show off his suspicious sarcomas. He works for an AIDS charity as well. Mind you, everyone I know that works for an AIDS charity is HIV-positive. It doesn't do much to reinforce my faith in safe sex.

Was I sitting grouching when he was telling me about his pal dying? Oh God, he's talking about Joy Division now. Simon always seems to bring every conversation round to bloody Joy Division or bands he thinks are trying to sound like Joy Division. The singer died about twenty years ago didn't he? They were crap anyway.

'Did I tell you about the time I saw them support the Buzzcocks at the Odeon?'

'I think you have, yeah, you definitely have.'

About a thousand times. I start checking out the bar for possible means of escape from misery-guts as there's no way I'm spending my night talking about John Peel and the cowie. The guy in the football shorts gives me a thin smile as I catch his eye. There's something really horny about ugly guys. They look like they're game for anything, and they're usually so grateful you're taking them on they go mad for it. I've seen him before a few times but I can't remember where.

I tell Simon I'm going to the cigarette machine and get up. The guy is still clocking me, blatantly, I love that. Pretending to put money in the machine, I push the button for Silk Cut. It rumbles, I slap it and walk back up to the table.

'They've run out, I'm just going over to the chippie.'

Simon has started chatting to a guy with fluorescent orange hair and merely nods in acknowledgement without looking round.

Walking out the pub I sense the guy with the shorts following me. My legs go a bit shaky, it's so fucking long since I've done anything like this. He comes out behind me, just like I expect him to. I don't know how you know, you just do. This surge of bravado just comes from nowhere. When I pretend to go back into the pub he blocks my way, grinning.

'You don't really want to go back in there, do you?'

'What would you suggest like?'

He shrugs his shoulders and we both walk back towards my new pad with his mutt. The last two days have had a dream-like simplicity about them.

6

His snoring wakes me in the middle of the night. I'm horrified to find him beside me and even more horrified to find his smelly dog squeezed in between us. How could a bottle of red wine and a vodka be so kind on the features of someone so grotesque? The snoring makes him doubly-unappealing. I stare at him for a minute with an uneasy mix of anger and morbid fascination till the sound of his honking drives me out the room. My rage is then propounded by a recollection of me not being able to get a proper hard-on when he tried to suck me off. I want him out of here, I wish he was dead. Did he say he was from Haymarket? That's where I've seen him before. Thank fuck I'm away from there now.

Stomping through to the living room, I attempt to roll a joint but my hands are shaking because I'm so annoyed. Just be assertive, I tell myself. Striding back through to the bedroom, I stand beside the bed looking down at him.

'Hey, hey pal. Wake up.'

He just lies snoring. I give him a gentle shake. 'Hey, come on, you'll have to go.' Still no response so I shake him more firmly. Surely that should have woken him up. Perhaps he's pretending to be asleep. I jostle him until he rolls onto his back. Still the awful noise continues. The anger is pumping adrenalin through my body. Lifting the quilt up, I grab his feet and pull him off the bed. As he thuds onto the floor his head cracks on the floorboards. Shit, I panic but the pain wakes him and he fumbles blindly for the duvet, wondering what's going on.

'I'm sorry but I'd rather you went home. Nothing personal you know. I just need some time on my own.'

He seems confused but ok about it all and starts stumbling into his ridiculous outfit again. Not knowing what to say, I go back through to my joint as the decisive action has curtailed my trembling. After a couple of minutes he comes through to say goodbye.

As I open the front door, I allow him to kiss me, just so he'll go away.

'Do you live here now then?'

Though I don't want him to know I do, the pose is almost irresistible. Compromising I give him a what-do-you-think shrug.

'Probably bump into you again sometime,' I say as I shut the door, knowing that life can sometimes be that cruel. Dammit, and the Phoenix is so convenient now.

Stripping the covers off my bed I stuff them in the washing machine. Remembering the joint, I take it through to my bedroom and start rummaging through one of my unpacked boxes of stuff. Why have I let that bastard get to me? I'm on a real downer now because I've sacrificed two years of celibacy for someone so inconsequential.

Hyper-alert through rage and remnants of the speed, I thumb through photos of myself as a teenager and think what a fat geek I was. I find a ticket for BB King at the Playhouse from twelve years ago and remember my hot date that night with a computer salesman I met in a toilet, who said he was going to take me away from it all. We snogged in the middle row. He told me I made him feel like James Dean. That was the last time I saw him. I hate BB King. My 1992 diary keeps coming to the top of the pile of junk but I'm trying to ignore it as diary-reading makes me feel like such an old fag. Perhaps one random page won't hurt.

Monday 7 May 1992
Mum lost her job. Wept a lot. Felt panicky and angry all day.

Tuesday 8 May 1992
Felt depressed in the morning but was unemotional by bedtime.

Wednesday 9 May 1992
Felt neither here nor there in morning. Threw a wobbly in a restaurant. Unemotional for the rest of the day.

Thursday 10 May 1992
Watched Taxi Driver. Felt mildly paranoid. Felt OK at night.

Friday 11 May 1992
Felt fine all day. Couldn't sleep.

Saturday 12 May 1992
Felt bad when I woke up. Didn't get Napier job. Thought when I was happy it was perhaps only mania. Felt better at night but couldn't sleep.

Jesus, have I always been such a sad bastard? I go back to bed but can hardly think for thinking about it.

7

Waking up in my new home is rather disorientating and my first thought is that I must have copped with some old poove or other. Once I've opened the shutters (yes, proper shutters, it's like fucking Paris), got Maria Callas blaring and christened my new toilet it feels significantly more homely. I devote most of the morning to swallowing strong black coffee (proper stuff, natch), smoking joints and nosing round the flat. Hope has some amazing clothes – as if Lena Martell, Quentin Crisp and the cast of *Shaft* maybe shared a wardrobe at some point. Everything smells of her, in a good way.

Rummaging through her drawers, I'm intrigued to find out what kind of knickers she might wear. The bland, pastel-shaded Marks and Spencer briefs, sort of disappoint me but are at least better than the shoulder-length passion-killers mum wears.

Noticing a *Miller's Antiques Guide* in the tightly crammed book-case I wrench it out and begin thumbing through it. Maybe I can identify some of the things she has stashed in here. It's tiresome at first having to negotiate the lop-sided weight of the flimsy pages. As I squint at the tiny print of the index and slowly begin to find things though, I start to really get into it. Hours pass as I study dishes, ornaments, side-boards, prints, totting up figures, not with any master-plan in mind, just because I'm enjoying teaching myself about it all.

By tea-time I'm bored with it though and exhausted by my own enthusiasm. Feeling listless and strangely alone I'm back in full-fledged sad bastard mode again in no time at all. When Hope's not back by seven I feel so frustrated I have to go for a lie down. I want to go out somewhere where there's no faggots, just for a change. Drawing a blank on suitable ideas I watch light dancing on the ceiling from the cars outside till I finally hear the door being unlocked. It's half eight. Hope drifts in singing 'Achey Breakey Heart'. Jumping out of bed, I rush into the hall to greet her like a dog that's been on its own too long. She does a bit of her line dancing for me and I'm so pleased to see another human being again, it seems good.

'Oh it's trite but I love it. Don't you get like that some-times?'

She hangs up her cape and I follow her through to the living room.

'No major disasters? No urban insurrection in Dublin

Street? My God, this place looks unnervingly pristine, my dear. Was it a wild party or are you a Virgo?'

'Just a Virgo, I'm afraid. I'm very anal about dust.'

She feigns horror.

'I'll try to be liberal about it, darling but I'm not allergic to dust, myself. Who am I to make spiders homeless?'

As she floats around the room, animated, I think how full of life she is and how empty of it I am. I think of my own mother – defeated, bowed and living for the bingo. Maybe energy is genetic. Hope tells me she has tickets for a whisky tasting at Waterstones and asks if I want to go with her. It sounds just about right. Maybe some of her will rub off on me.

8

The tasting is downstairs at the East End Waterstone's. A red-faced wag with a bushy beard describes each malt with such affection and desire that I almost manage to convince myself that I'm not only here for the beer. The really peaty ones are absolutely divine. My first two have me that safe, glowy way. Hope is circulating and seems to know everyone intimately. I've still no idea what her background is or where all the money comes from. It's too soon to ask her outright.

A few of the staff I know through Simon are buzzing around but I'm in one of my shy moods, so just stand in a growing daze, tripping-out over the whisky. My favourite is Isle of Jura because it smells like poppers and takes me from gloriously glowy to borderline pissed so beautifully. As I lean against one of the tables, a heavily made-up creature of indeterminate gender gestures to two measures at my side and stammers,

'Pleashe . . . away . . . I'm fucking guttered.'

Knowing that two more will probably push me over the edge I sniff both and knock them back. Jesus, whisky makes me feel really straight. It's such a manly drink.

By the time Hope gets round to me, queasiness is making the thought of a joint and an armchair very attractive. Arm-in-arm with the man who gave the talk, she introduces me as her flat-mate. Giving my hand a limp, clammy shake he begins quizzing me about what I do, where I come from, what I think of Edinburgh, how I know Hope, which I'm not really up to lying about. The way he launches at me and the intense eye contact suggest he's quite taken by me but he has terrible halitosis and I have to turn my head when he speaks to me. Hope observes with a worryingly conniving look. I'm starting to wish I'd stayed in. Why is it always the ugly blokes who go for me? If once, just once, a little *Death in Venice* chicken would return my glance, but no, it's always those seedy, cruisey types who don't wash their genitals very often. Why can't I force myself to like people? I don't really like anyone, particularly myself.

Hope though, I do like, but I don't want to be here. I always feel like a nonce unless I'm around people who seem less self-assured than myself. Oh God, Hope has just catapulted herself into a circle of luvvies and embraced everyone. The racket of their squawking and the fanfare of own trumpets being blown is grating on me. Now she's wittering away to the trannie-person that gave me its drinks, their faces almost touching as they converse. The spectacle upsets me somehow. What am I thinking? Why do I suddenly feel jealous about some old woman? I'm sick of this.

Barging up to Hope I tell her I'm leaving, I don't feel well. Her eyes try to speak to me out of the jumble of sycophants. Standing like a prick for a few minutes, expecting her to come over, she doesn't, so I make for the exit.

Walking out onto Princes Street, I feel like a Christmas puppy in March. The cemetery in Waterloo Place blinks seductively at me but I feel like I don't want that any more. I don't know what I want.

The walk back to the flat does nothing to lift a feeling of growing doom. I can't even be bothered to roll a joint when I get in. Besides, my chest is fucked because the blow at the moment is full of plastic. Home by nine on a Saturday night. It's fucking shocking. Lying fully dressed on the bed I listen to little cracks of noise outside. Am I destined to spend the rest of my life watching car lights on the ceiling? I just want Hope to come home, I'm lonely. I want to know that she likes me. I want to win her over. I'm still sitting waiting at one the next morning. Getting up, I close the shutters, undress then get back into bed. What a sad bastard.

9

Despite my early night, the blackened windows allow me to block out the world until well after noon the next day. Hope is back, as I can hear her singing about the flat. The sound is faintly erotic. It feels like we're lovers who've had a tiff. I worry about myself sometimes. Irritated by my feeling of non-specific mardiness, I force myself out of bed, stretching flamboyantly as I walk over to open the shutters. The streets below are that quiet, restrained Sunday way, as if the houses have all been abandoned. Perhaps I should do some sketches and flog them to the rich bastards that live around here.

Then I notice a figure opposite the flat, just standing against the railings. I look away, then back, to confirm the signal my eyes are sending to my brain. Jesus, surely not. It's the ugly bloke I brought back the other night, just standing there with that fucking stinky dog. What the fuck is he playing at? What does he want? Hope can't find out about Friday night, she'll think I'm such a scab. Fuck, fuck, fuck! Should I ignore him or go and see what he wants? How long has he been there?

Hurriedly struggling into my black Levis I look down again. What a fucking weirdo. He's just standing there smoking. The sight of such an eye-sore in my lovely new street offends me. Once I've finished dressing I go through to the living room and ask Hope if she needs anything from the shops. She points to a reading-room's-worth of newspapers on the coffee table.

'Most of the papers are there, dear. They keep me entertained until at least Wednesday. There's cholesterol in the fridge.'

'I'm just after some fresh air, really,' I blush. God, this is pathetic. How can leading a charmed life be so complicated? I've decided to take the guy for a pint as I don't want us having a barney in the street. We can go round to the New Town. It's usually full of creeps anyway. Christ, what if the bang on the head yesterday morning's turned him into a psycho?

He gives me a huge smile and starts walking towards me before I'm even out the stair. Jesus, I can't even remember his name. Standing stiffly, I allow him to kiss me then push myself out of his embrace and towards the pub.

'I was just trying to work up the nerve to come up and see you.'

Hell, no.

'Look, it's not convenient for you to come round the house. I live with someone. They were away the other night. We'll have a drink,' and I bluster onwards, unable to attempt communication again until I have a pint in front of me. He walks briskly at my side, gibbering away a lot of shite about the New Town, trying to impress me with historical details I couldn't give a toss about. Why am I even allowing this wanker the courtesy of giving him the brush-off face-to-face?

We sit at the back of the pub, me with a pint, he with a bloody Mary. As his arm sneaks round the back of my shoulders, I push him off.

'Look, pal, the other night, like. Is it ok if we just leave it at that? I shouldn't have taken you back, I'm sorry.'

'Did your mother never tell you not to go with strangers when you were little?' he smirks, refusing to take me seriously. Gulping back a third of my pint, I try again.

'Seriously though, you won't come round again, will you?'

Leaning back, he takes a contemplative sip of his vodka.

'Married, are you?'

'No . . . well, sort of . . . it's kind of complicated.'

He suddenly starts raising his voice. Thankfully it's empty up the back where we're sitting.

'Why do arseholes like you make yourselves available if you're not prepared to go all the way? Fuck, I must be some sort of magnet to bastards like you. You think you can just fuck me and forget it, eh?'

Now he's standing up, hands on hips, having a right queeny fit. What a mess.

'Ok, ok, I'm a bastard, I know. So will you keep away?'

Vodka and tomato juice are running down my face, my eyes smarting with Worcester sauce. Making for the bogs, I hear the pub door being yanked open violently. Fuck! Grabbing a toilet roll from one of the cubicles I feel something slimy on my fingers and notice come squirted across the tissue. Yelling, 'Bastard,' I kick the cubicle wall in anger and hear a terrified voice inside squealing, 'Fucking hell.' Heading for the exit, I see the barman surrounded by a little huddle of poofs, cackling away, watching where we'd been sitting on close-circuit TV behind the bar.

'You don't want to go upsetting that one,' someone laughs at me as I leave.

10

I almost expect him to be standing outside when I leave for work the following morning. Still feeling quite unnerved by yesterday's performance, I find myself checking behind me as I cut down through Canonmills. Once I'm inside the safety of the shop I castigate myself for my paranoia. As long as I avoid the Phoenix it'll be fine.

Once I'm settled with my coffee and a fag, I start reflecting on the previous night. Hope's sort of flirting with me, I'm sure she is. She put her feet up on my legs when we were sitting on the settee together. Her heel against my balls gave me a semi. If she noticed she certainly didn't seem to mind. What the fuck is going on there? I have to sort it out.

Every time the shop door goes, I jump. Shirley phones at lunch time to tell me he's coming round for a visit tonight. I find myself feeling strangely envious that he's known Hope all his life. I'm thinking about her a lot – about our conversations and her voice and her strong, intelligent face. It's almost like I miss her. This feeling intensifies as the day progresses until at three, I ring her on the pretence of telling her that her nephew's coming round, knowing they'd made the arrangement prior to him speaking to me.

'I've just got a few chums round for Canasta, they're leaving soon.'

'Erm . . . have you spoken to Angus?'

'Oh yes, round about eight, he said. Anyway, must dash. They'll be cheating next door.'

I'm just mumbling, glad to hear her voice.

'Ok . . . erm, yes, well, see you later.'

'Martin?'

'Yes?'

'I missed having you around today. It felt strange . . .'

Although I want to tell her I feel the same, I mumble a bit more then tell her I have to go. God! I bang my head off the desk. What an arsehole I am. I'm bewildered by my own emotions.

11

In the evening Hope cooks us up a Mexican sensation with tacos and nachos and lots of gorgeous little side dishes which

I force myself to eat some of. We drink tequila slammers and at one point the three of us are lying on the carpet, hysterical. Shirley is singing Ethel Merman numbers to himself, obscured by the table. As I roll onto my side to get up, my eyes meet Hope's and stay there for a few seconds. Despite a terrific urge to kiss her, I feel my face starting to flush and stand up.

'I almost thought you were going to kiss me, there,' she says, half-joking, half-serious. Laughing the comment off as ridiculous, I embroil myself in the rolling of a joint.

Shirley and Hope talk a lot about her husband and I insist she gets some photos out. He is a tall, elegant-looking man, chiselled bone structure, but despite his acute angular look, there's a gentle excitement in his eyes. Hope only shows me one wedding photo and shields her face in embarrassment until it's put away. They were married in a registry office in the Fifties which I think is quite cool. Hope is wearing a trouser suit, like a man's pinstripe, tailored and tapered at the waist for a woman. Her hair is short and her face is radiant and full of mischief. It's almost as if someone has cut a photo out of last month's *Cosmo* and pasted it on. Apparently, her family thought she was a lesbian prior to her wedding. The suit, Savile Row, was a stab at them.

'You've no idea how threatened a lot of people are by the sight of a woman in a suit. I still sometimes wear it for a lark.'

I'm sitting staring at her, as I can blame my fixed gaze on the cannabis. I'd really like to paint her in that suit. When I suggest it to her she seems utterly flattered and insists that I allow her to commission me. Unbelievable, getting paid to do what I feel compelled to do anyway.

Before long, Hope is lying on the settee with her feet on my lap again. As I massage her toes and soles, she writhes around beside me. 'You two seem quite taken with each other,' Shirley observes as we become increasingly touchy-feely.

Hope leans forward and kisses my cheek.

'Martin is giving me a new lease of life, not that I was ever as mothballed as you seemed to think. We plan to marry in the Fall.'

'What a riot, having old Dionne here as an uncle. Cool.'

'Watch your tongue lad or you'll feel my slipper on your arse,' I scold unamusingly, but we collapse into drug-induced hysterics none-the-less. I'm having my most relaxed time in ages but I'm also aware that it is getting on for midnight and Shirley is making no signs of leaving. I want to be alone with Hope in this state and see what happens. But then she makes hot toddies for us, and more joints are rolled, then at 1.30, Shirley's eyes start to flicker and he crashes sideways in the armchair. I try shouting over to startle him before he becomes unconscious but he's already started snoring. Hope swallows down the remainder of her toddy, then pulls herself wearily off me.

'I'm going to follow his example. Give me a knock before you go to work, would you, I'm playing golf at ten,' then she blows me a kiss and leaves me with the snoring bastard. The moment's gone now anyway. Perhaps it's for the best. I've probably just got a wee boarding school crush, you know, I shouldn't necessarily act on it. The sound of Shirley's snoring is reminding me of that little runt the other night. My eyes wince in recollection of the sting of Worcester sauce as I retire.

12

Hope gets up before I leave in the morning and makes me a coffee as I shave. She looks gloriously wrecked. Sometimes I judge people's beauty on how good they'd be to paint. Hope scores highly on this. Shirley has vanished, God knows when. I'm annoyed that he could plausibly have left shortly after we went to bed and I still could have made a move. Made a move, what am I on about? The new day has made me timid again. Perhaps it's better just to keep it all in my head. You can control situations if you keep them cerebral.

The doorbell goes as I'm about leave. A woman in her thirties stands behind an eruption of white roses. The lump of envy in my throat disperses when she tells me they're for Martin. The name on the envelope stuck to the wrapper confirms this but I still look at her as if she's joking, grab the flowers and in panic shut the door in her face. My immediate instinct is to open it again and apologise, but I'm too agitated. Hope is in the bathroom, thank God. Smuggling the rustling package into my room, I tremblingly tear open the envelope.

'Forgot to say. You sucked my cock beautifully. R xxx'

I feel sick, in fact I bring up and swallow a mouthful of coffee. My shoulders become very sore all of a sudden. Fuck fuck fuck. Tearing the remainder of the envelope from the wrapper, I stuff it, with the card, under my mattress. Grabbing one of my Lucien Freud postcards off the wall, I scrawl, 'Thanks. Last Present, honest!', regretting it immediately but throw it and the flowers on the telephone table regardless and run out the house. White roses are just so gorgeous. If they'd been tacky red they'd have gone straight in the bin.

Running round to Dublin Street, I hail the first taxi I

see. I don't want anyone following me to the shop. It's my safe haven.

13

I'm in pieces at work. He'll be standing outside the flat when I get back tonight, I know he will. I've never been violent towards another person but I've done some serious damage to inanimate objects in my time. Who knows how I'd react under pressure? It feels as if I'm being violated. What right does the ugly creature feel he has to hassle me like this? I'm an attractive guy. As if I'd get involved with that. Would I be letting it get to me as much if Hope wasn't in the equation? The fact is I would. When people try to invade my space and time it really pisses me off. I make my own decisions about if and when I see people and I hate anyone who tries to interfere with that. I'd get the police onto him but I realize I can't really. It would just bring it out in the open even more, besides, they'd piss themselves laughing.

I'm rude to the few customers we have because I'm so stressed out. At one point I put a 'back in 10 minutes' sign on the door and go to the back of the shop for a joint, but this just serves to make me even more tense. Sometimes I think I get no hit from cannabis any more, that I'm completely immune. Having a joint at work always dispels this theory though, as the surroundings really seem to intensify the hit. It also makes time drag something awful.

I'm kinder to the customers after the smoke, and end up

nervously raving to them about the books they're buying. About 2.30 a guy comes in with a large cardboard box. He looks like Paul Agutter the Safeway poisoner. Turns out he's flogging these extremely rare, immaculate art books – Lucien Freud, Bacon, Kitaj and one on the Scottish Colourists with actual prints by Cadell in it. Books I had no idea even existed. In Italian, mind you, but the sort of people that buy books like these are all cunnilingual anyway. I can tell that parting with them really pains the guy, something about the CSA being on his back. Business is business though and I tell him that my business is slow and hum and haw in my usual way till he's really desperate. After torturing him like this for a while, I offer thirty quid for the lot and he predictably jumps at it, looking thoroughly sick as he does. I can probably get that each for them. Entering them in the ledger as indiscriminate 'Art Books (several)', I make sure to leave plenty of space between the pound sign and the thirty. When he leaves I stash an amazing book of Egon Schiele plates in my bag at the back of the shop, make a coffee and settle down to look through the rest of them, feeling infinitely happier. A hundred pounds for two minutes' ham acting. Now I know how Tony Slattery feels.

I've only just started to price them when a woman comes over with a hefty tome on Raeburn that's been collecting dust since I started here. She spots the Colourists book and asks me how much. I've no idea what it's worth. It's a fucking antique – could be hundreds, could be thousands. As it's not even been named in the ledger I hazard a guess at ninety pounds. The woman's face lights up as she pulls twenty pound notes from her purse and I know I've made a huge boo-boo. Too late to worry about it now though and it means I've made a cool two hundred today including ten pounds on my first sale this morning. As I put the books in a bag for her, she thanks me profusely. The difference between her joy and the anguish of the guy who sold me them is striking. She's probably his ex-wife followed him here.

Buoyed by my burgeoning wealth I start thinking about holidays. Maybe Hope and I could go away somewhere together. I've only been out of Britain twice, to Paris, since I got my passport and it runs out in a couple of years. She'd be good, intelligent company to travel abroad with. She could teach me so much. Perhaps I should suggest it anyway, she'd probably insist on financing the whole trip.

About two o'clock a spotty bloke in a donkey jacket comes in with a holdall and tells me he has a few Williams first editions to sell. I can't believe it, 'Tennessee Williams?' I confirm. He looks at me blankly. 'Naw, Raymond.' I suppose one coup a day is enough.

After that, the shop is dead. Not that I mind, as I've had a good innings and I'm content to just put my feet up for the rest of the afternoon. Making a coffee I engross myself in my Egon Schiele book. The bell above the shop door tinkles and before I even look up, I get the strange sense that I'm not going to like what I see. First it's the horrible fucking dog, then the creep, smiling, coming towards me.

'Any nice surprises with the postman this morning?'

I'm dumbstruck. I can't believe he's found his way into my other world.

'. . . I'm a hopeless romantic, I just can't help myself. I hope white is your colour. I'm surrendering to you.'

I stand up to establish some semblance of power.

'Look pal, I don't want your flowers and I don't want you following me about.'

He looks genuinely offended.

'I'm not following you doll. I just popped in to see you.'

'How did you know where I worked? You must have followed me.'

He laughs now, as I erupt internally.

'Are you joking? This is where I first met you, remember, I used to bring in piles of uncorrected proofs when I worked in John Menzies.'

'I get a lot of people coming through here. I can't remember.'

'So you took a complete stranger home the other night, you dirty Scottish boy,' he drawls and tries to touch my hand. Pulling away, I fold my arms in front of me defensively.

'Look, please understand. I don't want to get involved with you. My life is complicated enough as it is. No offence mate but please, I'd like you to leave me alone.'

'I'm not averse to affairs. I'm terribly discreet.'

I don't believe this. How can I get it through his thick skull.

'I'm going away. My marriage isn't working out. I'm moving down to London.'

He keeps on.

'A long-distance love affair. I've never been further down than Manchester. Shocking, eh?'

I'm finding it very hard not to lose my cool as I imagine braining the bastard against the counter.

'Will you fucking listen to me? I'm sorry if you think I led you on but Jesus, you pick up a complete stranger in the street and fuck them, what do you expect?'

A blushing schoolboy appears from nowhere and purchases a book on Gallipoli. The creep stands smirking, intensifying the boy's discomfort. What if he tells someone? What if he tells his mother the man in the book shop picks up young guys? The door pings shut again. Creep leans on the counter and in towards me. I back away.

'So when are you leaving then? When can I visit you?'

No more.

'Look, will you fuck off? What do I have to fucking say to you? Get out my fucking face.'

The bastard's lip starts trembling, I don't believe it. A tear runs down his idiot face as he turns and makes for the door, roaring 'cunt' at me as he departs. Never has that word sounded so good.

14

There's no sign of him when I close up at five, so I walk home to reassert my freedom. A couple of times on the way back I imagine I see him in people who look nothing like him. When I turn into Northumberland Street and he's not there, I sense that he could finally have got the message.

As I enter the flat I hear Hope in the living room talking to someone. For a second I imagine the scene in *Fatal Attraction* when gorgeous Michael Douglas comes home and Glenn Close is there pretending she wants to buy the house. Then I hear another female speaking. I pop my head round the door and see Hope sitting with a woman in her thirties and a toddler. The roses are in a vase by the table. Hope gestures to them and smiles.

'Martin dear, this is my niece, Jacqueline, Angus's sister. Get that nice bottle of Chardonnay out the fridge and join us.

This is Angus's friend, he's flat-hunting at the moment and being an extremely pleasant house-guest in the meantime.'

Telling them I'll be through in a few minutes, I rifle my pockets for my gear as I walk up the hall to my room. I need a joint before I'm subjected to fucking babies.

As it turns out, the child is not too bad. Jacqueline is a crushing bore though. Nobody else wants a drink so I pour myself one and sit in a glorious little stupor, watching the kid doing its kiddish things. It is into everything. Hope seems unconcerned as it staggers around pocketing keys and trying to chew everything in its wake. Is he hyperactive or are they all like this? Jacqueline seems very experienced in the art of sustaining a conversation whilst running about fretting over the wee monster. Jason (and the Argonauts? The Golden Fleece? Surely not Donovan), is playing to an audience and throws a tantrum every time our attention wavers.

After about an hour, and three-quarters of a bottle of Chardonnay he starts getting a bit tired and greety. He keeps lolling about the room then crashing into his mother for a cuddle. Hope looks pretty irritated by now. Jacqueline tries to calm him down by shyly singing 'Mockingbird' to him and rocking him gently in her arms. I love croaky, nervous voices like hers, they're so human. 'No sing mummy, please no sing,' the child pleads. Hope hoots with laughter and the rest of us are soon infected by it. Jason is annoyed that we seem to have got something over on him and starts crying again. Jacqueline notices the renewed look of subdued displeasure on Hope's face and begins getting her things together and squeezing into her coat.

Hope beckons to me as Jacqueline crawls around on the carpet looking for discarded toys. I follow her through to her bedroom. She goes to the other side of the bed, rummages around, puts a bit wood against the wall and pulls out a wad of notes, counting through them, 20, 40 . . . 180, 190, £200. She slips it in the pocket of her blouse, then tears another twenty off and hands it to me.

'You wouldn't be a dear and pop out and get me a bottle of Ten Year Old MacAllan would you? I need to have a word with Jacqueline on her own . . .' she gestures to the money in her pocket, '. . . man trouble,' and winks at me.

She squeezes my hand as she sees me out the flat. Jesus, why was she so obvious about where she keeps money? Is she testing me or something? And £200 to a niece she never sees, just like that. I don't need her money, I don't want it. There's no way I'd steal from her, she's too kind. Stealing is a form of revenge.

As I open the stair door my suppressed trepidation hits me again but the street is still clear. Once I'm sure that nonsense is behind me, I'll be able to put my real feelings for Hope in perspective. It was funny, just the look she gave me tonight when she was telling Jacqueline about me flat-hunting. There are strange erotic sparks between us, I'm sure of it.

When I get back, Jacqueline has gone and Hope is lying back on the settee with *La Traviata* blaring. Her arm rises like a charmed snake and she points at two tumblers on the table. Pulling the MacAllan out the bag, I pour us a couple of measures.

'Straight tonight, madam?'

'Indeed, but twist up one of your little mary-janes as a chaser.'

We lounge back on the settee together, tingle with the whisky and pass the joint to one another as Maria Callas bangs it out. In a matter of days, without trying, our friendship has deepened to such an extent that we feel completely at ease without having to say anything to each other. Nuzzling closer to Hope, she drapes her arm across my shoulders and I snuggle against her upper arm. Her skin smells of talcum and fresh air. The heat where my head touches her arms feels like it's buzzing. I feel utterly replete.

We lie huddled up like this for ages until the CD player clicks and the chorus bursts into '*Dell'invito trescora e' jia' l'ora'*, for what must be the second time. Hope clambers up from the settee and switches it off.

Pouring us both another whisky, she gestures to my blow and I obligingly begin rolling another joint.

'Have you ever been to Italy?' I ask as she sits down again

'*La dentro non ci andrei, e pieno d l'Italiani,*' she says incomprehensibly in a thick Italian accent. '. . . My husband worked in Rome for a while before I met him but we never made it over together somehow. Maybe he had another wife over there.'

The mention of her husband, that tiny part of the vast life she had before I met her, gives me a little twinge of jealousy.

'I'm very backward as far as foreign travel is concerned. Holland once, Greece once, France a few times. I've a couple of pals just outside Paris I see every now and again (eight years ago!). It just seems such a lot of money to spend before you buy your first pint.'

Hope becomes animated.

'Oh I love France – Paris, Fontainebleau, Marseilles . . . Provence used to be lovely too until they BBC'd it and attracted all the riff-raff.'

'I'd love to go there with you sometime. I could save up.'

Hope waves her hands in front of her like she's doing the Charleston.

'That's a wonderful idea. I'd love a little break. When could you get time off work?'

'I'm owed loads of annual leave but I'm always afraid to take it in case the place goes to pieces without me. Plus, he doesn't pay me when I'm off.'

'Pah, don't worry about money, for God's sake?'

'I'd like to take you, though. If I put a bit away each week we could go there for the millennium. The next one that is. But you know, I like to pay my own way. I feel bad enough as it is about you not taking anything off me for staying here.'

She dismisses me with a wave of the hand.

'Pay me back a pound a month if it bothers you that much. I'm not going to go hungry without it, put it that way.'

'Oh but that's terrible.'

She looks at me as if I'm mad.

'What's terrible about it? Is the thought of setting Paris alight with me so awful? Don't be so bloody silly, when could you get time off? A month? Next week?'

'Whenever, I just need to give a couple of days' notice and my boss can get his wife to watch the place.' I also need time to go through the books with a nit-comb.

She bangs her glass against mine.

'Leave it to me. *Vive la France.*'

We say good night at the living-room door. Thoughts of a possible free holiday and all the lush times we might have, keep me awake for hours. I'm also dying to see Roxanne and Jonathan. We shared a flat for two years when I was studying in London. There's been an open invite since I was last over eight years ago. Something else always comes up though and work's usually good in the summer as the tourists are such idiots with money.

15

I'm woken up at 2.34 by a right racket out in the street – loud voices, lights flashing through the chinks in the shutters and the roar of machinery. It better not be those cable TV bastards digging up the road at this time of the morning. I stumble out of bed and over to the window. It's a fucking fire engine, putting out a fire in one of the bins. Such an unbelievable amount of noise for a pissing little fire in a bucket. As I slump back to bed I feel wide-awake with anger.

Once I'm back under the duvet, I realize I've left the shutters open but by then I'm getting the fear and don't want to go back over to the window again. Why did a bucket go on fire in a New Town street at half two on a Wednesday morning? It had to be deliberate. Surely that wanker wouldn't pull a stunt like that. The bucket is only about fifteen feet away from the steps up to the flat. He wouldn't, would he? Why am I imagining this? There's been no sign of him since yesterday afternoon. He would have rung the buzzer or been outside when I got home from work. Oh fuck. I bet he's been along at the Phoenix. Fuck fuck fuck. Wild imaginings about the bastard keep me awake for most of the remainder of the night. When the alarm goes off at eight I feel like I've only just shut my eyes.

16

Hope phones me about eleven to say she's booked two open-ended flights to Charles de Gaulle. We can travel any time after tomorrow if there's space on the flights. It's off-peak so we shouldn't have any trouble getting a hotel at the last minute. This time of year it's probably only people going over to look at Diana's blood on the road. Hope wants to keep our holiday a secret until we get back in case anyone else tries to get in on the act at the last minute. I can't wait for us to be alone together, to be forced to really get to know one another. If we get on, I am definitely going to go for it.

When I try to phone my boss, I discover he's been in hospital for the past three days, the cancer's gone into his stomach. What'll happen to the shop if he dies? I'd never get another job where I made so much for doing so little. It's almost like this place is part of my identity now. Maybe I should visit him before we go away, see what he's saying before he pops his clogs. Maybe Hope would buy him out. Mmmh. His daughter Angela can't cover for me until next Tuesday though, which is a pain in the pisser. Does he have to fucking die when I get the chance of my first holiday in years? I don't tell her where I'm going as I don't want her asking about it when I get back.

I've just put the phone down when it rings again.

'Look Martin, I'm sorry, ok.'

'Who is this?'

'Raymond,' says a hurt-sounding voice.

'Raymond who?'

'The person you told to fuck off yesterday. Have you forgotten me already?'

Oh Jesus, I don't believe it. My heckles are up immediately.

'. . . Look, can I see you? Just once more, please? When are you going away?'

Fuck, how does he know? Then I remember my lie about London. 'Tomorrow, after work, so I really don't have time to meet you.'

'But I need to, sweetheart. You don't understand, I can't see past you . . . I can't think straight.'

Oh, for heaven's sake.

'Look, I'm sorry mate but there's nothing I can do. Give me your address and I'll get in touch when I'm settled.'

'Really? You won't though, will you? I'll never hear from you again. Please Martin, let me see you. I could pop along now. I could help you take your stuff to the station tomorrow . . .'

'No, please, don't come along here. I don't want you in here. Just leave it, for fuck's sake?'

'What time's your train tomorrow? I could meet you at the station. Just five minutes, please?'

It goes on and on like this for about ten minutes. I tell him to fuck off and die and put the phone down on him a couple of times but he just rings back immediately. Why am I tied up in knots by this stupid lie now? Fuck. In desperation, I tell him I'm leaving at six, going from work so I'll be straight on the train. He insists he's going to be there though, no matter what I say he insists and finally hangs up.

Now if I'm not there at six he'll know it was a lie. This will just go on for fucking ever. I'm actually toying with the idea of saying goodbye, getting on the fucking train for one stop, then coming back again but it seems an absolutely ridiculous thing to have to do for that cunt. If I can just get his focus off Northumberland Street, stop him lurking around so near to Hope. Apart from my idea with the train, I can think of no other solution. It is utterly flawed, however, as I'll no doubt bump into the bastard the next day.

Perhaps if I can keep a low profile till we go away next week. Jesus, I can always just take a sickie off work. My attendance record is understandably impeccable and they can't sack me anyway, who would take over? I'm sure Angela would just love to commute from Stirling every day, not. She hates it when she has to cover for me. If they have to close the shop and ugly boy goes round there looking for me it'll make my story more convincing.

Spurred on by my own resolve, I phone the Waverley and book a day-return to Berwick on Switch which I've to pick up at 5.30 tomorrow. I just want this sodding saga cleared up before we go away.

As I close up the shop at five I realize I've forgotten to pilfer anything with all this shit to think about. Hastily scribbling a few books through the ledger that have been on the shelf for months, I take £30 for blow. My booty from yesterday's still in my back pocket and I can go daft for holiday money tomorrow.

Having left the safety of the shop, the unguardedness of the street summons feelings of acute anxiety akin to a massive whitey. Escaping into a taxi, I get him to take me to Davie's in Whitson for some gear and to get me out of the stress of the city centre for a while. Fucking £7 as well, I must stop jumping in and out of cabs or else steal my old dear's disabled pass.

Out of politeness I have a couple of joints with Davie, but my nerves are so shot I can only manage a few grunts of conversation. Davie's not much of a talker anyway, it's way too much effort for him. Thank God we have *Hollyoaks* to sustain us. Then I start getting these involuntary spasms in my left leg and it starts shooting out in front of me. Davie just looks on impassively as if this happens to him all the time. Before long the lack of communication is depressing me so I leave.

As I open the stair door, I see a 21 coming and sprint to the bus stop just in time to save myself from phoning 999 again. As we pull away I see more satellite dishes than I ever have in my life.

Hope is out at a writing workshop when I get back. I'd forgotten all about it but it's convenient. Half-filling two hold-alls with books, I stick a few shirts on top, just to give the impression they're full. To avoid having to get them out the house without Hope seeing me in the morning, I put them in the cellar at the bottom of the stair. Although this is probably the stupidest idea I've ever had I'm trying very hard to get into it, just to see if I can pull it off.

Hope's left me some casserole which looks gorgeous but my hunger is making me nauseous so I place it tactfully in an old bread bag at the bottom of the bin. When was the last time I actually ate anything? I've no idea. I occasionally have a Mars bar with my coffee at lunch-time but I didn't even manage that this morning. The bottle of Chablis in the fridge, however, is another matter.

It's times like this, I really miss having a telly. Without such a distraction I'm soon worrying about everything again and my proposed plan of action seems sillier, the more I think about it.

When Hope comes in at midnight, I'm sitting dozing on the settee, exhausted by my procrastination earlier. Leaning over me, she kisses my forehead. The smell of whisky on her breath explains her wide-awake radiance.

'The tutor didn't turn up so we all went to a pub, I'm quite pissed. A real man's bar, it was . . . I liked it. Real people can be frightfully entertaining sometimes. They just come out with it, don't they?'

The chorus of Pulp's 'Common People' bounces around inside my head amongst feelings of animosity towards whoever she's been out with. Why didn't she phone to say where she was? I'd have phoned her and invited her to join me. Stop it, stop it. Why am I getting like this? I've not even shagged her yet.

'I'm on annual leave from tomorrow night,' I lie, whitely.

Hope claps her hands together.

'That's wonderful.' She looks at her watch, 'Oh, I suppose it's too late to phone the airport now, isn't it?'

And whose fault is that?

'There's a couple of things I have to do before we go anyway. How about Saturday, if there's flights available?'

'Fine by me. I'll call a couple of hotels I know in the morning. Super. Anyway, you're not going to believe some of the things I overheard in that pub . . .'

I've no desire to hear about her new pals. Her enthusiasm for them is stressing me out. I stroke my temples melodramatically.

'Sorry, Hope, I've had this migraine coming on for the last half hour. I'm going to have to lie down. Tell me tomorrow, eh?'

She pretends to pretend to look hurt. God, I hate the mind fucks you give yourself when you're emotionally involved with someone.

'Poor dear. There's some out-of-date DF118s in the bathroom cabinet if they'd help.'

DF118s! I don't really have a migraine but I help myself to six, swallow two and put the rest in a little ink-well in my room.

It feels wonderful to be in bed. If I could just stay here for a few months. That's what I'll do on Friday, keep a low profile. Will she book single rooms or a double I wonder? She didn't even ask me. If I just think of it all as an adventure. It is an adventure. The thing at the station tomorrow is part of it. It's sort of exciting, I suppose. The DFs start to take hold really quickly. I'm having really disgusting fantasies about Hope by the time I fall asleep.

17

In the morning, she's not up (no doubt hungover) by the time I go to work. I leave a note on the telephone table saying, 'Back late' – deliberately unspecific to get her back for not calling last night. Only taking enough money with me for a taxi, I count through the rest – £440. That's not forgetting the two grand in my Investment Account. This is going to be some fucking holiday, I think as I stuff the wad in a sock.

Having retrieved my hold-alls from the cellar, I struggle out with them, feeling stupider by the second. As I turn into the positively mountainous Dublin Street, my arms are aching from the ridiculously heavy bags. Taxis are whizzing by on Queen Street but I have to scale the worst of it before I finally manage to stop one.

Work is a nightmare, as I have to square the place up, make the accounts looks semi-respectable, run through loads of fucking figures to make sure I've covered myself on everything. Every time the door goes I feel like Anne Frank.

There's loads of students in during the morning, giggling, talking very loud and constantly asking for things, making me work my arse off for piddling little £1.50 paperbacks.

By mid-afternoon I've not managed to make a penny for myself. A guy comes in with a carrier bag full of photography books – Ansel Adams, Weegee, Cartier-Bresson, but I can't find a fucking pencil anywhere. He lends me his pen and I know I'm going to have to make at least £100 or nothing at all on the deal. Utterly offended by my initial offer of a tenner, he says something like £90. Although the books are worth five times that, this could be my only chance of the day. It takes me about twenty minutes to haggle him down to £25. I respect him for holding out so long but business is business. I'm wasted in this job, I should be on Wall Street.

Any empathy I had with the guy disappears when I notice he's put the figure in the book himself, when he was signing it. Fuck, there's barely room for a 'one' in there and I was counting on a 'two'. I'll need to watch him if he comes in again. He's probably worked in a bookshop and knows the form. It's nearly half three by the time he leaves and I still have to do something with all the books I've been buying and not bothering to display for the past few months. I'm sweating like a bastard by the time I close up at five, a mere hundred pounds richer.

The stupid bloody bags mean I have to get yet another taxi to the station. It'll be worth it though, if it gets that bastard off my back, at least until he's calmed down about the whole thing. It should flatter me that someone's so into me, but I'm from Edinburgh, you know, I hate people invading my space.

There's a long queue at the booking office. I should have told the bastard to stand in the queue for me while he was waiting, although he doesn't seem to be here yet, anyway.

That's fine though, the less time I have to spend with him the better.

I'm in a queue for ten minutes before I realize there's a separate desk for previously paid for tickets. They serve me immediately as apparently no-one else has the savvy to pay in advance.

Leaving the booking hall, I walk down to the platform, but still can't see him. In John Menzies, I thumb the glossies for ten minutes, then for extra authenticity, buy a copy of *Time Out*. Still no sign. It's now 5.45. Walking round to the Rendezvous Point, I scan the crowd and sit down. The smell from the bin next to me turns my stomach. I walk back over to the platform. The Tannoy announces that the train is arriving. Lots of people waiting, but not him.

At 5.52 I walk back over to the shop, then have another quick look in the booking hall. Jesus, I don't believe this, I'm going to fucking Berwick for his benefit and he's not even here. What will I do? I've wasted £11 on a fucking ticket. This isn't on.

5.58 and people are getting on the train, doors are being slammed, the engine is starting to roar. Will I just go home? Stand in that fucking queue again to get a refund on my ticket? What if he's watching me? That's it, he's fucking watching to see if I go or not.

The guard asks me if I'm getting on. I stand like a bewildered prick for a few seconds, then he asks me again. Utterly humiliated, I jump on. The door is slammed behind me and the fucking train is off before I even have time to think about it.

Clambering up to the smoking carriage in complete shock, I drop into a seat and light up a Silk Cut. As Edinburgh slowly disappears, I still can't quite believe what I'm doing. The whole journey down I'm raging at myself for doing something so fucking idiotic. It's an hour's wait at Berwick to get the train back, and once I'm on it I crash out, sick of thinking.

It's only thanks to some noisy squaddies getting on at Waverley that my evening doesn't end in Aberdeen. Then I'm howking those bloody bags back down the bloody platform again, thinking that if I see him now I'll fucking kill myself. I try phoning the flat but there's no answer.

It's nine o'clock by the time I get my third taxi of the day. I must learn to drive, I hate having to rely on these fuckers. As I get dropped off I'm relieved to see that the lights are all out in the flat, so I can get the bags in again undetected.

My note to Hope has gone from the telephone table, but there's an envelope with my name on it – just 'Martin'. It's definitely not Hope's flamboyant script, in fact I know exactly who it's from the second I see it. He must have put it through the fucking door. Please make Hope have been out when he turned up. There's no note to say where she is and it makes me feel stupid for bothering to tell her I'd be late. Taking the envelope through to my room I need a joint before I can face it.

There's a flimsy bit of lined paper, torn out of a notebook inside, folded once. All that is written on it is '*Vous l'avez voulu.*' What the fuck does that mean? Why didn't I nick a French phrase-book from work for next week? Has he found out about Paris? How long has it been lying there? Maybe he couldn't make it to the station. Why would he bring it here though, if he thought I'd be gone? Please don't let Hope have met him. I don't want to have to explain him to her.

Looking out onto the empty street as I finish the joint, it begins to really irritate me that Hope hasn't left me a note. Maybe she phoned while I was out. Going into the hall, I do a 1471 but its the fucking pay phone I called from at the station.

Thinking she might have left a note in the living room, I open the door. A black shape lunges at me from nowhere. The shock knocks me over. The next thing I'm aware of is something licking my face. It's his dog. It's his fucking dog. He's fucking in here.

Thrusting myself into the room, I expect him to be sitting there with a fucking smug look on his face but it's empty. There are cushions all over the floor and it smells of piss. My whole body begins trembling, like I'm going to have a fit, as I stagger up and check the kitchen, then the bathroom.

They are both in Hope's bed. As I walk round taking it all in, it seems strangely normal. Hope's skin is yellow and plastic-looking, her throat discoloured by what looks like a string of lovebites. They are the same colour as the inordinately large tongue which lollops at the side of her mouth. Her eyes are open and pleading with me to do something. I close them.

Raymond is lying sideways over her. His skin is much darker than hers but yellow still seeps through. A huge, wet, purple carnation blossoms out on the blue sheet beneath his hand. The dog jumps up on the bed and tries to lick the death from his face. It is like something out of the Sensation exhibition. I think about the air tickets on the mantlepiece and the money under the floor. I think about calling Shirley, or dialling 999. Then I think about me being just another cunt getting carted into a prison van on the Scottish news. Nah, I don't think so.